THE ONLY ONE LEFT

A Neema Mystery

Pamela Beason

WildWing Press

This is a work of fiction. Names, characters, places, and incidents are products of the author's imagination or are used fictitiously and are not to be construed as real. Any resemblance to actual events, locales, organizations, or persons, living or dead, is entirely coincidental.

WILDWING PRESS
Bellingham, Washington

Copyright © 2018 Pamela Beason
ISBN 978-0-9983149-0-7
www.pamelabeason.com

Cover design by Christine Savoie

Printed in the U.S.A.

I dedicate this book to all those who stand up for the rights of women and children

THE
ONLY ONE
LEFT

Chapter 1

Monday

Detective Matthew Finn had never before been kissed by a gorilla.

When Neema wrapped an arm around his neck and pulled his head close, he shut his eyes so he couldn't focus on the big ape's giant teeth or her piercing red-brown eyes that seemed all too human. After brushing his cheek with her huge rubbery black lips, she ran her thick black fingers through his hair, grooming him. He took a deep breath, willing himself not to flinch.

He should have known better than to accompany Grace into the barn where her gorillas lived, let alone agree to sit with them in what Grace called an "unstructured period." Normally, during these periods Grace introduced something new to the gorillas, an exercise ball or a set of pink plastic flamingos or a pair of binoculars, just to see what would happen next and whether they'd use their signs to communicate with one another. Today, she had shanghaied Finn into being the variable in their ape play. He was grateful that Gumu, the massive, unpredictable silverback, had stayed outside.

"Be gentle, Neema," Grace warned from her seat several yards away. "Matt is still new to ape affection."

"Why does she even want to—"

Finn completely lost his train of thought as Neema stuck a finger into his ear. He jumped to his feet.

With a soft hoot, Neema leapt back, then sat on her haunches a few yards away. The gorilla squashed a pair of sunglasses onto her face and then made a pinching sign next to her broad nose.

"Hey! Those are *my* sunglasses!" He tapped his chest, signing *mine*, one of the few American Sign Language words he knew.

Neema stared at him, her maroon-colored gaze intense over the dark lenses perched on her broad nose.

He repeated *mine*, then copied the gorilla's pinching sign, which had to mean *glasses*. And then he held out his hand.

Grace broke into laughter. "I *so* wish I had the video recorder running. Neema's *teaching* you signs!" She scribbled a note into the tablet she held in her lap.

Dear God, it was true. He'd just learned a new sign from an *ape*. "I'm glad you didn't get it on tape, and you'd better not tell anyone that. She stole them right out of my shirt pocket! I want my sunglasses back."

"Neema." Grace put down her pen and notebook to sign as she spoke. "Give the glasses back to Matt."

Finn knew she actually signed *to Dog Gun Man*, which was the complex sign the gorilla had invented to name him because of the Glock he usually carried in his belt holster and the animal hair he perpetually wore on his pants. At least his name had been shortened now from *Dog Cat Gun Man*. Neema liked cats and didn't complain about the feline scent any longer. He hoped in time his gorilla name would become only *Gun Man* or at least something a little less laughable.

He signed *glasses mine* and then held his hand out toward the gorilla again, sighing. Why couldn't he have fallen in love with a normal woman who had normal pets? Although the gorillas were not precisely pets; they were Dr. Grace McKenna's research subjects, and seemed to be the only close family she had, as well.

Kanoni, the baby gorilla, climbed his leg, took an object out of her mouth and placed it in his outstretched palm. Then she launched herself from his thigh, making him stagger backward as she bounded over to her mother. Snatching the sunglasses from Neema's face, Kanoni raced away with them to a dark corner of the barn, whooping loudly with glee.

"Yuck." Finn groaned. His thigh smarted from baby-gorilla toenails and his hand was slick with ape saliva.

Grace dissolved into guffaws.

"You're not helping," he complained, dumping the slimy object from his hand into the sawdust at his feet. He dried his palm on his pants leg.

"That was one of the most entertaining observation periods I've had in a long time." She stood and walked to him, wiping tears from her eyes with the collar of her shirt. "I'm sorry." Pulling him into her arms, she excused herself with, "It's just so damn funny."

"If you say so." Her kiss was much gentler and more welcome than Neema's, and Grace smelled better, too. He stroked her shoulder-length black hair. Today she was wearing it in the loose waves that he loved to run his fingers through.

She pulled away, sweeping her hair back from her face with both hands. "Are you wiping gorilla spit off on my hair?"

It was his turn to laugh. "No, I . . ."

She combed her fingers through her tresses.

He grinned. "Well, maybe a little."

Abruptly, Grace's face sobered. She closed her eyes and flattened a hand on her stomach, swaying slightly on her feet.

He clutched her arm. "You okay?"

"Yeah." Opening her eyes, she gave him a light smile. "Just a little dizzy for a second. Stood up too fast, I guess. What did Kanoni give you?"

Finn checked the ground at his feet, then picked up a gray-white object a little over an inch long. He turned it over several times, then measured it against his index finger. It was slightly shorter than the space between the first and second joints, a little smaller in diameter. "Do you give the gorillas bones?"

"Never." She took the object from him. "But this barn was originally part of a working farm, and the farmers kept all sorts of livestock in here. I have found a few chicken bones, and once a leg bone from a calf."

She peered at the bone carefully. She turned it over a couple of times, inspected the ends. "I hope I'm wrong. It's been a long time since I took basic anatomy. This looks an awful lot like . . ."

As a homicide detective, Finn had seen quite a few skeletons. He finished the sentence with Grace: ". . . a bone from a human finger."

Chapter 2

Monday

"Here we go again," Finn groaned. Having a love relationship with a scientist who studied interspecies communication was full of weird happenings no normal man could anticipate. The last "incident" had involved the disappearance of all three gorillas, leaving behind a huge, mysterious pool of blood in this very barn.

Grace glanced frantically around the barn, which had been remodeled to provide a jungle-like habitat for gorillas. Leafy broken branches and bunches of straw and stuffed toys littered the dirt-and-sawdust floor. Several tree trunks were propped into various positions against the walls. The original hayloft had been removed, and now the building was open all the way up to the roof, which rose to a peak more than thirty feet overhead, supported by a massive beam that ran the length of the entire building. The main beam was in turn held up by four vertical posts as thick as telephone poles. Dominating the space was a manmade "tree" of platforms that radiated out and up around one of these posts in a spiral formation, like leaves sprouting from a vine. Finn knew the gorillas often slept on the platforms. He'd also seen them chase one another up and down the structure, leaping from one platform to the next.

"I've never found anything like this in the barn," Grace said. "Surely this bone can't be human."

"Well, it definitely did not come from a chicken. Or a calf."

Holding the bone between her thumb and index finger, she twisted her hand to study it from a new angle. "You know, bear paw bones are frequently mistaken for human hand bones. Someone could have butchered a bear in here."

"Let's hope for that." He'd heard of a couple of cases where officers had embarrassed themselves by identifying bear bones as human remains. How was he going to sort this out? Maybe someone at the local college could tell the difference?

"But Matt, you have to keep this to yourself, for now."

He raised an eyebrow. Last time Grace asked him to keep an incident secret, all hell had broken loose.

"Please." She put her hands together in a praying gesture. "I have an inspection coming up in a few days. If anything out of the ordinary happens, the county might revoke my permit to keep the gorillas. You know a lot of people think they shouldn't be here."

Finn was well aware of the Evansburg citizens who were opposed to apes in their neighborhood. And so far, there was no evidence a crime had been committed, so he didn't have much to report, anyway. "Where could Kanoni have picked up that thing?"

"Kanoni!" Grace yelled. "Come!" She gestured the baby gorilla away from a plush toy monkey the little ape was busily covering with a blanket.

Kanoni barreled over to them, stopping at Grace's feet, suddenly intrigued by the laces on her keeper's running shoes. She pulled on one, hooting happily when it came undone.

"Where did you get this toy, Kanoni?" Grace held out the bone and gestured with her other hand, ending in the extended thumb and little finger that was either the sign for "Hang Loose" in Hawaiian or the letter Y.

Finn frowned. "Toy?"

"Well, they don't know the word for bone." Grace demonstrated a disturbing combination of tapping her forearm and then making crab claws with both hands crossed.

How the heck had *that* sign come about? Something about an arm being picked clean by crabs? Or crossed skeleton arms? How macabre.

Kanoni untied Grace's other shoe. Grace repeated the question and again held out the small bone.

The swish of feathers drew the attention of both apes and humans to the roof peak overhead. A small bird swooped from the louvered air vent in the wall to the massive main beam that ran the length of the barn.

"There are birds inside your barn," Finn observed.

"No kidding, Detective? They have a nest up there, I think."

Now that Grace mentioned it, Finn thought he heard faint cheeping sounds.

"I should find a way to clear it out because birds attract mites. But that beam is thirty-four feet from the floor."

Finn studied the barn's architecture. The highest platform on the "tree" stopped about twelve feet below the roof, but the vertical supporting pole was bolted to the main beam. Maybe the pole could be climbed or reached by a ladder set on the highest platform, but he was not about to volunteer. "How'd you bolt that pole to the main beam up there?"

"I didn't. They were already connected. The construction team used one of those lift trucks like the line workers use to attach the platforms. I'd have to rent one of those again, or maybe get an extra long extension ladder or something. I can't justify that expense just for a bird's nest."

The bird flew back to the air vent and squeezed out between the louvers.

"Besides, I like swallows. They are beautiful birds." Grace looked back at the baby gorilla. "Now—"

Kanoni grunted and pinched her fingers together beside her mouth.

"That's right, that's a bird, Kanoni." Grace repeated the bird beak sign. "But where did you get this toy?" She again held out the bone and shook it in front of the little ape's face.

Kanoni raked both hands down through the air, then moved one hand at the side of her face as if pulling on whiskers.

"Snow cat is not here," Grace responded, signing back.

Finn grimaced. Over the past two years, he'd learned that conversation with apes was riddled with non sequiturs, but he still found it disturbing. "Why is she mentioning the cat?"

"Snow is her favorite. And he's been missing since yesterday afternoon, so she's thinking about him. Or maybe she's trying to say that Snow brought her that bone."

After spending more than two years with Grace and her menagerie, Finn knew that the apes often made up stories to shift blame. Or just because they thought the lie was funny. He'd been the focus of ape humor more than once.

Grace turned to the mother gorilla. "Neema, where did that toy come from?"

Snow cat, Neema signed.

"I don't believe that, Neema." Grace shook her head. "Where did the toy come from?"

Neema raised her face toward the ceiling, signed *bird*.

"Neema." Grace's tone was exasperated. She jabbed her index finger at the bone in her other hand. "Where did this come from?"

Nest, Neema signed, naming the calico cat that looked like the multicolored blankets the gorillas wove into sleeping nests each night. Finn glanced around the barn. Nest was nowhere in sight.

Grace frowned. "No. Cats don't carry toys like this. Tell the truth."

Tree candy juice yogurt, the gorilla signed, bartering.

Finn groaned. "Do you think Neema even knows the answer to that question?"

"Probably. But that doesn't mean she'll tell me, even if I give her food." Grace turned back to Kanoni. "Did Snow bring you this toy?"

The baby gorilla slapped her chest in a *mine* sign, snatched the bone out of Grace's hand, and popped it into her mouth. Slapping her chest *mine mine mine* as she loped away, she fled to the lowest platform and quickly scampered up to the highest.

Finn put his fists on his hips. "We're gonna need that bone."

"I'll get it. Somehow. Eventually."

"And my sunglasses."

"I'll find them, Matt, I promise. I'm sorry."

He sighed. "It's a good thing I have another pair in the car."

Neema signed, *Give Neema tree candy good eat now tree candy*. The big gorilla swung forward on her knuckles, gazing hopefully into Grace's eyes.

"No lollipops," she said sternly.

Neema sat back and signed *yogurt juice*.

Finn was reminded of his frustration when he'd first met Neema. Questioning a gorilla was only marginally more informative than conversing with his dog Cargo. He was glad nobody at the Evansburg Police Department was witnessing this interaction. He could imagine Sergeant Greer's snide commentary about talking to apes.

His cell phone chirped from his back pants pocket, and he pulled it out. Neema abruptly switched her focus to the phone, her gaze dangerously intent. Finn tightened his grip on the phone, turned his back to the gorilla, and walked a few steps away. "Detective Finn."

"Where are you?" Greer barked, startling him.

Had he conjured the stout desk sergeant out of thin air? He wanted to answer, "It's none of your business," but diplomacy won out and he merely said, "It's my day off, Sarge. Today's Memorial Day. That's a national holiday, in case you hadn't noticed."

"Crime doesn't take holidays. And it's afternoon already, so you had half. You'll get comp time for the rest."

Finn frowned. He had nearly six weeks of comp time in his account, but never had the opportunity to take more than an hour or two. One of the many joys of working for an under-funded small-town police department. "What's so urgent?"

"Missing young woman, age seventeen, last seen in Bellingham three days ago. Her car was left at the Gorge Amphitheatre. The Sasquatch Festival there ended over two hours ago. The managers of the Amphitheatre called earlier when the car and the tent were left abandoned in the campground."

"The Gorge Amphitheatre is not even in this county."

"No shit?" Greer retorted. "Dawes and Larson are out, so we're down two detectives, as you well know. You've got the most experience, and you're available. Grant County Sheriff requests mutual assistance, and we aim to deliver."

Finn wondered when the mutual part of the quid pro quo assistance agreement between local law enforcement units was going to kick in. It was about time one of the others volunteered someone to help out the Evansburg department.

When he took the senior detective position in Evansburg, he had expected to be revered for his expertise as an experienced homicide detective from Chicago. Instead, all the police and sheriff organizations in the area seemed to view Detective Matthew Finn like a piece of department property they could borrow at will for cases that ranged from cattle rustling to drug deals. He checked his watch. "It's a quarter to three, and the Amphitheatre is about a one-hour drive from here."

"The parents were notified around one p.m.; they're on their way. The missing girl is Darcy Jeanne Ireland, from Bellingham, driving a red 2018 Ford Edge registered to her parents."

What sort of parents gave a brand new car to a teenager and then let her drive on her own from Bellingham to the Gorge? His parents had certainly never been that generous or lenient. He wouldn't have been, either, if he'd had the chance to be a father.

He hated cases involving missing people. In his experience, most missing adults had ditched their everyday lives to take off somewhere with a new companion. Most missing teenagers were runaways, hell bent on punishing their parents for reasons the parents usually didn't divulge. But then there were the few horrible, genuine cases in which people vanished because of abduction or murder or accident. And as long as the individual was listed as missing, the department and the media and the relatives and even his own conscience would hound him, because there was always the chance that minutes could mean the difference between life and death.

Greer broke into his grim thoughts. "I'm sending the particulars to your phone right now, Detective."

Rowdy ape hoots erupted behind Finn, and he turned to see Grace chase Neema across the barn, threatening to tickle the gorilla. The Sasquatch Festival was probably tame compared to this gorilla circus.

On the platform high above, Kanoni bounced and screeched in excitement at the activity, adding to the cacophony. The doorway to the exterior enclosure darkened as the big male, Gumu, peered in to see what was going on.

"Where the hell are you?" Greer snarled.

"On my way to the Gorge Amphitheatre." Finn tapped the END button.

Chapter 3

Monday

Finn knew two things about the Gorge Amphitheatre: One, with sunset views over the Columbia River and the Cascade Mountains and incredible natural acoustics, it was ranked a premier venue for outdoor concerts. Two, it was in the middle of nowhere.

He did not plan to spend an hour driving from the small town of Evansburg to Nowhere, Washington, without some guarantee of results. So he tracked down the managers of the Amphitheatre, a married couple who lived not far away, near a tiny settlement named George.

"Rex and I are on our way to the venue now," Brynne Brady, the wife, told him. "Meet you at the main gate at four p.m.?"

Finn checked his watch. "That should work."

On his drive through the Columbia Gorge canyon, he considered Kanoni's bone. Where the heck had the baby gorilla picked up that gruesome treasure?

He hoped the bone belonged to a bear. But even if it was human, it didn't necessarily indicate any kind of foul play. The land around Evansburg had been settled by farmers and loggers since the 1860s, long before public graveyards and cremation services were available. Rural families often simply buried their dead on their property. Neema and Kanoni occasionally accompanied Grace on walks through the local hills, which was a disturbing image in his mind: two gorillas out for a stroll in the woods. Still, *that*, he decided, was the most likely explanation for the finger bone; it had somehow been exposed from a dearly departed in a historic grave, and the baby gorilla had picked it up. He'd have to ask Grace if she'd found any sign of burial plots on her land or on the surrounding national forest land.

To say that the Gorge venue was out of the way was an understatement. There was not much of anything except desert scrub and wind turbines lining high bluffs along the Columbia River after he turned off Interstate 90. The area was home to petrified wood, rattlesnakes, and coyotes, and probably not much good for anything else. A bit farther east or west, with irrigation, this arid landscape became farmland for hay and potatoes. Oddly enough, in recent years, low energy prices and cool winds from the plateau had also made the nearby town of Quincy an attractive site for huge computer server farms. Finn wondered how the hi-tech set mixed with the farmers in that small community.

Brynne and Rex Brady turned out to be younger than he had imagined, probably in their late thirties at best. For some reason, he'd expected them to be aging hippies in tie-dye T-shirts. Clearly he needed to update his mental vision from the Deadheads he'd pictured.

"We just manage the location," the woman explained. Her sand-colored hair was cut short in a boyish style, and silver rings fringed the edges of her ears.

"It's more of a massive handyman position than anything having to do with music," Rex Brady told him. "The bands bring their own technicians to handle all that." He was the one with the ponytail and a ragged reddish beard.

Finn watched the wind blow a seemingly endless wave of trash across the fields. A group of men and women dressed in jail uniforms with GCDC prominently displayed across their backs chased the bits and pieces with long claw-handled sticks, then stuffed the trash into bags slung over their shoulders. "I see there's a janitorial aspect to the job," he commented.

Brynne rolled her eyes. "You have no idea. Most of the concert goers stay in the campgrounds, and believe me, they are pigs."

He was surprised to see the inmates handling sticks that could potentially be used as weapons. Not to mention that this was a privately owned venue, so he hoped they weren't doing court-mandated community service. "You have inmates pick up trash?"

"We pay 'em," Rex said. "They're cheaper than anyone else, and since they're supervised"—he jerked his chin toward a couple of armed Grant County deputies observing from the sidelines—"they actually do a great job. If I was locked up for months, I'd sure welcome the opportunity to get outdoors, wouldn't you?"

Finn couldn't argue with that. But now he'd need to talk to the deputies and the Grant County Sheriff, too. He counted the inmates—nine in all—and made a note on his pad. "Do they work during the concerts, too?"

Rex nodded. "A few of 'em. Just specific hours during daylight, hauling out trash and stuff like that."

"Do the same ones come every day?"

Brynne turned her head toward her husband, who shrugged and said, "Damned if I know. You'll have to ask the Sheriff's Department about that."

The wife looked back at Finn. "Are you asking because of

that car? You want to see it now?"

"Please."

They led him down a gravel path to the trashed campground. A Grant County Department of Corrections van and a Sheriff's Department cruiser were parked in the middle of a huge field that was labeled STANDARD CAMPING on the map they handed him. No picnic tables, no cement pads, just grass and dirt.

"Looks a little bleak," Finn observed.

"Try to imagine it with hundreds of tents and cars and thousands of people," Rex told him. "Then it's just one humongous party."

That image was even more disturbing to Finn than the current barrenness of the site. The red Ford Edge occupied a lonely position next to a tent made concave by the blowing wind. Three plastic bags were stuck on the car's windward side.

With the massive number of people involved and the wind that had blown steadily for the past few days, the general area was not likely to yield much of interest as a crime scene. But maybe the car would prove more informative. He bent at the waist to peer through a window.

"It's locked," Brynne told him.

He straightened. "You tried the doors?"

She studied her hands for a quick second, seeming embarrassed. "Sorry. Never thought about fingerprints. I'll give you mine, of course."

Rex said, "The festival ended at noon today, but sixty percent of the crowd left yesterday evening. When everyone was cleared out, we noticed the car and tent were still here. We called in the car license to the Sheriff's Department; they said they'd call the owners. If they don't show up in a day or two, the Sheriff will send someone to tow it."

Finn walked around the car. The Edge looked brand new except for a long scratch in the paint across the driver's door. From what he could see through the windows, the glove box was shut, the driver and passenger seats empty. The back seat held a tangle of clothing. Four crushed diet cola cans littered the floor.

"Why would someone just walk off without their car?" Rex pondered.

Finn shook his head. "The Grant County Sheriff's Department contacted the owners, who live in Bellingham. They claim their daughter drives it. She's seventeen. Her parents last saw her on Friday morning." He brought up the photo of the missing teen on his cell phone and held it out to the Bradys. "Darcy Jeanne Ireland."

Brynne's hand flew to her mouth. "Oh, no."

"Seventeen? Crap." Rex frowned.

Rex's reaction could have meant any number of things: crap, there's a child in danger, or crap, there shouldn't be teenagers on the loose here and there's going to be trouble.

In her driver's license photo, Darcy had long, curly black hair, a square chin, and sturdy looking shoulders. According to the accompanying information, she was five foot eight and weighed a mere 115 pounds. Finn found the weight a little hard to believe, but then the DMV didn't ask license applicants to step on a scale.

He asked the couple, "Have you seen her?"

Both shook their heads.

"But then we wouldn't have." Rex ran a finger over his bearded chin. "Like we told you, we really don't have much to do with what goes on at the concerts. Our events coordinator hires subcontractors to handle security and supplies and stuff like that, and we contract with food trucks, but all those people are on their own. We're mostly caretakers, I guess you'd say, coming in to clean up and fix anything that needs fixing." He made a face. "And believe me, a *lot* of things need fixing after Sasquatch. It's always a total mob scene."

"Sasquatch is the worst, since it runs Friday evening through Monday morning," his wife added.

It was a multiday festival? Finn gritted his teeth. That would make everything so much harder. The list of people he'd need to interview kept getting longer and longer. "I'll need the names of subcontractors, along with the names of everyone you know who was working over the course of the Sasquatch Festival."

He eyed the grounds. Only a few light poles were scattered throughout the campground, and none of them sported video cameras as far as he could tell. "No security cameras?"

Rex turned toward the huge amphitheater area. "There are a couple focused on the backstage area and on the aisles, one near the concession stand and another near the ticket sales booth. We don't have any in the campground. Privacy issues, you know."

Finn didn't know, but he supposed there could be issues with people crawling in and out of tents. As far as he was concerned, that was all the more reason to have security cameras.

"The security staff could tell you more about all that," Brynne suggested.

"Any of those folks likely to be here right now?"

"I think Vaughn's in the office," Brynne told him. "Vaughn Boylan. We're in charge of the facilities, but Vaughn's the general events coordinator, in charge of bringing it all together. Vaughn would know who worked security during the festival."

Finn wrote down the name. "I'll need to talk to Boylan, and I'll want to see whatever video is available for the last few days."

Brynne and Rex nodded in unison and then turned, presumably to lead him to this Vaughn guy. But a gray Highlander careened into their path, slamming to a stop only a few feet away, dragging a cloud of dust that rolled in their direction.

When the dust cleared, a man and woman stood in front of them, posture tense, faces taut. "Where is she?" the woman wailed, holding her curly, dark hair away from her face with fingers sporting cherry-colored nails. "Where's Darcy? She's in so much trouble . . ."

The man held out his hand toward Rex Brady. "Paul Ireland. This is my wife Andrea. Have you found her?"

"Uh . . . well," Rex stuttered. He shot Finn a hopeful look.

The parents must have driven above the speed limit if they'd come all the way from Bellingham this afternoon. Finn stepped forward and thrust out his hand. "Detective Matthew Finn. I've been assigned to this case."

"*Detective?*" The mother's hand landed on Finn's jacket sleeve. "Oh my God. What *case*? They only told us that Darcy's car was here."

"That's it," Paul Ireland said needlessly, pointing at the red Edge. "But that's not our tent."

"Then you know as much as I do at this point," Finn explained. "Nobody has seen your daughter since the festival ended at noon."

"Oh." Andrea moved her hand from his sleeve to her throat, anxiously glancing around the area as if she might spy her daughter somewhere close by.

A tumbling wad of paper smacked Finn in the leg, but the

wind whisked it away before he could grab it. Turning to the Bradys, Finn asked, "Is there someplace we can get out of this wind and sit and talk?"

The caretakers looked at each other, blinked. "Admin trailer," Rex said. "C'mon."

The Bradys led their party down a gravel path to a white single-wide trailer hidden behind a privacy fence that was vibrating in the stiff breeze. Inside the trailer was an empty desk with a nameplate—Vaughn Boylan—and a small break area filled with folding chairs and a battered round dining table. The place smelled of burned coffee.

Brynne lifted the scorched carafe from the machine on the counter and waved it at Finn. "Shall I make fresh?"

"Please." Finn slid into a chair. "We may be here awhile."

At that, Andrea Ireland glanced at her husband and crossed her arms, hugging herself as if she were afraid she might fall apart.

Paul Ireland worked as a public relations consultant. Andrea was a paralegal. They'd been at home the entire weekend, going out only for local walks and dinner at a brew pub in Bellingham on Friday evening.

"And you took that trip to the hardware store yesterday," Andrea reminded her husband.

Paul's jaw tightened. He turned from his wife to look at Finn. "Yes, I went to Lowe's on Sunday," he said in a dry tone. "We needed a new garden rake."

Andrea continued, "The kids were gone. Samuel, our son, was competing in the Ski to Sea relay as their mountain biker, so he and his buddies were busy with that. And Darcy had volunteered for an all-girls team. Not competing, but hauling gear and helping and stuff like that." She frowned. "Or so we thought. That's what she told us, anyway."

Paul slid into a chair across from Finn. "Why do I know your name? Was there some write-up on you a while ago? Some case you worked on?"

Finn didn't want to introduce the old article about his involvement with a signing gorilla into this discussion. "So the two of you were home the entire holiday weekend, until you were called today. And Darcy was staying with this girls team?"

"We—" Andrea began. The door banged open as she finished, "—thought Darcy was at Mia's house."

As they all turned toward the entry, Finn asked, "Who is Mia?"

Chapter 4

Monday

"*Our* daughter," announced the blonde who stepped inside. "Mia Valdez."

The woman was petite, no more than five two, with a delicate frame to match her small stature. The man who accompanied her was a full head taller with a square, muscular build. His hair was more silver than dark brown.

Brynne turned away from the coffeemaker toward a nearby cabinet. "I'll find two more cups."

Finn stood up to greet the couple.

The new man, presumably Mr. Valdez, ignored him and glared at the Irelands. "How could you let this happen?"

Andrea pushed to her feet. "How could *we*? Darcy told us she'd be at *your* house."

The blond woman shot back, "And Mia told us you were chaperoning both of them when they weren't at Ski to Sea."

"Ski to Sea?" Finn was perplexed why everyone was talking about this event with the weird name.

Mr. Valdez frowned at Paul Ireland. "What is our tent doing out there? How could you let Darcy drive Mia all the way here? They both still have restricted licenses."

Finn's teeth began to ache. There were *two* missing girls?

He held out his hand. "I'm Detective Matthew Finn." Gesturing to the chairs along the wall, he said, "Please pull up a seat, Mr. and Mrs. . . .?

The couple introduced themselves. Robin and Keith Valdez, also from Bellingham, sixty and sixty-three years old, according to their drivers' licenses. On reading Robin's age, Finn had to stifle an urge to do a double take. She had blue eyes and a spatter of freckles across her nose and cheeks. Her ash-blond hair was cut in a short, layered style that framed a pretty, heart-shaped face, but as he studied her more carefully, he noticed telltale wrinkles in her lips and forehead.

Keith Valdez was handsome and olive skinned with a moustache that held even more silver than his hair. "This is what happens when you give a seventeen-year-old a car," he said to Finn, shooting a scowl sideways at Paul Ireland.

"Darcy never did anything like this before she met Mia," Andrea Ireland shot back.

Robin Valdez clutched at Finn's arm. "Detective Finn," she said. "We would never let Mia have a car at such a young age. She's allowed to drive only when one of us is in the car with her."

Finn looked at the manicured fingers on his sleeve. What was with these women grabbing him, anyway? He gently slipped his arm away to pick up his pen. "Tell me about Mia."

Robin sucked in a breath, then said, "Her full name is Miracle Luisa Valdez."

Andrea jerked her chin up. "Miracle?"

Ignoring the younger woman, Robin told Finn, "She was a miracle baby. You know, an unexpected gift. But she hates to be called Miracle; she insists on Mia."

"I see."

"Coffee?" Brynne interrupted, waving the pot of dark liquid in one hand and clutching a stack of Styrofoam cups in the other. When they all nodded, she handed the cups to Paul, who stared at them for a second, then slipped one off and handed the others around the table.

Brynne poured coffee for all five of them, then placed sugar, powdered creamer, stir sticks, and napkins in the center of the table. Catching Finn's gaze, she tilted her head toward the door, and when he nodded, she slipped outside.

Removing a billfold from her purse, Robin flipped it open to a photo and held it out to Finn. "Here she is."

Finn took the billfold from her. The girl took after her mother in coloring. Her shoulder-length blond hair was carefully smoothed in the straight, flat style favored at the moment by most teen girls. Her face was heart shaped, her eyes were blue, and she had Cupid's bow lips.

"Pretty girl." He handed back the billfold.

Robin carefully deposited it back into her purse. "She is. She's our baby."

Both girls attended a private, all-girls high school north of Bellingham called the Stanton Academy. Neither set of parents had seen their girls since the previous Friday morning.

"But Mia texted me every day," Robin assured him, "telling me what a great time they were having, being part of Ski to Sea."

"Oh, God." Andrea Ireland buried her face in her hands. "Darcy did exactly the same thing."

"Ski to Sea?" Finn asked again, taking a sip of his watery coffee.

Keith Valdez nodded as if that answered the question. "The high school division. The girls are not athletes, but we thought it was nice that they were supporting a local-area team."

The story that both Mia and Darcy had told was that they planned to help out with the Ski to Sea Parade on Saturday, and then they had volunteered to assist a team that was competing on Sunday.

Ski to Sea turned out to be a relay race from Mount Baker to Bellingham Bay. Both couples made it sound like a really big deal.

"Ninety-three miles in one day," Paul told him. "I did the downhill run a couple of decades ago, and Andrea did the road bike section." He put a hand on his wife's shoulder as if to congratulate her.

Finn wondered why he'd never heard of the event, but the race seemed likely to be irrelevant now. The basic fact was that each family clearly thought their daughter was with the other girl. Which, apparently, they were. Just not anywhere close to Bellingham.

"When was the last time you heard from your daughters?"

"Mia texted on Sunday around five p.m." Robin tucked a wisp of pale hair behind one ear. "That's the day of the race, by the way. She said that their team didn't win but they were planning to have fun at the after party and then go to bed because they'd been up since dawn."

Andrea jumped in. "And Darcy texted that they'd be out of cell range most of today because they had to go back along the race route and pick everything up, but they'd be home tonight."

Robin stared at the other woman. "Mia sent the same message."

"So none of you were worried when your daughters didn't show up for a few days," Finn summarized.

Realizing they'd been played, all four parents now wore miserable expressions.

That was both the blessing and the curse of cell phones, Finn thought. Unless you continually tracked them on GPS, you never knew where the callers actually were. Texting was even worse, because you didn't even have a voice to analyze. Anyone could text from someone else's cell.

Both fathers studied their wives. The men were probably thinking that things would have gone differently if they'd been in charge, but they were smart enough to keep their mouths shut under the circumstances.

All four adults claimed they'd never heard of the Sasquatch Festival.

Finn took down the names and numbers of the girls' friends, praying he was not on the verge of discovering there were more than two missing teens. "Do Darcy and Mia have boyfriends?"

The Irelands supplied the name of Sean Torqhart for Darcy's love interest. Andrea obviously felt compelled to add, "He's a nice boy who lives in our neighborhood, same age as Darcy. His family goes to our church. I know he didn't have anything to do with this. I saw him yesterday out mowing the lawn."

"I'll still need his number," Finn said. "Darcy might have told him about her plans."

"Mia's only been out on a few dates. She doesn't have a boyfriend," Robin Valdez assured Finn.

Blocked from Robin's view, Andrea Ireland rolled her eyes. Finn made a mental note to separate the sets of parents and ask about the other family's daughter.

He ushered the parents back to the campsite. While they'd been inside the trailer, the trash strewn over the site had been captured and stowed somewhere; the prisoners and their van and guards were gone. Only the flattened grass and the lone tent testified to the campers who had been here for the festival. From what Finn could see from the opening, the tent appeared to contain only two sleeping bags and pillows, a flashlight, and a used tissue. He pulled on latex gloves before taking the car key Paul held out. He asked the parents to stand back, and together they did a visual inspection of the car, the mothers identifying various items of clothing as belonging to their daughters. Finn separated them into two piles on the back seat.

"Do the girls have purses?" he asked over his shoulder.

"Mia has a couple, but she hardly ever uses them," Robin told him. "She has a little black leather backpack she uses instead."

"Darcy, too," Andrea said. "Those backpacks are all the rage right now. Just big enough for a comb and lipstick and a bottle of water. They usually carry their cell phones in their back pockets."

The glove compartment held the car registration and insurance forms, a hairbrush and lip gloss, and two cell phone cords. He showed them to the parents. Glancing around, he noticed a lack of electrical outlets in the immediate camp area. "Probably not much opportunity to recharge a phone out here."

"Shoot." Andrea moaned. "No wonder Darcy's not answering her phone. It's probably dead."

Robin nodded, her lips grimly pressed together.

Backing out of the car, Finn straightened. "Do the girls have credit cards?"

"Debit cards." That came from Paul Ireland. "It's pretty standard to give teens a pre-loaded debit card these days."

"I'll need those account numbers." Finn looked at both men.

"I can just tap into Mia's and show you. It's connected to our account." Keith Valdez turned in place, studying the surrounding area. "Maybe they went hiking?"

Finn rubbed his chin. "I'm not aware of any hiking trails around here, but I will check." It was a worrisome thought, that the girls could be wandering in the surrounding countryside. Then again, that was a more optimistic scenario than other possibilities that were snaking through his imagination.

"Where do you think they are?" the men demanded from Finn.

"No clue yet," he murmured, blinking into the sun that was already descending toward the mountains to the west. "Maybe they met some friends and took off with them?" His stomach growled, and he realized that he hadn't eaten since breakfast. He waved his notebook at the foursome. "I have all your information. I think we're done for today."

"What?" Robin Valdez yelped. "We need search parties now!"

For once all the parents were in agreement, nodding enthusiastically.

Finn promised, "I'll get the girls' descriptions and driver's-license photos into the police networks tonight as soon as I get back to the station. All local law enforcement will be on the lookout for Mia and Darcy. And I'll work on getting Civil Air Patrol volunteers in the air tomorrow."

"Why not tonight?" Paul Ireland demanded. "We need a ground search, too—immediately!"

Resisting the urge to heave an exasperated sigh, Finn told them, "You might notice that this is a very rural area. None of the local law enforcement agencies have much in the way of resources." Hell, their radios didn't even work in many locations. But these parents were desperate. "I promise I'll muster what I can, and I'll get back to you as soon as I have any news to share."

"And you'll send out an Amber Alert right away?" Andrea asked.

Finn narrowly managed to suppress an eye roll. The instant anyone went missing these days, everyone requested an Amber

Alert. It was nearly as bad as the CSI effect, with everyone expecting instantaneous DNA results and fingerprint matches. He explained, "We can only issue Amber Alerts when we have a reasonable suspicion of a specific individual the missing child is likely to be with or a description of the vehicle the child is likely to be traveling in."

All four parents stared at him, their expressions wavering between anger and frustration.

He added, "You can imagine the resulting phone calls if we issued Amber Alerts every time anyone went missing."

He knew they were hoping for more. More sympathy. More action. Welcome to the country, he wanted to tell them. Instead, he told them about hotels in Quincy. "Those are the closest accommodations. Or if you want to return home, I promise to keep you informed."

Andrea Ireland shook her head and folded her arms across her chest. "No way are we going back to Bellingham while our daughter is missing."

Throwing an arm around his wife's shoulders, Keith Valdez added, "The same for us."

Paul Ireland, keys in hand, reached for the door of the Ford Edge. Finn blocked him. "Sorry, I can't let you take the car. Or the tent." He looked at each parent in turn. "Our team needs to inspect them tomorrow."

"You mean a crime scene team," Keith Valdez stated bluntly.

Finn swallowed. The crime scene "team" was one guy in his county, and he didn't know if Grant County had one at all. If he were still in Chicago, he'd be able to muster experienced evidence collection techs within an hour, but here, it could take days. He still couldn't believe he'd so blindly followed his ex to this backwater.

Robin Valdez began to cry. "Mia's our only child," she choked out between sobs. "She's all we've got."

The words seemed overly dramatic, but the woman's distress was real. "I promise we will do everything we can to find Mia," he told her. "It's entirely possible the girls caught a ride with someone to continue the party elsewhere."

"Oh, God!" Robin Valdez flattened a hand against her chest.

The Irelands exchanged anxious glances.

Clearly, partying elsewhere was not a comforting suggestion. Finn was afraid to offer another possibility. "Please, all of you." He met each parent's gaze, glancing from one to the next. "Make some notes on the girls' associates and get me their contact information. Write down anything Mia and Darcy might have told you, or that you might have seen or suspected. You never know what might be useful. And meet me back here at ten tomorrow morning."

Keith touched his wife's shoulder. "Robin and I will have some flyers made up right away so people will know the girls are missing."

"That's an excellent idea," Finn told them, although he had no idea if they'd find a copy shop open in Quincy.

Glad to have a mission, the Valdezes left first.

Finn stopped Andrea Ireland before she got into her car. "Mrs. Ireland, I couldn't help noticing that you looked like you wanted to say something when Mrs. Valdez was saying Mia had no boyfriend."

"Well, I probably shouldn't talk." Her eyes darted toward her husband and then back to Finn. "As far as I know, from what I've seen and what Darcy has told me, Mia doesn't have a boyfriend, but she's looking for one." Andrea leaned closer. "In other words, Detective Finn, that girl is hot to trot, if you know what I mean."

"Okay." Finn didn't know what else to say to that comment.

He waited until the Irelands drove away, then found the Bradys sitting in folding chairs in front of the closed concession stand. "Do you keep records of who reserves which campsites during festivals?"

"Of course," Brynne said. "Well, not us, but whoever was in charge of reservations for the site. Vaughn Boylan would know."

"I never caught a glimpse of Boylan this afternoon."

Rex shrugged. "I guess Vaughn didn't come in today after all. It was a *very* long weekend, and the next concert isn't for two weeks."

"Give me Boylan's phone number. I'll set up an appointment." Finn jotted down the number on his notepad. "Don't touch the car or the tent. We'll do a more thorough inspection tomorrow."

Finn's stomach growled again. Rounding up a deputy to camp here on such short notice seemed unlikely, and anything could happen if the site was left unguarded. "Can you have someone stay here overnight in case the girls turn up?"

Rex and Brynne studied each other for a long moment, seemingly annoyed at his request.

"Two teenage girls are missing from your campground," he reminded them.

Rex sighed. "Hon, can you go home and bring the camper?" Turning back to Finn, he explained, "We have one of those teardrop trailers. I'll park it near that car and sleep in the trailer overnight." He glanced at his wife. "Don't forget a comforter and pillow. And our good flashlight. And the shotgun." He flashed a sideways glance at Finn. "Just in case."

Finn nodded. "Good idea. Make sure your cell phone is on, and call me if anything happens."

Brynne told her husband, "This is too creepy. I'm staying,

too. I'll bring some supper when I come back." She turned away.

Rex stuck his hands in his pants pockets and rocked back on his heels. "I just flashed on where I know your name. Aren't you that gorilla guy?"

"Unless the girls show up overnight, I'll talk to you tomorrow. Thank you for your help." Pushing his notebook and pen into his jacket pocket, Finn headed for his car before Rex could ask about gorillas again.

Chapter 5

Monday

Some *thing* was strolling across her right cheek. Darcy Ireland woke with a start, frantically brushing the thing away with her fingers, but it came right back, now tickling her chin. She blinked hard. All she could see was green. Tall grass curved over her, brushing her face as if checking to see if she was still alive. Pushing the grass away with both arms, she sat up.

The world lurched violently. She closed her eyes to make it settle down again, and raised her hands to feel her scalp, checking for a lump on her head to explain this concussion. Her fingertips identified clumps of dirt and shreds of grass, but no bump. *Contusion.* It had been a vocabulary word on the English final only a week ago.

Memory slowly came back. The motorcycle guys. Comet. The picnic. The sunset. The beer had tasted funny. What the hell was in that beer?

Suddenly remembering lectures on date-rape drugs, Darcy fingered her jeans. The snap was undone, but her zipper was still pulled up. She didn't *feel* like she'd been raped. She wasn't a virgin, but she would know if anything had happened down there, wouldn't she?

A motorcycle track looped away from her feet and

disappeared into the grass. She stood up, and saw nothing but waving grass for at least a half mile in every direction. Barren hills bordered the hayfield. She brushed her hand over her back pockets and then over the pockets in her denim jacket, turning in a slow circle and surveying the ground around her feet. Nothing but dirt and grass. The motion made her feel like she might throw up.

Damn Comet. He'd dumped her in a hayfield and taken off. With her backpack and cell phone.

The sun was high overhead. Her phone would have been able to tell her the time, the direction she was facing. Why was this happening to her? Tears pooled in her eyes, but she angrily wiped them away. There wasn't time for self-pity. Damn Comet. Damn Mia for wanting an adventure. They were both going to be in such trouble.

She cupped her hands around her mouth. "Mia!"

Her only answer was the wind that rippled the thigh-high grass around her. "Mia!"

She'd been away from the campground for a whole night. She was ravenous. And so thirsty. The Sasquatch Festival was probably already over. Would the car get towed? Oh, jeez. She'd be grounded for a year. She'd never hear the end of this. And Mia's parents would be even more freaked than hers.

"Mia!" She stared at the motorcycle track ripped through the field. One track. One motorcycle. Her stomach clenched. What had happened to the other motorcycle? Where was Mia?

Swallowing her panic, Darcy followed the track, shoving her way through the sea of waving grass. This trail had to lead to a road eventually.

It was harder working her way through the tall grass than she would have imagined, and she was amazed that Comet had been able to plow through all this hay on a bike. It swirled around her and then arched back, so thick that most of the time she couldn't even see her feet. The sun was over the hill now, and she missed her sunglasses, which Comet had probably stolen along with her phone. Plus, she really needed sunscreen. She was going to be deep-fried by the time she got back to her car.

She put her hands to her face. Her cheeks were hot and sore. Shit, she was already deep-fried. How long had she been lying there? How much drug had been in that beer?

Her throat was so dry it felt like it might crack. Now she understood why they called those shoe flaps tongues, because her own tongue felt like it was made out of slick nylon like the ones in the dusty running shoes on her feet. Wouldn't it be nice if there was a convenient drinking fountain at the edge of the field? Didn't farmers have to provide water for their field crews? They usually had water stations for the fruit pickers at the farms she'd visited in Whatcom County.

Oh, yeah. No pickers here. No fruit. Just an ocean of grass.

A loud buzz startled her. Her cell phone? Coming from the ground, but she couldn't tell exactly where. It was angry-sounding, a continuous buzz-rattle, didn't really sound like a cell phone. Sounded more like . . .

A chill cascaded from the crown of her head to her toes as she remembered that, unlike her home west of the Cascades, eastern Washington had rattlesnakes.

Chapter 6

Monday

Mia was lying in a strange bed, her face pressed into a soft pillow. Her head throbbed, and her mouth felt like mice had made a nest near her tonsils. She pushed herself to a sitting position, and ran her dry tongue around her mouth, nausea swimming through her gut. A quilt slid off her shoulders and pooled around her feet. No, not a *bed*, really, just two mattresses stacked up.

The room she was in was small, enclosed by rough wooden walls. The door was closed. What time was it? Where was she? Inside a shed, or maybe a barn? The light was dim in here. A bulb on the ceiling was enclosed in a metal cage contraption, but the light wasn't on. Sunlight leaked in through a slender crack in the gray-brown wall, and one knothole near the ceiling streamed a shaft of brightness, a miniature spotlight that illuminated the far corner.

So it was daytime. Crap, they'd missed the concerts last night?

This was beyond embarrassing. Was she such a baby that a couple of beers knocked her out? Had they affected Darcy like that? They had to get on the road. It was almost a four-hour drive back to Bellingham.

Where was everyone, anyway? She studied herself, running

her hands over her jeans and T-shirt. Her jacket was laid across the foot of the mattress. Her socks were still on, but her shoes rested neatly, side-by-side, next to the bed.

She slid her feet to the floor, which was, surprisingly, only packed dirt. Where the hell was she? This was a weird guest room—there was only the frameless bed, made up with pink sheets and a flowered comforter, and a small wooden table next to it. A granola bar and a bottle of water lay on top of the nightstand, if that was what it was intended to be, along with a single pink rose in a beer bottle.

Across the room was a big plastic paint bucket, upended, with a roll of toilet paper on top. She hoped that didn't indicate the use planned for that bucket. The public toilets at the campground had been gross enough.

Mia stood up and padded to the door, her hands held out in front of her in the dim light, fighting dizziness that threatened to make the walls undulate around her. She flipped the light switch near the door. Nothing happened. Next, she tried the doorknob. Locked. She searched for a button to release the lock. There was none. Using both hands, she twisted the knob with all her strength, rattled the door again.

The door was locked from the outside. A stab of alarm tweaked her gut. It was a metal door, the kind her dad called a security door.

She searched the walls. There was no other light switch in the room. Just the one that didn't work.

Had Darcy left her here, locked in, in the dark?

Was that a footstep she heard outside? "Hey!" she yelled. "I'm awake. Come let me out!"

There was no answer. She clenched her hand into a fist, pounded three times. "Hey! I really have to pee! Open the door!"

Holding her breath, she listened for a moment. What was

that creaking noise? It might have been only the wind, because a puff of air whistled in through the knothole at the same time. "Darcy?"

She remembered now that Darcy had begged to go back to the Gorge. That had been irritating. Why did she want to cut short the first real adventure Mia had ever been on? The wind in her hair, her arms around the cute guy, racing down the highway on a motorcycle like a scene out of that old hippie movie, *Easy Rider*.

Born to be wild . . .

What was her guy's name? Rusty? No, Dusty, that was it. Dusty and—what was the name of Darcy's guy?—something weird like Commie, no, Comet—had invited them on a picnic. A bike ride, food, beer. The guys were both clearly older than high school, but that was okay; everyone knew that girls matured faster than boys, and she wanted a man, not one of the pimply boys her parents were always trying to warn her away from.

Dusty was a handsome dude in a clean-cut-farm-boy sort of way. He looked like a guy she could lose her cherry to and not pick up some disease. And best of all, nobody at school knew him. It was so mortifying to still be a virgin at seventeen. She was pretty sure she was the last virgin in Stanton Academy.

Mia had instantly been ready to hop on the back of Dusty's motorcycle, but Darcy hadn't been sure it was a good idea. Probably thinking of Sean, the neighbor boy she was hooking up with. He was still a kid. Mia was pretty sure Sean had never done anything interesting. And probably never would.

But there'd been no point in worrying about Sean. Sean wasn't at Sasquatch. And those two boys who bought them snacks had taken off, too.

There were just these two smiling motorcycle riders

standing in front of them, promising them a good time.

"We'll be gentlemen," Comet had promised, holding up his arms in an "I'm unarmed" gesture.

That clinched the deal. Most boys they hung out with probably didn't even know the word *gentlemen*.

The ridge where the bikers had taken them was sweet, overlooking the valley and the hills beyond that rolled out as far as you could see, with fields of gold and green and brown like a patchwork quilt. So different from Bellingham, where basically all you saw was trees and mountains and once in a while, water and the San Juan Islands out to the west.

They'd watched the sun go down as they ate cold fried chicken out of a box and sipped those beers. Hers hadn't tasted as good she expected, sort of sour and bitter at the same time, but it was her first and everyone said beer was an acquired taste. Plus, there were hundreds of kinds of beer, and you had to try a lot to find the kind you liked. Bellingham was like the brewpub capital of the United States.

Then Darcy had wanted to go back to the festival, telling Comet, "We want to hear the last concert, and we have to get up early in the morning and drive back home."

Mia wasn't really ready to go, but Darcy had the car keys, and she probably wouldn't think twice about leaving Mia at the Gorge. "Yeah," she had agreed, "We'll get busted if we're not back by dinnertime tomorrow."

"Sure thing. It's not like we planned to keep you prisoner or anything." Dusty had smiled at them and then shot a look at the other guy. "You'll see how sweet it is to ride under the stars out here in the country; you'll love it."

"It's like flying," Comet added.

Mia flashed back on her brother Jared riding his motorcycle. That was exactly what he had said: "At night, it's just like flying."

At five years old, she'd had a vision of Superman flying through the sky under star-spangled heavens, but of course Jared had meant riding his bike at night. Probably speeding way too fast down some lonely highway. She liked to imagine Jared that way, riding free and happy.

It wasn't really a memory, because she'd never actually seen her oldest brother take his bike out after dark, but that mental picture of him was so much better than the real memory that was seared into her brain. When she thought of her sister Julie, she liked to imagine her riding a palomino horse bareback through a field of flowers, the blond mane of the horse and her sister's dark hair floating in the breeze. Justin was a bit harder to envision, but she imagined him sailing on a yacht somewhere. He'd always been quiet, but he loved the water.

After the beer and the chicken were gone and the sun had set behind the Cascades, Mia and Darcy—Sunshine and Blackbird—had mounted up again behind Dusty and Comet. On the way back to the Gorge Amphitheatre, Mia had started to feel so sick that she was afraid she'd spew down the collar of Dusty's leather jacket, which would be absolutely mortifying. The world was spinning. So she'd shut her eyes, held on tight, and put her cheek against Dusty's shoulder. She didn't remember seeing the stars.

Actually, now that she examined her memory, she didn't remember anything after closing her eyes on the back of that bike.

"Darcy?" she yelled again. "Dusty? Comet?"

As she pounded again on the door with her fist, dust shimmered down from the ceiling above. "This is *so* not funny!"

Chapter 7

Monday

Where was the rattler? Darcy could see her feet but not more than an inch in any direction around them. She wanted to run, but which way? If she tried to push away the grass with her hands, the snake would bite her for sure. So she stood, paralyzed, holding her breath, her heart pounding, anticipating the deadly sting of fangs piercing her leg at any second. She had dressed in her favorite jeans for the motorcycle ride, but they were skin tight, practically an invitation to an angry snake. Darcy Ireland was going to die alone in this field in the middle of nowhere. Her body would swell up and turn black and putrid like a rotten potato, and they wouldn't even be able to have an open casket at her funeral. If they ever found her at all.

The buzzing stopped. Which was almost worse than before, because now all she could hear was the galloping rush of blood in her head. Then she heard the faintest of rustling noises, moving away. She waited until she couldn't hear anything but the wind, then she sucked in a giant breath and screamed as she ran down the motorcycle track as fast as the tall clutching grass would let her.

Finally reaching the edge of the field, she stood, breathing hard, trying to let her nerves settle. He head ached, and her stomach was doing somersaults. Her toes were on a gravel road that stretched endlessly in both directions. Which way should she walk? Why wasn't there a person or a house in sight? A tractor, some sign of human activity? There was only a long-armed watering machine on giant wheels. Would it have water? But it was at least half a mile away, and if that reddish color was rust, the contraption might not have been used in a decade.

The motorcycle track curved out of the hayfield off to the right, which, by her reckoning, was east. Or maybe south? If only she had her phone to point her in the right direction. Or better yet, to call a Lyft or Uber. Which probably didn't exist in Hay Land, not to mention she probably couldn't get any bars here, so she probably couldn't call for help even if she'd had the phone.

This made the third phone she'd lost this year. How was she going to explain that to her parents? She rubbed her forehead, and then started to laugh. Really, worrying about the dang phone? What a doofus. A lost Android was the least of her problems right now.

She'd follow Comet's track. As near as she could tell from the marks where the darker field dirt met the gravel, the motorcycle had gone back in the same direction it had come from. She walked down the middle of the road in case more snakes were lurking in the grass near the edges, scuffing her running shoes in the gravel. If she saw a decent-size rock, she intended to pick that up. In case Comet came zooming back down this road, she wanted to have something in hand to hit him with.

Was Mia traipsing down some other farm road right now, too? No, she'd probably already talked Dusty into taking her back to the campground and had even gotten him to buy her a drink and ice cream. Mia was like that—pretty and persuasive. Too persuasive. And Darcy had fallen for the Valdez charm again. "You have a car! Sasquatch Festival—I'll pay for both of us."

Look how *that* had worked out.

It seemed like it took hours of walking before Darcy reached another road. But still it was gravel, and obviously not a well-traveled route. Not a car in sight. And no clue here which way led to anywhere, either.

Par for the course, as they said. Where did that stupid expression come from? Sounded like something to do with golf, maybe. But who cared, anyway? She needed her phone to keep her brain from veering off on lame thoughts like that. Turning right, she kept walking, moving her wooden tongue around in her mouth to work up a little saliva.

Was that the sound of a car coming up behind her? She turned, shaded her eyes with her hand. Yes! A dark-colored pickup was coming her way. She moved to the side of the road and stuck out her thumb. As the truck neared, the driver veered to the opposite side of the road.

Darcy frantically waved her arms. "Hey!"

The pickup roared right on by, the black dog in the bed barking and snarling at her, showing his teeth as truck passed, leaving a cloud of dust in its wake.

"No!" she screamed, coughing. Then she held up her middle finger. "Fuck you!"

Those words rarely came out of her mouth, and certainly never at that volume, but if any situation deserved a good F-U, this was it. She coughed in the dust for another minute and then started to trudge down the road again.

It was at least another half hour before a second pickup

came by, this one an ancient turquoise truck heaped with bales of hay. Darcy stepped into the road, jumping up and down, waving her arms.

Mercifully, the truck stopped. A plump woman with graying brown hair rolled down the window and then leaned toward the opening. Two brown paper bags rested beside her on the passenger seat, a plastic package of hotdog buns spilling out of one. "Where you off to, darlin'?"

"The Gorge, where the Sasquatch Festival is."

A puzzled expression took possession of the woman's face.

Maybe nobody here called it the Gorge. "You know, the Amphitheatre."

That got through. "Oh, way down by *George*." She shook her head. "Sorry, hon, I'm going the opposite direction. You'll have better luck if you walk on the other side." She jerked a thumb back behind her.

"But where—"

"Well, I've got to get these groceries home." She tipped her head toward the paper sacks. "Good luck, honey!" The woman stepped on the gas, pulled around Darcy, and took off down the road.

"Shit!" Darcy pounded her fists on her thighs. "Shit! Double fuck!"

What did the woman mean by "way down by George"? Was the Amphitheatre ten miles away? Hundreds of miles away? And did that backward thumb jerk mean that Darcy was walking the wrong way? Had she just walked for half a freakin' day in the wrong direction?

"Shit, shit, shit! I hate this place!" she yelled. "I hate you people! You deserve rattlesnakes!" Then her throat practically cracked open, and she bent over, coughing. When she was finally able to breathe again, she straightened, crossed over to the other side of the road, and started walking back in the direction from which she'd come.

A little ways down the road there was a damp spot by the side, bordering another giant field of the damn hay. A clump of green plants were clustered in the wet soil. She didn't know what they were, but she plucked a few of the soft green leaves, wadded them up, and pushed them into her mouth. At least they were moist.

She wondered how many steps she could walk in an hour. She'd always made fun of her parents, wearing their clunky watches, when everyone just checked their cells. Now she wished she had one of those handy things on her wrist. A Fitbit. Anything.

Was it her imagination, or was the sky getting darker over there behind the hills? Was the sun *setting*? No, that couldn't be right. It couldn't be that late, could it? It seemed like hours before another vehicle came humming down the blacktop. It was going the other direction, but it slowed. A monster truck this time with a double row of seats, jacked up on giant wheels, radio blasting, coated with mud. The two windows facing her slid down, and a puff of smoke rolled out. Weed.

There were at least four boys inside. They appeared to be about her age or maybe a little older.

"Baby, baby!" The driver waved a beer at her. "Where are you going all by yourself?"

The guy in the back made a smooching gesture with his lips, then stuck his tongue out and waggled it. Disgusting.

"Don't you want to come with us?" The driver slugged down the rest of his beer, crumpled the can in his fist, and then dropped it to the ground.

"I need to get back to the Amphitheatre," she croaked. "You know, down by George."

"Wrong direction," the driver told her.

"Do you mean I'm walking in the wrong direction, or you don't want to take me there?"

Another face appeared over the driver's shoulder. "Why you want to go there? You'll have a better time with us."

The driver opened his door and slid out onto the road. So did the guy behind him. Both wore cowboy boots, something she'd didn't often see in Bellingham. The driver jerked a thumb up behind him, indicating the back seat. "C'mon, babe, we got space. Hop in."

"I need to go to George," Darcy insisted.

"I know what you need." The guy from the back seat grabbed his crotch. And then he made a kissing noise and took a step toward Darcy.

She bolted down the road. Behind her the doors slammed, and then she heard the truck turn and roar in her direction. She leapt over the ditch at the side of the road, and launched herself between two strands of barbed wire fence, catching her jacket on the bottom one. After what seemed like an eternity, she ripped the fabric away and dove into the tall vegetation, crawling as fast as she could away from the road, her breath snagging on her tonsils as her gaze flitted from side to side. *Please God no snakes shit, shit, shit.*

The radio blasted from the road through a commercial about tires and then a whole song, something about a girl "shaking it." The greenery she was tunneling through was not hay this time. The plants didn't look like anything she'd seen in grocery stores. She was grateful that this crop had rows and had more leaves on top than down toward the roots. Better for hiding and better for watching out for those damn snakes.

Darcy could catch only snatches of conversation from the boys on the road.

"See her?" one yelled.

She stopped crawling and flattened her body against the ground, praying she was far enough away.

Something about one of them going first.

A lot of F-bombs.

Just as the "Shaking It" song ended, one finally said, "Fuck it."

Doors slammed, and the monster truck roared away.

Was this happening to Mia? Darcy had a vision of her tiny blond friend running from a gang of redneck boys. She'd be screaming, and then she'd trip, and they'd be on her like a pack of hyenas, just like those boys from the monster truck would have been on Darcy if they could have caught her.

Darcy was a track star. Mia wasn't. Had she learned enough karate in her secret lessons to defend herself? Could any girl defend herself against a whole pack of boys?

Had a gang of rednecks caught Mia? Was her friend already dead?

Would she be next?

Darcy pressed her face to the ground and cried.

Chapter 8

Monday

Mia was asleep again when a noise woke her up. The door swung inward. A bright light blinded her and she put a hand up in front of her eyes. The light shifted away. Dusty stepped in, carrying a paper bag and a small cooler under one arm and a metal flashlight in his other hand. He gave her a big smile as he bumped the door shut with his hip.

"Hi, darlin'." After setting the flashlight and the bag down on the makeshift nightstand, he perched on the edge of the bed and stroked her arm. "Feeling better?"

She sat up. "What the hell, Dusty? Why am I locked in here? What time is it?"

Running her fingers through her tangled hair, she realized she didn't even have a comb. And she'd had to pee so badly she'd used the stupid bucket, but she wasn't going to point that out. "Where's my backpack and my cell phone?"

He pushed a wisp of hair from her brow. "You were pretty out of it. I just wanted to keep you safe. And I had to get to work. But hey, I brought dinner." He gestured toward the paper bag. "Burgers and fries."

They did smell wonderful, and she was starving. She felt like she hadn't eaten for days. Saliva pooled in her mouth as he ripped open the bag, spread it across the bed to use as a plate. He handed her a foil-wrapped burger and a grease-stained envelope of fries.

"Okay, that's great," she said. "But after we eat, you've got to take me back. And where's Darcy?"

"Darcy's fine."

Naturally, the beer hadn't hit Darcy like it did her. That figured. Darcy was always lording things like that over Mia. Being the first to smoke a joint, describing the hot sex she had with Sean, having her own car. It was mortifying.

Mia unwrapped her cheeseburger and bit into it, then grabbed a fry. "Is there ketchup?"

He handed her a packet, and she ripped it open and drizzled it across her fries.

"Slow down, darlin'." He nudged the cooler closer with his foot, bent, and opened it, came up with two beers in his hand. "I brought brews, too."

After setting one bottle on the nightstand, he twisted the top from the other and held the bottle out to her.

She stared at the label. Some brand she'd never heard of, with a long scratch through the paper label. She licked her lips uncertainly. "Oh, I don't know, Dusty. I'm not sure I like this kind of beer. That one I drank last night really gave me a headache." Or maybe even a hangover. Did anyone get hung over from one beer?

"This is a different brand than we had before. And it's all we've got." He waggled the bottle in front of her. "Hair of the dog that bit you, my dad used to say."

That was a reference to drinking more alcohol to fix a hangover, she knew. She took the bottle from him. "Maybe just a sip."

It didn't taste any better than the one she drank last night, but it was cold and it was liquid and made the fries and burger slide down easier. After a big swallow, she put the bottle on the nightstand next to his. "Is this your house, Dusty?"

He chuckled and half choked on a bite of burger. "You think I live in a house with a dirt floor? This is my grandpa's old barn. This was the tack room, where all the bridles and saddles and stuff like that were stored. I used to sleep here sometimes. I fixed it up some for you. I figured you wouldn't want anyone to see you . . ." He hesitated, picked up his beer, and twisted the cap off, grinning as he turned back to her. "I mean, well, the way you were. Really out of it."

She felt her cheeks flush. "Thanks for looking out for me." To cover her embarrassment, she quickly finished off her burger, snagged another fry, and gulped down three swallows of beer. Dusty was down to a couple of bites, too. "We really need to hit the road, Dusty."

"Soon, darlin'." He chewed and downed half his beer in one long gulp, then wadded up the greasy papers on the bed and moved them to the nightstand. Leaning forward, he gently stroked her chin. "You're so beautiful, Mia." His breath smelled of beer as his lips brushed her cheek. "We're going to be great together. Just one little kiss, okay?"

His lips crushed into hers. She knew she should protest, but the beer was already starting to make her woozy.

He pressed her back into the pillow, one hand gently rubbing her breast. She stared at his face, noticing for the first time that he had a hole in one earlobe where an earring should have been. Why wasn't he wearing one now? He said he had been working. Maybe his boss didn't like it. Closing her eyes, she hoped he would be gentle. After all, this was what she had wanted, wasn't it? She'd just get it over with, and afterward he'd surely take her back to the campground. She'd never have to see him again, but she'd know what all the sex talk was about.

The hand on her breast slipped inside her shirt. Wasn't she supposed to feel something? If not love, then at least lust? Did she really want this? All she could think about was how much trouble she was going to be in if her parents found out she and Darcy had come down here. And if Darcy left her behind? She couldn't even imagine that.

His tongue wormed its way into her mouth, and his fingers rubbed across her nipple. She didn't enjoy either sensation. Did she even *like* this guy? She didn't even know his last name. And it didn't seem like he intended to use a condom, either.

As he moved his hand down and popped open the snap on her jeans, panic surged up from her gut, filling her chest. Twisting her head to the side, she said, "No, Dusty! I don't want—"

"Ah, honey, don't be like that." He slipped his fingers around her chin, tried to pull her face back under his.

Those fingers hurt. How dare he treat her like that? "No! I said no!"

He put a knee on either side of her hips and reached for her zipper. "You be sweet to me, Darcy, and I'll be sweet to you."

"No! You have to *stop*!"

At age fifteen, she'd grown to be only five feet tall. The last two years hadn't added even a fraction of an inch. Nice boys saw her as some sort of cute blond pet, and the sleazebags regarded her as easy prey. She was determined not to be anyone's toy poodle, and certainly not any boy's prey. That was why when she'd discovered that Toshi, the Japanese boy she was tutoring, was a black belt, she'd made a deal to swap karate sessions for English lessons.

Dusty wasn't stopping. He ground his lips painfully into

hers, and she could feel his hard-on digging into her abdomen.

Toshi had taught her to fight back. Closing her fist, she whacked Dusty on the side of his head. When he rose to his knees, rearing back in shock, she brought her knee up between his legs as hard as she could.

His cry of pain was choked off as he tumbled sideways onto the floor, both hands clutched around his crotch. He rolled back and forth in the dirt, groaning.

She should run for the door. Basic rule of self-defense: get up and prepare for the next move! But her arms and legs felt like they were made of concrete. Just rolling to her side seemed nearly impossible, and she couldn't shift her weight to move her feet to the floor.

After a few terrifying moments of swearing and moaning, Dusty finally rose to his knees beside the bed. Spittle splattered her face as he snarled, "You're gonna be so sorry you did that."

What was wrong with her? She was paralyzed. What was she going to do when he crawled back on top of her?

He swayed to his feet, grabbed the flashlight and the cooler, and then staggered, bent over like an old man, to the door. Shining the light viciously into her eyes, he growled, "*So* damn sorry . . ."

Behind him, the door lock snapped into place like an exclamation point. With the flashlight gone, the room was lit only by the fading streaks of sunlight that pierced the walls.

What had she done? Why couldn't she move? All she could do was stare at the ceiling as the room grew pitch black. She could practically hear her mother now.

"Miracle Luisa Valdez." How she hated that name; who wanted to be called *Miracle*? "You realize that riding off on a motorcycle with a perfect stranger is not only foolish, but also incredibly dangerous."

Dangerous. That's what her parents always said about practically everything. Although sometimes they substituted the word *"sketchy"* if they thought she was proposing something that might *eventually* turn dangerous. Whatever. The upshot of it all was that she never got to do anything cool.

"You're our precious jewel," her mom always told her. "Our little Miracle." Yeah, she was *precious* all right, a jewel locked in a safety deposit box inside some bank vault. What good was being alive if you didn't get to *live*?

Jared, Justin, and Julie would be old now, probably with kids of their own, but in her imagination they were always joyful teenagers. Just like in the photos around the house, all proudly displayed in her mom's artsy hand-crafted frames. Her sibs had been stars. Photos of Jared in his track uniform, proudly holding ribbons for races he'd won, decorated the mantel in the living room. In the hallway, Justin marched in his band uniform or played his trumpet in a brass ensemble. The dining room wall belonged to Julie in all her dance costumes, tapping in a spangled pink number, throwing long ribbon wands in the air while gracefully twirling, and even balancing on her toes in a pale lilac tutu. Always smiling, all three of her sibs, in those pictures.

Would they be proud of their baby sister now?

No way.

Her memory of the crash was more audio than video, of all her sibs screaming so loud, over and over, as the car flipped around and around. Just like the walls were doing now. She closed her eyes so she wouldn't have to watch the nauseating movement.

After the screaming and the horrific screech of metal, there'd been only the sounds of her own cries. Until finally there were sirens and then so many people talking at her. She couldn't see anything but red, and her left arm had hurt so bad. She still had a big scar between her elbow and shoulder where the bone had come through the skin, and a little one near her hairline above her right eyebrow. Any time she doubted the nightmare had actually happened, she looked at those scars to remind herself it had all been too real.

Jared. Justin. Julie. Just . . . gone. Nothing left but pictures. And memories. She'd heard all the stories so many times that she felt like she remembered all the birthday parties and awards and adventures, when for most of them, she hadn't even been born.

She was so . . . nothing . . . by comparison. How had she made it to seventeen without ever accomplishing anything? It was no wonder there was only one photo in the house of her beyond the age of five, last year's school picture, sitting on the table in the entry hall, in a cheap, gold-toned frame from a discount store.

Stupid was not a strong enough word for what she'd done, riding off with a stranger. She should have died instead of her sibs.

Now, maybe she would.

Chapter 9

Monday

During his drive back to Evansburg, Finn's hands-free phone system chimed. He pressed the button on the steering wheel. "Detective Finn."

"We were going to have dinner with Tony and Heather," Grace reminded him.

Damn. He knew she'd been counting on an outing. He slowed down, checked his watch. Quarter to eight. He was already too late, and he was still twenty minutes out of Evansburg.

The hour didn't really matter. He didn't have time to do anything other than his job. He pulled over to the side of the road next to a power pole to give Grace his full attention. "Sorry. I totally forgot. I'm on my way back from the Gorge Amphitheatre."

"Okay." After a brief hesitation, she added, "I'll get that bone back from Kanoni. I'll save it for you."

"Good," he said.

Silence reigned for a long minute between them.

"Sorry," Finn said again, trying to fill the void. "I found out there are *two* teenage girls missing."

"Oh, no. Those parents must be in agony."

"They are. All four of them are here. Well, in Quincy now, actually. I've got to go back to the station and file reports and make a hundred phone calls."

"I understand, Matt. Rain check. But since Z's ape-sitting, I'm going, regardless. Who knows when I'll get another chance? And I'll be late if I don't leave right now." She hung up.

He couldn't blame her. After the novelty of working with gorillas wore off among the locals, Grace's staff had dwindled down to only Jon Zyrnek—Z—who worked a full-time job in town and slept at his girlfriend's house most nights. He showed up several evenings a week for a few hours, and occasionally a handful of her former volunteers stopped by to lend a hand. But most people were not willing to go through the training and stick with gorilla care for little to no money, so Grace was stuck at home with the gorillas most of the time these days. Which also meant that Finn was stuck there, too, if he wanted to spend time with her.

The power pole in front of his car had three flyers stapled to it. LOST: SAMSON, a gray tabby cat, according to the photo. HAVE YOU SEEN KATIE? A goofy looking mixed breed dog grinned from that page, one ear up, one sticking straight out. MISSING. Another dog, this one some kind of spaniel.

He sighed, pulled back onto the road. So many lost beings in the world. He hoped the dogs were off on an adventure together and the tabby was just out hunting. Grace had a missing cat, too. Snow. All the gorillas were complaining about that.

There weren't nearly enough notices labeled FOUND. Maybe he should post a flyer about the bone. FOUND: DO YOU KNOW WHO THIS FINGER BONE BELONGS TO?

Grace's disappointed tone haunted him all the way back to town.

The Evansburg police station was switching to night shift by the time he arrived, lugging a grease-stained bag from the Burger Shack. He could feel the cholesterol clogging his veins as he munched his way through the cheeseburger and fries while typing his report. Thank God he managed to snag Micaela d'Allesandro, better known as Miki, the only clerical aide employed there, before she walked out the door. Miki was studying for her associate degree in criminal justice, and planned to go to the police academy as soon as she had her diploma in hand. She was always eager to win points with the officers. She agreed to stay late to scan the girls' photos for Finn and type up a list of contacts from his notes.

His first call was to Vaughn Boylan, the events coordinator at the Gorge. There was no answer. Finn left a voicemail identifying himself and listing what he needed: contact information for subcontractors, videos from all security cameras, names of everyone working during the concert. He closed by saying, "I'll meet you at nine a.m. tomorrow, at the admin trailer. I asked the parents to come in at ten."

He uploaded the girls' descriptions and details to the network and blasted them out to all the police and sheriffs and highway patrol computers in the state.

The clock read 11:25 by the time he'd finished. When the door opened to the detectives' shared office, Finn was surprised to see the bedraggled figure of Detective Sara Melendez limp in, accompanied by a stench of smoke.

He eyed her smudged face and wild hair. "Have you been chasing cars again?"

She collapsed into her chair at the next desk, grabbed a water bottle from a drawer and took a long pull. Sliding down in her chair, she rested her gaze on the ceiling. "Another arson."

"Anyone hurt?"

She shook her head and then took another swallow of water. "This is the third barn. Miller place this time. Not one hundred percent abandoned, though. The owner came running when he saw the flames, along with everyone else for miles around. No animals inside, thank God, but Miller claimed there was about five hundred dollars of hay stored there. Total loss. Plus at least a quarter acre of pasture burned before the volunteers managed to put it out. Shit, if that had really gotten started . . ." She made a clucking sound with her tongue.

A grass fire was always a frightening thought in this dry country. He worried about Grace's compound, surrounded by fields and forests.

Arsonists had targeted two unused buildings so far, and now a barn that was used only for storage. The gorilla house was a remodeled barn. It did not exactly appear to be abandoned, but still . . . He didn't want to think about the near-impossibility of evacuating three freaked-out apes during a conflagration. The volunteer fire department certainly hadn't trained for *that* contingency. He snorted at his mental image of gorillas and firefighters racing around, each group terrified of the other. "Any clues who's behind these fires?"

Melendez sighed and closed her eyes. "I have my suspicions. A few of the local boys. I got film of the crowd and license numbers of all the vehicles. But since pretty much everyone in the vicinity shows up to watch the show, it's kinda hard to separate possible dirtbags from excited bystanders. When the roof caved in, I thought they were all going to applaud."

She set the water bottle on her desk and slid upright again, swiveled in her chair to face her computer, and switched it on. "Anyhow, I'll call Rodrigo and get him to rake through the debris after it cools off. Maybe we'll find a clue of some kind."

"He's not going to be happy. I just talked to him and he needs to be at the Gorge Amphitheatre first thing to check out a car and tent left there."

She turned toward him. "I heard Sarge sent you to the Gorge to check on an abandoned car. What's up with that?"

It was his turn to sigh. "Two missing girls. You'll see the report in your inbox."

"Shit."

"Let's hope they're just out partying and come back on their own. In any case, I've got to be back out there first thing, too." He pushed himself up from his chair.

"Night, Matt. Better luck tomorrow."

"Same to you, Sara."

As he drove up to his house, a bulky figure rushed out from his front porch. He'd only begun to open the car door when Cargo leapt up on it, smacking Finn's leg back into the car frame.

"Good Lord, dog," he complained, rubbing his shin. "Settle down. And how the heck did you get out of the back yard again?"

The gigantic dog, some unholy mix of Newfie and God knew what else, pawed him and crisscrossed his path all the way to the front door, threatening to trip him. The canine antics were accompanied by loud groans and whimpers.

"You are *not* starving," Finn told him.

The dog continued his whining chorus and leapt repeatedly against the front door as Finn twisted the key in the lock. "I'll write down the number of the SPCA," Finn told the beast, who regarded him woefully with one blue eye, one brown. "Feel free to call and tell them how badly abused you are."

The dog raced ahead of him through the dark house to the kitchen, where he frantically pawed a cabinet door that had long ago lost its finish to canine toenails. Opening the cabinet, Finn slid out a massive bag of dog chow and pulled the scoop out of the sack. When he bent to reach for the dog dish, Cargo jumped against the sack, knocking it over. A wave of kibble splashed across the tile floor.

Cargo fell on it, inhaling bits and pieces, crunching and slobbering. Finn snorted. "Congratulations, mutt. Objective accomplished." He leaned back against the counter, crossing his arms. "And slow the heck down—if there's dog barf on the rug tonight, you're going to the pound tomorrow."

Claws snagged his sleeve above his elbow. Finn turned toward Kee, an orange tabby sitting on the counter behind him. His brother Lok sat beside him, his expression equally annoyed. *Maaow,* complained Lok. Kee joined his more mellow meow to the refrain, but raised his paw to claw at Finn's arm again.

The menagerie had not been Finn's idea. Shortly after she'd convinced him to move from Chicago, his ex-wife Wendy had left him the house, her pets, and all the bills. Evansburg is a great place to raise a family, she'd told him. Evansburg was an even better place to hook up again with her old flame, as it turned out. Now she was in Spokane with her new husband and their new baby, and Finn had somehow become hopelessly entangled with all these animals. Even with gorillas, for God's sake.

After the animals were fed and watered, he poured himself a finger of whiskey, moved to his study, and stared longingly at the watercolor he had only just begun. The photograph he was using as a reference sat to the side of the painting: a weathered, half-collapsed barn a few miles from town, surrounded by a field of wildflowers. His faint pencil sketch on the watercolor paper was complete, and his fingers itched to pick up a brush and fill it with color.

He despised missing cases. There was always a ticking clock, always the thought that if he were clever enough, fast enough, he might find the victims alive. And if he didn't measure up, if he was even a few minutes too late, it would be his fault.

Sighing, he shut off the overhead light, showered, and set the alarm clock for five hours later. Then he fell into bed. Less than a minute after he stretched out, a canine sandbag settled over his legs, pinning him to the mattress. Then a cat draped itself across the pillow above his head. The other watched from the headboard, flicking its tail.

Finn closed his eyes. While he wished for a phone call telling him that Mia and Darcy had returned during the night, he also worried that any sudden noise would unleash pandemonium and he'd end up in the emergency room trying to explain how he'd broken his leg falling out of bed and why he had claw slashes across his forehead.

Chapter 10

Tuesday

The next morning, as Finn drove to the Gorge venue, he noticed a new flyer on the utility pole where he'd briefly parked the night before. MISSING, screamed the headline, in bright red capitals. From a photo below, Darcy Ireland and Mia Valdez smiled at the traffic on the road. Beneath the picture was a paragraph of smaller text that he supposed contained a description of the teens. At the bottom was the Evansburg Police Department tip line number, again in red. He was grateful the parents hadn't posted his cell number.

Another poster greeted him as he drove through the gate to the Amphitheatre. The department's evidence technician, Jaime Rodrigo, accompanied by a Grant County Deputy, was already examining the girls' Ford Edge when Finn drove into the campground. A Grant County Sheriff's Department cruiser was parked near the girls' campsite, along with Rodrigo's SUV.

Rex Brady watched from the open door of his camper. As Finn approached, a dog bounded out the camper, barking. Baying was a more accurate description. It was a basset hound.

"Wolf!" Rex reprimanded the hound.

Finn raised an eyebrow. "Wolf?"

The other man grinned. "Well, *he* thinks he is. But in any case, it's short for Steppenwolf."

"Aha." The basset sat in front of him, and Finn held out a fist for him to sniff. "Any movement here last night?"

"A couple of coyotes trotted through. Wolf let us know about that at three a.m. That's it."

The dog stood up and began sniffing Finn's trouser legs, no doubt smelling a giant mongrel and a couple of orange tabbies. Finn glanced around the area. "Where's your wife?"

"She's with Vaughn." Rex inclined his head toward the trailer in the distance, and Finn noticed a small fleet of vehicles parked outside the structure. Finn winced when he saw the logo of the local TV station on the side of a blue van. "The news crew—a cameraman and a reporter—are in the trailer, too. And the parents."

Finn grimaced. "All of them?"

"Yep."

This was going to be a circus. "I told them ten a.m."

Rex shrugged. "Could you sleep if your daughter was missing?"

After a word with Rodrigo about when he'd be ready to release the car and tent, Finn reluctantly turned toward the administration trailer.

"Hey, Detective!" Rex yelled. "Can we sleep at home tonight?"

"I'll let you know," Finn yelled back.

Inside the trailer, Brynne was pouring coffee for the Irelands and Valdezes, who had all taken the same seats they'd occupied the day before. An additional chair had been pulled up, and an African-American woman sat in it, holding a portable microphone in front of Andrea Ireland's nose as Andrea said, "No, we've had no news about the girls as of this morning."

The cameraman leaned over Keith Valdez's shoulder, filming from the other side of the table.

As Finn shut the door behind him, heads swiveled and all eyes focused on him. So did the camera.

"Detective Finn!" The reporter leapt up from her seat. "What can you tell us about the search for Darcy Ireland and Mia Valdez?" She shoved the microphone in front of his face.

Finn hoped his hair was lying down and he didn't have any shreds of his breakfast burrito stuck in his teeth. "We are pursuing every angle to find the girls," he said.

The reporter peppered him with questions. "Do you have search parties out? What do you think happened to Darcy and Mia? Do you have any suspects at this point?"

"That's all I have to say at the moment. Now please let me do my job." He waited for the camera to turn away, but when it didn't, he held a hand up in front of the lens and stepped away toward the desk.

The reporter made a slashing motion across her throat to her cameraman, who shut down the camera.

"I think we've got all we need for now," she told him. Then she turned to the parents. "This report will be on the six o'clock news in Spokane and maybe even Seattle." She strode toward Finn and pressed a business card into his hand. LULU HENDRIX, BROADCAST JOURNALIST. "If anything breaks, Detective, you'll inform me?"

"Check with the Evansburg Police and the Grant County Sheriff's Department," he told Lulu. "I'll be a little busy."

After an annoyed intake of breath, the reporter turned to Brynne with a beatific smile. "Thank you, Mrs. Brady."

"We will do everything we can to help find the girls," Brynne answered.

The TV news team swept out the door.

Behind the desk, a woman with short brown hair typed on a keyboard, her eyes fixed on the computer monitor in front of her. As Finn approached, she held up a finger toward him, her gaze never shifting from the screen. Behind her, on a table, a printer hummed to life and began to spit out pages. The woman directed her gaze toward Finn, stood up, and extended her hand. "Vaughn Boylan."

Vaughn was a woman?

"Detective Finn." He did his best to cover his surprise as he took her fingers in his. He'd thought because Boylan was in charge . . . The voices of a thousand women shouted inside his head: *Never . . . make . . . assumptions, you—!* Fill in the blank: *dolt, nincompoop, sexist jerk*. He could never admit this to Grace or Melendez or the department's other female detective, Kathy Larson. He'd never said the word *he* in the same sentence as Boylan's name, had he? He hoped not.

Boylan turned and grabbed pages from the printer, then twisted back and handed the printouts to Finn. "All the contractors are listed here, along with their contact information, their tasks, and the locations they occupied." She pointed out the column headings on the spreadsheet. Pulling out the page beneath the top one, she said, "These are the names of all parties renting campsites."

"Wow," he responded.

"Names and credit cards of ticket purchasers." She handed him several more sheets of paper. "The numbers with checkmarks beside them are charges that are being challenged by the credit card owners."

His face must have shown his confusion, because she added, "It happens, a few with every event. It's a risk of online transactions. Parents don't know that their kids used their cards for a concert, people get confused by seeing 'Gorge

Events Inc.' instead of the name of the event, and a few might actually be stolen cards."

"I see."

"And . . ." Boylan picked up three thumb drives from the desktop and thrust them in Finn's direction. "The security camera videos from the festival. They're all time-stamped."

The drives were neatly labeled by location. Boylan pushed a map of the site across the desktop. Several slashes of highlighter colored the page. "Here are the locations of the cameras."

The woman's efficiency was almost overwhelming. "Can you come to work for my department?"

For the first time, Boylan cracked a smile. "Now, can I leave on vacation, Detective?"

He eyed the small office. A laptop was closed on top of a file cabinet. "Any chance we can use both your computers?"

"Passwords." She handed him an index card. Nodding toward it, she said, "Guard that with your life. The financial info and contracts are all in special locked folders with different passwords. If you really, really, really need to see any of that for some reason, give me a call. I may not answer right away, but leave a message and I'll get back as soon as I can." She added a business card to his pile.

"Thank you so much, Miz Boylan. Have a great trip. I'll call only if I need your assistance."

Vaughn Boylan plucked a jacket from a hook on the wall and swept out the door. Finn turned in place to watch her go, the printouts and cards still in his hands.

Behind him, Brynne laughed. "Vaughn has that effect on everyone. Coffee, Detective?" She waved the nearly empty pot in his direction.

All four parents stood up from the chairs, talking

simultaneously. The girls' mothers, Andrea and Robin, flapped pieces of paper at him.

Finn set his piles of information down on the desk and held up his hands. "Stop!"

Jaws tightened. Foreheads wrinkled into frowns. Keith Valdez's hands clenched into fists at his side.

"I wasn't expecting you all to show up so early," he explained.

That was an understatement. He'd expected to have time with Vaughn Boylan to develop an investigation plan before being besieged by the foursome. He wished Boylan had stayed; she seemed like the type to maintain order no matter what.

Finn gestured at the chairs. "I know you have a million questions for me. Please have a seat and let me fill you in on what has been done so far."

"Excuse me?" Brynne Brady waved a hand, interrupting. "Can Rex and I go home?"

"For now," Finn told her. "I'll call you later if I need you."

She turned toward the door.

"Thank you for all your help," Finn remembered to say at the last minute.

He turned back to the parents and collected their bits of paper listing additional contact names and numbers of Darcy's and Mia's friends. After answering their questions with the little info he had, he set them to examining the videos from the Sasquatch Festival, the Irelands at Boylan's desk and the Valdezes using the laptop on the table.

Taking a breather from the tense atmosphere of the trailer, he walked back to the campsite.

The deputy from Grant County—the nameplate on his uniform read WILDER—agreed to stay in place for the duration of his shift. "If nothing breaks today, I'll stay tonight, too, just in case the girls—or other visitors—come back."

Finn was relieved. "That's great."

"I could use the overtime." Wilder hooked his thumbs in his duty belt. "Say, you got any new info on these arsons?"

Finn shook his head. "My colleague, Detective Melendez, is following up on those. You know anything?"

"We've only had one, and as far as I know, there's two kinds of gossip going around about it: fun by some local kids, or the owner did it for insurance."

"The owner? Wasn't the Grant County barn the second place to burn?"

The deputy quirked an eyebrow at Finn. "Maybe the first one gave him the idea. Wouldn't that make a second burn in a string of arsons even more plausible?"

"Yes, I guess it would. Which theory do you lean toward?"

Wilder shrugged. "Could go either way, I guess. Although the owner of our barn is eighty and hadn't used that barn for decades, so it can't be worth much. So it's probably the kids. They just don't have enough to do around here." He focused his attention on the MISSING poster near the entrance gate. "I sure hope those girls are okay."

Finn studied the guy's worried expression. "Do you have any suspicions about what might have happened to them? Any bad actors in your jurisdiction you want to tell me about?"

The deputy thought for a minute. "We have the usual domestic disputes and thefts, and of course we got the same drug problems that everyone else has. But really, nothing memorable since Sutter got locked up."

"Sutter?"

"Todd Sutter. You know."

Finn shook his head. "I don't. I'm from Chicago. I've only been out here for a little more than three years."

"Chicago?" Wilder's expression brightened. "I knew it—you're that gorilla guy, aren't you?"

Finn snorted and rubbed a finger across his chin. It would be pointless to deny it. "I've had a couple of cases involving apes in my county, because there's a research facility just outside of Evansburg."

Wilder snapped his fingers. "Yeah! You're the big-city detective who got clues from a gorilla to find that missing baby."

"It was a little more involved than that." Why was Neema the only thing people remembered about the Ivy Morgan case? All the credit for finding that baby went to the darn gorilla.

"Cool!" Wilder rocked back on his heels. "Wish I'd get to work on a case that interesting sometime."

Finn briefly considered telling the deputy about the bone the gorillas found in Grace's barn but said instead, "Hang in there. I'm sure you will. But back to this Sutter?"

"Todd Sutter, serial rapist and murderer, multiple victims across two counties."

Finn whistled. "Jesus."

"Convicted in 2006; serving life if I remember right." Wilder glanced toward the car and tent. "But the county's been pretty quiet ever since he got caught."

"Finn! Detective Finn!"

Finn turned to see Paul Ireland trotting their way, waving an arm in the air. "We got something on the video!"

"Coming!" Finn yelled back. Turning to Wilder, he flipped a business card out of his pocket. "Here's my cell. I'm expecting a canine unit to arrive sometime soon. Give me a call when they show, okay?"

"Will do."

Chapter 11

Tuesday

Grace McKenna stood in the middle of the gorilla habitat, trying to envision it from the eyes of a suspicious inspector who would want to know that the "wildlife" in her care was safely contained and humanely treated.

That wildlife was, at the moment, scattered around the former barn building. Neema sat on the second level of the aerial platforms, a children's picture book about Africa open in her lap, paging through photos of wildebeest and elephants and lions. The gorilla had learned the signs for some of those animals, and when she crooked a finger in front of her broad black nose, Grace guessed Neema was studying a photo of an elephant. If only she had insight into Neema's mind; who knew what a captive gorilla actually thought about an animal she'd never witnessed in real life?

Kanoni sat by her mother's side under Neema's left arm, alternately sucking on Neema's sagging breast and tapping the book pages with her feet.

Gumu was hunched in a corner of the barn, fascinated by a bug in a beer bottle that Grace had brought in. Picking up a piece of straw from the dried grass scattered across the floor, he inserted it into the neck of the bottle and tried to dislodge the bug—a black beetle—from the side of the container.

Grace hoped the gorillas would be this calm when the inspector came.

Where could Kanoni have picked up that bone? And what the heck had she done with it? Grace walked outside the barn into the exterior portion of the gorilla habitat, where a large net stretched upward to the fencing that enclosed the area. She walked a zigzag pattern, scuffing her shoes in the dirt beneath the rope net. She found a few small sticks and some bird droppings, no doubt left by the crows that sometimes came in through the fencing overhead to see if the gorillas had left any food out. There were no bones and no holes where the apes might have been digging in the dirt.

She walked back into the barn. Toys and blankets and pinecones, straw and leaves and small branches and other natural debris were scattered across the sawdust floor. She bent to pick up a clown mask from the dirt, along with an ostrich feather. She carried them toward the basket by the wall where she kept the gorilla toys.

Kanoni, bored with "reading," abruptly slapped the book pages hard with both hands, slipped from Neema's arms, leapt to the ground, and raced to her father, leaping onto his outstretched leg. Gumu gently elbowed the baby away, but Kanoni grabbed for the bottle in his hands and a brief tug of war ensued. Gumu grunted and bared his impressive canines at Kanoni. The baby hooted in dismay, then scampered to Grace and clung to her leg.

"Well, you asked for it, didn't you?" Tucking the mask under one arm to free up a hand, Grace patted the baby gorilla on the head.

When the inspector showed up, she'd need to lock Gumu in the outside enclosure to be sure that teeth-baring gesture was not repeated. Most people who had seen the silverback's sharp fangs never felt safe in the same room with the massive male gorilla again.

Kanoni was obviously bored. Grace felt a flash of guilt, as she often did when she was with her apes. In the wild, a baby gorilla would most likely have multiple playmates in her troop. Truth be told, Grace was a little bored herself. Last night had been a welcome break, a rare chance to spend time with adult humans. Heather and Tony and Tom had talked of movies and books and classes they'd taken, and Grace realized how much of the larger world she was missing.

Her gorillas could use a larger world, too, or at least more varied activity. She was grateful that Brittany Morgan, her teen mom volunteer, occasionally brought her three-year-old daughter Ivy to play with Kanoni. Grace pulled out her cell phone to review the amazing video she'd filmed of a playdate a couple of weeks ago.

Along with Ivy, Brittany had brought Sophia, another three-year-old she'd been babysitting, and they'd all spent the afternoon in the gorilla enclosure. The scene was hilarious, with Neema giving two tiny humans and one baby ape rides on her strong back and then the three youngsters competing to see who could spin themselves like whirling dervishes for the entire length of the barn floor. Kanoni always won, twirling long after the girls had collapsed. Short legs and long arms were clearly advantages when it came to spinning.

Grace smiled at the twirling playmates on the video. Even Neema and Gumu joined in for a few whirls before regaining their adult dignity. Then little Sophia collided with one of the many tree branches that littered the floor, tripped and fell onto her back, and started screaming.

At this point, the video footage swung wildly as she and

Brittany had leapt to their feet, but after a few seconds, the camera focused again on the scene. Neema was first to reach Sophia, and the mother gorilla scooped up the wailing little girl. Neema gently cradled Sophia against her chest, while Kanoni clung uncertainly to her mother's leg. Sophia hiccupped, staring in wonder at the huge gorilla face so close to hers, and then, when Neema pressed her rubbery lips to the little girl's forehead, Sophia laughed out loud.

It was a precious moment, and a dynamite video. Grace needed to get Sophia's mother's permission to post this on the gorilla website; the clip would help with donations for gorilla care and maybe even with sales of the apes' artwork. Yes, she really should encourage those sort of playdates more often, while the few human children she knew were still young enough to accept apes as playmates.

Neema had been born in a zoo, but she had lived with Grace from the time she was an infant. Kanoni had been born in this barn. Gumu had been born in the wild, but his mother had been killed and he'd been captured as a baby. Grace had no idea if the silverback had memories of being a free ape in Africa.

Would her gorillas be happier in a zoo with a larger band of apes? Grace was never sure. She didn't know how to play the "what if" game with apes who had only experienced captivity with one another in her small compound. How could they even understand the choice?

Much as she loved them, she'd never intended to keep the gorillas forever. This was an unnatural life for great apes. And now that most of the educated world had accepted the idea that apes had thoughts and feelings, it was nearly impossible to get grants from educational institutions to continue her language research. But her gorillas didn't know how to live in the wild, and she didn't know of any place in the natural world where wild gorillas were safe. And she couldn't just sell them to a private collector, because who knew what might happen after that? She couldn't bear the thought of saying goodbye to Neema.

Kanoni noticed the clown mask in Grace's hands and stretched her hands toward it. Remembering her goal for coming into the barn, Grace held the mask out of reach. "Bring me a toy, Kanoni." Tucking the feather duster under her arm, she signed *toy*. "A small toy." She made the sign for *small* and then *toy* again. "Trade."

The baby gorilla had never made the sign for *trade*, but Kanoni knew the basics of this game and raced to the toy basket. Plucking out a black object, she barreled back to Grace to offer it up.

Matt's sunglasses. Grace took them, pushed them inside her shirt for safekeeping.

"I want a smaller toy," Grace told the little ape. "A tiny one." She doubled the sign for *small*.

Kanoni raced back to the basket. She pulled the basket over onto its side, dumping toys onto the sawdust floor, and then sorted through them, picking up several and biting them. Finally, she came loping back.

Climbing Grace's leg, the baby gorilla again reached for the mask, and Grace had to stretch her arm up to hold it out of Kanoni's reach. "Trade," she repeated. "For small, small toy." She held her thumb and index finger close together to demonstrate the size.

Wrapping both legs around Grace's waist, Kanoni leaned back and pulled an object from her mouth, offering it.

Grace took it. Yes! It was the finger bone.

"You want this toy?" Grace waved the mask above her head.

Give me, Kanoni signed, and then slipped another object out of her mouth and held it up toward Grace's face. Taking the second object from the baby gorilla, Grace briefly held the mask over her own face to tease the little ape. Kanoni hooted and grabbed for the mask, and then leapt down and scooted away, holding the clown face in front of her little gorilla face.

Placing the new object in the same hand as the bone, Grace examined them carefully.

Uh-oh. Kanoni had given her another bone, this one fatter and shorter than the finger bone. Maybe a toe bone?

Where was the baby getting these?

She went to Kanoni, who was examining the mask, touching her lips to the red clown lips as if kissing them.

"Kanoni." When the little ape looked up, Grace held the bones out in her hand. "Where did you get these toys?"

Kanoni grabbed for the bones, but Grace closed her fingers in time to keep them out of reach. Kanoni gave up and put the clown mask in front of her gorilla face, hooting loudly in excitement.

Grace feigned fear, waved the feather duster in the air, and allowed the baby to chase her around the barn with the mask for a few moments. In any case, it was probably useless to ask Kanoni where the bones had come from. Her sign vocabulary was so small.

After the little gorilla tired of the game, Grace approached Neema, who had climbed down to investigate the commotion.

Holding the bones out on the palm of her hand, Grace asked the mother gorilla where they'd come from.

Neema studied her keeper's face for a long moment, then sat back and signed *juice*.

"After you tell me where these came from," Grace insisted.

Yogurt, Neema signed.

Grace groaned. The big female gorilla loved nothing better than a good bargain. "Where, Neema?"

Neema plopped her rear end down in the dirt and crossed her hairy arms over her breasts, the epitome of ape stubbornness.

"I'll give you juice *after* you tell me where," Grace repeated, signing as she spoke.

Neema uncrossed her arms and signed *up*, jabbing her hand toward the roof.

"Up?" Grace asked, raising her eyes to the roof where the swallows were nesting. "Up?"

Bird, Neema signed.

Grace supposed it *was* possible that a bird had brought in the bones. Crows and seagulls had been known to carry objects long distances. But barn swallows? She'd never seen one with anything bigger than an insect in its beak. She'd have to ask an ornithologist.

Neema clutched at Grace's thigh with one hand and signed with the other. *Give juice hurry Neema good.*

Juice, Grace agreed, nodding. Neema had been known to make up stories when she thought it would benefit her, and Grace wasn't at all sure that Neema was telling the truth now, but it was nearly lunchtime anyway, so she slipped the bones into her back pocket, closed and locked the gate behind her, and strode toward the staff trailer to get juice for all three gorillas.

Two bones. Found somewhere in the barn, or brought in by a bird? When the agricultural inspector showed up, it would probably be best to keep this a secret.

But Matt would certainly be interested in this development. She sighed and rubbed a hand over her stomach, thinking about their times together, remembering the way he laughed as he ran his fingers through her hair. He was an entertaining companion, a tender lover. And he was the first man who was willing to accept her life as it was; her gorillas and her constant anxiety over money to care for them. But when Matt was on an important case, he lived for that case. Then he was simply gone.

And the search for two missing girls was certainly an urgent case. She wished Detective Matt Finn had more time to spend with her, but she recognized that he had an important career, a vital job in the community. Frankly, she was more than a little jealous of that.

Chapter 12

Tuesday

All four parents were clustered around a single laptop, studying the grainy security video of their girls in front of the concessions booth. With no sound, it was like watching a silent movie.

Darcy was wearing a skin-tight black T-shirt with a rose on the front of it over black tights with mesh inserts, and Mia sported a crop top that didn't meet her low-cut jeans. The girls were bracketed by two young men. The encounter appeared friendly. All four of them were laughing as they approached the counter. One of the men had long hair and wore plugs in his earlobes; the other had tight curls of dark hair and a beard that needed trimming. The men bought flavored waters and French fries for the girls, soft drinks and fries for themselves, and then they all wandered away.

"Who the hell are those guys?" Paul Ireland asked the others.

"They're not the ones I'm worried about," Robin said. "Rewind, please." She watched as the video backed up a few frames to the scene where the girls were standing in front of the concession counter. "There! Stop!" She poked a finger at the screen.

Finn focused on an inmate in the background. He was carrying a trash bag over his shoulder, his upthrust arm obscuring part of the GCDC lettering on his shirt. His head was turned toward the camera, his gaze aimed at the concession stand.

Robin wasn't looking at the inmate. "I don't know the boys on either side of the girls," she said. "But that guy in the back, the one with the earring? He looks familiar to me." She pointed.

The grainy video showed a youth waiting in line behind the girls. He was of average height with light-colored, cropped hair. The only distinctive feature was a blobby earring dangling from his right ear. Finn guessed that the blob might be a silver skull, but the video was not clear enough to determine that for sure.

Andrea shook her head. "Doesn't look familiar to me. He looks older than our girls." She leaned forward to peer closer. "Is he staring at Mia?" She turned to the other mother.

"Give me a minute," Robin muttered, turning away from the screen to stare at the wall.

The two husbands exchanged blank looks.

After a few more seconds, Robin snapped her fingers. "I've got it. That boy *is* older. He was a senior at Stanton when Mia and Darcy were in ninth grade. He had darker hair, then. He was kind of a scary kid."

Finn raised an eyebrow. "Scary?"

Robin met his gaze. "See, I volunteer-tutor special needs students. Back then I had this one really pretty girl, Taylor, a junior at the time. Very sweet and very naive. She was extremely dyslexic; that's why I was working with her. That kid"—she pointed to the screen again—"stalked her. Taylor didn't like him, but he wouldn't stop leaving her candy and notes, and she told me he'd hide behind corners and jump out to surprise her. She was really scared of him. He was reprimanded multiple times but never seemed to get the message. After he keyed her car because she wouldn't go out with him, the parents transferred Taylor to another school."

Interesting. Finn turned to the Irelands. "Was that scratch on Darcy's car when you last saw it?"

"I honestly don't remember," Andrea murmured. "Darcy never said anything about it."

Paul remarked, "It seemed fresh to me, like it might have happened in the last few days."

Andrea raised both hands to her face. "Oh my God, why didn't I know any of this? That *creep* was at the festival with the girls?"

Robin glanced at the other woman but then continued her story. "After the problem with Taylor was solved, I thought it was over. But then, in a couple of later photos from school events, I noticed his eyes were always on Mia. I was just getting ready to complain to the principal when his family moved away, thank God." She drummed her fingers on the desk. "What *was* his name?"

She moved her focus to the wall again for a long moment as she thought, muttering, "Connor something . . ." She abruptly snapped her fingers and swiveled back to Finn. "No, it was Cooper. Cooper Trigg! T-R-I-G-G."

Finn glanced at Keith Valdez.

The man held up both hands. "Don't look at me."

Finn made a note on his pad, did the math in his head. "So this Cooper would be around twenty-one now?"

"Or maybe even twenty-two or twenty-three, depending on when his birthday is. A lot of parents hold back their boys for a year," Robin informed him. "Boys are less mature, and Cooper certainly fit into that category." She chewed on her thumbnail and stared at the computer screen, a worried expression on her face.

Stifling the urge to defend the males of his species, Finn wrote down the information. "When did you last see this Cooper Trigg?"

"Oh, gosh, his family moved away at least three years ago," Robin told him. "I'm not sure Mia really knew him. Cooper was an oddball at the Academy; there on some sort of hard-luck scholarship." She glanced again toward the image frozen on the screen. "I hope the girls didn't run off with *him*."

"Do you know where the Trigg family moved to?" Finn asked.

Robin shrugged. "No. I just knew Cooper was gone and I didn't have to worry anymore."

"But he's here," Andrea interjected. "And he keyed Darcy's car."

Her husband, Paul, rubbed her arm in sympathy or comfort. "Maybe he thought it was Mia's."

Robin frowned at him.

"We don't know for sure that this guy is Cooper Trigg or that he keyed the car," Finn reminded them.

"Maybe Mia and this boy are online friends?" Keith Valdez suggested.

"Maybe." Robin nodded. "If he reached out to her. I don't think she ever noticed him when they were both at Stanton."

"Maybe Instagram?" Andrea said. "Darcy uses it nonstop. Oh, God. Do you think the girls are with this Cooper guy? Or whoever these two in front are?" She turned to Finn for an answer.

"No way to know for sure, but it's a place to start. The girls probably met them here. And at the time of this video, it doesn't look like either of the girls have even noticed

Cooper. Can you get into your girls' Instagram accounts?" Finn asked all of them.

Furrowed brows all around. Clearly, none of them knew how to do that.

"We could create our own accounts and follow them," Paul Ireland suggested, pulling a cell phone out of his pocket.

Finn thought that would likely be a waste of time, but these parents needed something to do. "Might be a good idea," he said.

His cell phone buzzed.

Deputy Wilder told him, "Your canine crew is here."

"I'm on my way." He pocketed the cell phone again. Bending down to squint at the computer screen, he made a note of the time stamp on the video. "This is from Saturday, so there may be more. Keep watching." He pushed the notebook back into his shirt pocket. "I'll let you know when I locate Cooper Trigg."

Both sets of parents returned to their respective areas and focused again on the security videos.

The canine Search and Rescue teams were not what he'd expected. A chunky, middle-aged woman named Suzanne, dressed in jeans and a blue SAR T-shirt, held a beagle on a leash. A younger man, Tim, wore a matching shirt, and was partnered with a black Lab.

After taking one glance at Finn's skeptical expression, Suzanne chuckled. "Quit worrying, Detective. Maggie and I are the best tracking team east of the Columbia, and Tim and Shade here are a close second."

"Hey!" The man elbowed Suzanne. "If we can't find 'em, no dog can."

The beagle uttered one sharp bark, as if to emphasize the

point. The Labrador retriever glanced sideways at the beagle like he was appalled by the noise.

"Okay, then," Finn said. "We've got two missing teenagers."

"When did they disappear?" Tim asked.

"Most likely around forty-eight hours ago."

The dog handlers glanced at each other, their expressions grim. Then Suzanne said, "That's a long time. Hundreds of people could have crossed this area since then, right?"

Finn nodded glumly. "That's certainly possible."

Tim met his gaze. "We'll try, but the odds are against us."

"Understood." Finn snapped on his latex gloves and pulled open the car door. "I presume clothing is best?"

"The smellier, the better." Suzanne stepped forward.

He found two pairs of panties and two T-shirts so stained and wrinkled that the girls might have been living in them. "I can't remember what belongs to which girl."

"Doesn't matter since we're searching for both." Suzanne took the items from him and held them out toward her dog.

The beagle pushed her nose into the bundle of clothes, still wagging her tail, and then made a soft noise that might have been a groan of satisfaction. The Lab was slightly more dignified, but thumped his tail and made an excited huffing sound, his eyes focused on his handler.

"Find, Maggie!" Suzanne ordered. "Find!"

Tim echoed, "Find, Shade!"

The beagle gave a yip of excitement and tugged at the leash. Tim shoved the clothing back into Finn's hands.

"Okay to let them off the leads?" Suzanne asked.

Finn didn't see any reason why not.

Tim and Suzanne unsnapped the leads from their dogs' collars. All four of them took off, the handlers trotting after the dogs down a gravel pathway that led from the campground toward the amphitheater. Finn placed the clothes back into the car and then followed at a slower pace, keeping the dog teams in sight as he talked on his cell phone, asking Miki back at the station to locate Cooper Trigg and find out if he or his parents owned vehicles.

The beagle was in full bugling mode now, and Finn stopped to watch as the canine teams jogged across the grassy area above the amphitheater. At one point the beagle hesitated and zigzagged across the ground for a few minutes, then took off again down a sidewalk toward the concession stand. The Lab cruised the aisles of the amphitheater for a bit, then also headed for the concession area.

He'd worked cases where dogs had found corpses and hidden suspects, and in one rare, happy event, an autistic teenager who'd wandered away from a train station while his family was traveling.

He wondered if his own dog Cargo would be able to find someone. He couldn't envision the giant mutt zigzagging around on a mission like Maggie and Shade were now. Cargo could probably locate someone only if that person had dog chow in his pocket. The dog didn't even fetch. Lok and Kee were actually much better at that. The cats were also experts at locating spiders and insects in the house, and they'd once imported a small garter snake that had freaked him out when it emerged from beneath under the coffee table.

Finn hoped the dogs would indicate that the girls had walked away from the festival grounds, perhaps toward the Columbia Gorge, but after nosing around the closed concession stand for a few minutes, the two teams headed back toward the camping area, where they circled a bit more. Finn got tired just watching the handlers jog behind their dogs.

Finally Maggie's hindquarters dropped to the ground only a

few yards from the abandoned car. Fixing her soulful eyes on Suzanne's face, the beagle barked twice. The Lab, too, stopped but remained standing, staring into the distance toward the road and then looking back to his owner.

The woman turned to Finn. "Clearly the girls, or at least one of 'em, walked all over the place here, and probably sat or laid down there on the grass." She pointed to the general area where the dog had zigzagged. "But now Maggie's telling me that the scent trail ends right here around the campground. Shade agrees."

"Which means that the girls most likely did not leave here on foot," Tim summarized.

Finn rubbed his chin, realized he'd miss a patch of whiskers while shaving this morning. "I was afraid of that."

"Now you know for sure," Tim concluded.

Finn stared toward the entrance road as if he could conjure the girls. "I don't suppose Maggie or Shade can give me a hint about the type of vehicle they got into?"

Suzanne laughed. "If only."

"Thanks." As he watched the canine teams depart, Finn felt a new appreciation for Grace's signing gorillas. Neema had originally described Finn as Dog Cat Gun Man because she'd smelled cat and dog essence on his clothing and noticed his gun. If she had seen a vehicle, the gorilla might be able to describe the color, and maybe even a distinguishing feature or two. Maggie's bark and Shade's body language provided no clues other than that the girls had vanished from the campground in a vehicle, which he'd already suspected.

In the distant hills, he spotted a line of horseback riders. When the news broke about the missing girls, the local 4H horse club had volunteered to search the area around the amphitheater. He was grateful they were already on the job.

This afternoon, another club had promised to launch drones and film the area. Since the girls seemed to have left in a vehicle, he wasn't hopeful, but it would make his life easier if the volunteers could find a clue or two. *Please*, he thought, *don't let them find a corpse.*

His phone buzzed. He was surprised to see the caller identified as "Alice Foster, FBI." He'd worked with Foster before, when Ivy Morgan had been abducted as an infant. "Hello, Agent Foster," he answered. "Detective Finn here."

"I see you filed an alert for two missing teenagers in your area?"

The FBI trolled all of Washington's law enforcement sites? "Unfortunately, yes."

"Can you give me an update?"

Her tone, which seemed to imply that she perceived herself as his boss, grated on him, but his irritation was eased when almost instantly she added, "I'd like to help if I can. The girls vanished from a big music festival at the Columbia Gorge, correct?"

"Yes. A multiday event called the Sasquatch Festival. I'm still collecting information. We have identified a person of interest on a security video."

"Do you suspect the girls may have been kidnapped?"

He sighed. "That's one possibility. They left a car and a tent in the campground here. But they might have just gone off partying, too. The caretaker tells me that happens from time to time."

"Big concert events like that can be hunting grounds for human traffickers. Multiple abductions have happened in other states at similar venues. And the proximity of the Gorge site to a major trucking route like Interstate 90 makes it even more attractive to traffickers."

He gulped. That possibility of human trafficking hadn't even occurred to him. Two pretty young women would be prime targets. "I'd appreciate your assistance, Agent Foster. Are you still in the Los Angeles office?"

"I'm in Seattle for a seminar. I can be in Evansburg tomorrow morning."

He was grateful she hadn't mentioned anything about gorillas. They arranged to meet at the Evansburg Police Department at nine a.m.

When Finn told the Valdezes and the Irelands that the FBI was sending an agent to assist, their faces registered even more alarm.

"Trust me," he told them. "This is an excellent development. The more resources and personnel we have working on this case, the faster we'll find Mia and Darcy."

Chapter 13

Tuesday

Mia was so ravenous that if a mouse had wandered into her cell, she might have eaten it.

She had no idea how long she'd lain there on that cot, paralyzed, until she finally passed out. What the hell had Dusty done to her? He hadn't left her any water, and she was desperate for liquid. She poured the remaining beer in the bottle with the scratched label out onto the floor, but dared to take a tentative sip from the bottle Dusty had drunk from. The brew was flat and warm but it didn't make her dizzy, and at least it wet her mouth and tongue. She'd eaten the crumbs of burned fries from the greasy paper when she'd woken up this morning. Or afternoon, or evening, whatever time it was. The light streaming in through the little knothole had been gray and then pitch black, and now it was gray again in the room. Did that mean two days had passed? She thought it was still daylight outside now, but maybe it was cloudy? Her world had been reduced to a dim twilight when the sun shone outside the building, and after it set, a blackness so thick she couldn't see her hand in front of her face.

With a crack and a knothole in the barn wall like that, she imagined she'd be able to break through the wood. Using her best karate moves, she'd kicked it. The only result was that her leg now ached all the way from the ball of her foot up to her hip, and her hair was full of dust that had showered down from the ceiling. The planks in the walls seemed more like iron than anything that could have once been a tree; she couldn't even press a fingernail into that grainy concrete. The wood was BP, as her mother would say; "before plywood," when pioneers used anything they could get their hands on to build with. Her mother had once tried to fashion some grayed scrap wood into picture frames but had given up after trying to cut it, saying the wood was probably a hundred years old; so dry and weathered that she'd dull saw blades on it.

So she was in an ancient barn. The metal door was scarred with dents and scratches, but it clearly wasn't ancient. And she was willing to bet that the lock was brand new. Dusty, the sicko bastard, had planned this. Did Comet have Darcy in another cell somewhere?

She'd thought this kind of thing happened only on television. Were she and Darcy about to be sold to some fat toad of a sheik in the Middle East to become part of his harem?

She'd tried to dig into the dirt floor next to the wall, but the ground was so hard it might as well be cement, and all she had were her fingernails and the beer bottles. She'd barely scraped out a depression an inch deep next to the wall, and she hadn't even found the bottom of the wall boards yet. Her hands were black with grime, and the ends of her fingers were bloody. She couldn't believe this was actually happening to her; it was like some sort of horrible nightmare. She contemplated crying, but she was too angry for that, and sat on the bed fuming to rest for a minute.

"Loser," she said aloud, tapping a big letter L against her forehead with her thumb and index finger. "Loser, loser,

loser!" She raised her voice, shouted as loudly as she could, "Loser alert! There's a loser trapped in here! Help! Help me!"

She banged on the wall twice for emphasis, although she knew it was hopeless; she'd yelled herself hoarse hours ago. Or was that yesterday? She was locked into an antique barn in the middle of nowhere. Her mouth was so dry she couldn't even work up a drop of spit, and the beer was gone.

She was a fool. A total fail. How could she have fallen for this? A handsome stranger on a motorcycle. *Wanna go for a ride?* What a cliché. She should be featured in warning films; they could show them in elementary school. *Remember what happened to Mia Valdez. Stranger danger! Inappropriate touching! Beware!*

At least she'd kneed Dusty good. He'd practically crawled to the door. But the way he'd snarled *You'll be sorry . . .*

She got the shivers just thinking about it. When he came back, would he bring a gun or a baseball bat to kill her?

Or maybe he'd just leave her here, locked in to die from thirst and hunger. That would be even worse, because that would be pathetic. What a legacy. *Did you hear about Mia Valdez? She got kidnapped because she did something truly stupid, and then she died all alone in a really pathetic way. Don't you pity her family? That has to be so mortifying.* She chewed her thumbnail, envisioning all the sad social media posts.

You'll be sorry.

Throughout history, women had been beaten, raped, imprisoned, and killed, all because they'd trusted some man to be a decent human being. And here she was, joining the ranks of foolish girls, locked in a converted tack room inside a barn that nobody ever used, waiting to be attacked again. She had been drafted into the army of lame women.

She ran a hand along the rough boards of the wall, wondering what kind of horses might have lived in this barn. When she'd gone to riding camp, the instructor had explained that horses were naturally skittish because they were prey animals. At the time, that had seemed a weird concept, because horses were so big and so strong. But after she imagined herself as a wild horse out on the plains, constantly watching for a mountain lion or a bear or a pack of wolves to spring out of the bushes, she understood. From then on, she had always tried to show her horse that she meant no harm before she climbed into the saddle.

Women were prey animals, too. Especially small, pretty women with curves. Boys were always trying to pick her up, pull her onto their laps, toss her into their cars. She wished she had a kind person here to reassure her that no harm would come to *her*. Instead, she had exactly the opposite.

You'll be sorry.

She gritted her teeth.

You'll be sorry.

A wave of rage abruptly flooded through her, and she clenched her fists. She was sick of being manhandled, sick of having to be careful, sick of being a prey animal. *No,* you'll *be sorry, Dusty.*

She would think of a way out of this; she had to. The instant she heard any movement outside that door, she was going to position herself beside it so she could jump Dusty as he came in. But he was at least a foot taller than she was and probably fifty pounds heavier. She needed a weapon, and a beer bottle wasn't going to help much unless she could somehow break it, and she'd already tried that, banging the bottle into the walls and the bedside table. She needed concrete or metal to break that thick glass. All she'd accomplished was to cause more dust to shower down. She probably looked like a zombie that had just climbed out of the grave.

A weapon, a weapon . . . Toshi had said anything could be a weapon. But not much in this room could be an *effective* weapon.

She eyed the bedside table. It was too big to throw and too small to block the door. The dark wood was heavy and dense, maybe oak, held together with plates and screws.

If only she had a screwdriver, she could take off a leg and wield it like a baseball bat. But Dusty had left her nothing except the mattresses, the table, and the disgusting bucket, which already reeked. At least in a real prison cell, she'd be able to flush.

Was Darcy in another barn somewhere? Was she dead? No. Mia wiped that idea from her brain, replaced it with the story that her friend had escaped and was bringing help right now. But how long would that take? Dusty would come back any minute, and he'd be looking for revenge.

Or he'd never come back, just leave her to die alone. Either way, she couldn't sit here feeling sorry for herself. She didn't want to be a victim. That's why she'd made the deal with Toshi for karate lessons.

She stood up, grasped the top of the little table. After pulling it away from the wall, she climbed up on it. When it didn't even creak, she jumped. Still nothing. The damn thing was solid. She climbed off, tipped it upside down, and stood on the underside between the table legs.

Pushing on the legs did nothing except make her arms ache. She set it against the wall and tried a couple of karate kicks, but that hurt so much she was afraid she'd break her foot.

She remembered once seeing her tiny mom brace her back against a wall and shove a heavy dresser with her legs to reveal

Mia's pet hamster hiding beneath it.

In an attempt to copy her mom's move, Mia sat down on the upside-down top, wedging herself between the upthrust legs. Placing her back against one of the legs, she put her knees against her chest and her feet against another leg. Taking a deep breath, she pushed as hard as she could with her legs. The table leg moved a fraction, and the one digging into her back seemed to slant a bit. Yes! After resting for a few seconds, she tried again. More movement. When she let up the pressure, she could see that the table leg was slightly askew now.

This just might work.

Was that a scuffling noise outside the door? She bolted up from the ground and quickly flipped the table upright, nudging it against the wall on its now wobbly legs.

She flattened herself against the wall next to the door, a beer bottle in her hand. She sucked in a breath. Could she kick Dusty in the balls again? She drew her right leg back like Toshi had shown her. Fight position.

A footstep. A swish of clothing. The click of a key against a metal cylinder.

The door swung open. The flashlight poked into the room, and she blinked quickly to adjust her eyes to its sudden brightness. She launched her attack, but Dusty was ready this time; dropping the flashlight, he quickly jerked the door back. Her foot hit the edge of the door. A jolt of pain shot through her foot and up her leg. She fell to the floor.

Dusty stepped in and shoved the door closed behind him, picked up the flashlight. Just like yesterday, he was dressed in a button-down shirt and khakis, and his hair was neatly combed. *Such a nice-looking young man*, her mother would say. He looked like the neighbor boy you would trust to carry your groceries or walk you to the bus stop.

Bending over her, he focused the bright beam directly in her eyes and then grabbed her shoulder. "Why won't you be sweet to me? All you need to do is be sweet." His breath smelled like spearmint.

"Get that light out of my face." She shoved his hand aside and then tried to push her feet back under herself. A lightning bolt hit her just below her collarbone. Every muscle in her body clenched. Stiffening into a rigid plank, she fell backward onto the floor, whimpering like a wild animal in pain.

Her gaze traveled from Dusty's face to the black plastic object in his right hand. Shit, he had a stun gun.

Leaving the flashlight on the floor, he picked her up as if she weighed no more than a housecat and tossed her onto the mattress, then climbed on top of her and ripped open the zipper on her jeans.

"No!" she yelled, bucking beneath him. "I am not a prey animal!"

She felt the bite of the stun gun against her neck. The pain surged through her again, freezing all her muscles. Jerking her jeans and panties off, he gave her another jolt of electricity as he unzipped his pants and then he forced himself inside of her.

It hurt. A burning, tearing pain that went on and on, shredding her like used Kleenex, scraping away her insides. The worst part was that she was completely helpless but totally aware of the smallest details. The cheek he pressed against her temple was clean-shaven, and under the spearmint breath, his skin smelled like the same aftershave her father used. The fingers of his left hand were knotted through her hair behind her right ear; she was afraid he'd rip out a piece of her scalp with each tug.

"Damn, girl, damn, girl, damn," he moaned, his words and

his burning, scouring thrusts getting faster and faster until he spasmed. It was over in seconds, and then he collapsed, his full weight pressing down on her. She could barely breathe.

Bending his head, he ground his lips into hers, stealing what little air she had left. Then he rose up on one elbow. "*Now* you're going to be sweet to me, aren't you, Mia?"

She closed her eyes so she wouldn't have to see him. When she didn't reply, he blew a wisp of hair away from her damp forehead, his breath now surprisingly gentle. "*Aren't you*, Mia?"

The stun gun was still pressed against her neck, and now he twisted it into her skin even harder. She was sure his finger was near the trigger. Her eyes snapped open. "Yes, Dusty."

"Say it." He twitched the stun gun against her neck.

She could barely hear his voice above the roar of her blood in her head. "I'm going to be sweet to you."

Raising her chin, she kissed him, loathing herself all the while. Then she tried for a laugh, but it got caught in her throat and came out sounding more like a whimper. "I just went a little crazy there, Dusty. Thirst can do that to you, you know? Could you please give me some food and water? Please?" She pressed her lips to his again. "It's so hard to be sweet when I'm dying of thirst."

He grinned. "Now that's more like it." Rolling off her, he stood up and zipped his pants, then waved the stun gun at her. "You made me use this, you know. I'm not a bad guy. I'll be sweet to you if you're sweet to me."

She gave him a weak smile, her lips trembling. Her whole body was trembling. Was that the result of being electrocuted or being raped? A shameful wetness trickled from her vagina onto the quilt between her legs. Her blood, or his semen?

"Don't try anything." Dusty aimed the stun gun at her as he

backed toward the door.

With a quivering hand, she pulled the quilt over herself to hide her nakedness. The door closed, and she dared to take a shuddering breath.

Then she startled as his hand slid back inside the door. He grabbed the flashlight from the floor and deposited a paper bag and a can of Coke into her cell. "See? If you're sweet, you get a reward."

The lock clicked.

Lying in the dark, with the pain burning between her legs, Mia felt as if she'd been sanded inside. No, branded, that was a better description, branded with a red hot poker, like a piece of livestock.

After what might have been ten minutes or two hours, her hunger and thirst overcame the pain. She pushed herself to her feet and pulled her clothes back on. Sitting on the bed, she wolfed the cold burger and fries and gulped the Coke in the dim room. Her brain felt numb, and she was almost grateful he'd brought her food and drink. Almost. Tears streaked her cheeks at the wrongness of it all.

She choked down the last swallow of lukewarm cola. There was a fruit turnover in the bag, too. She'd save that for later. Who knew when he'd be back? But she knew he would be.

She'd wanted to lose her cherry, and now she had. She was no longer a virgin.

She was a piece of meat. A rape victim.

Damn Dusty to hell for making her a victim.

So it hurt. It still hurt. She'd battled her way through pain before, after the wreck. And she'd been only five, then. She fingered the scar on her arm.

She couldn't let Dusty win. He couldn't take her *soul*.

No, she wasn't going to lie back and be a prey animal,

begging for the mercy of a predator. She wasn't going to be a timid *victim*. She was a rape *survivor*, and she would find a way to be strong, even if it killed her.

Tremors overtook her body again, and she was angry that she couldn't control the shaking. She wiped away her tears with the back of her hand. It was so unfair. She'd wanted to meet a hot guy, have romantic, passionate sex with multiple orgasms, like in the books. Instead, she'd been kidnapped by a sadistic rapist.

"Be sweet to you, Dusty?" She squinted her eyes at the locked door. "Not on your life."

Taking a deep breath, she went back to the table, flipped it, and worked on the legs some more. By the time it was so dark that she could no longer see anything in the room, she was drenched in sweat and two table legs were so wobbly that she was reasonably sure she could break off at least one of them tomorrow.

She might not get out of this stupid horse barn alive, and maybe she didn't even deserve to, but at least she'd go down fighting.

Chapter 14

Tuesday

According to the records Miki had sent him via email from the station, Cooper Trigg was twenty-two, and in the last three years he'd accumulated quite a rap sheet, including B and E, a couple of DUIs, car theft, and two assault charges, the most recent only three months ago, and that one on a girl of nineteen. The kid currently had a bench warrant due to failure to appear in court. Finn could easily believe that he was also a stalker. But according to the mothers, the girls probably didn't know Cooper, or at least, they didn't know his reputation.

The driver's license photo for Trigg showed a youth with dark hair and a soul patch, very different in appearance from the boy Robin had named on the video. The license was three years old, though. The eyes and earring were similar, and boys used hair color nearly as often as girls did these days.

He called the phone number listed for Trigg's address in Moses Lake at the time of the kid's last booking. A tremulous female voice answered, "Taylor residence."

After identifying himself, he asked to speak to Cooper Trigg.

There was a slight hesitation, and then the woman exclaimed, "Oh lordy, what trouble has that boy gotten himself into now?"

"I don't know that's he's in trouble, ma'am. To whom am I speaking?"

"Dorothy Taylor. I'm Cooper's grandma."

"Cooper may have information about a missing persons case I'm working on."

He heard a quick intake of breath. "The two girls from the Gorge?"

"May I please speak to Cooper?"

"I'd certainly let you if I could, Detective. But I haven't seen that boy since Christmas, and I'm not sure I want to again until he straightens himself out. I've had no end of trouble since he listed my address the last time he was arrested."

"Do you have any idea where he might be? Do you know any of his friends?"

When Dorothy's answer was no to both questions, he gritted his teeth. "Do you have a phone number for him?"

She rattled one off, then said, "But it's no good now. I tried to call him after the last time the police were here, and the recording said it was disconnected."

"Does Cooper own a vehicle, ma'am?"

"Oh, who knows?" she said. "That boy is driving something different every time I see him—cars, motorcycles, you name it. I don't know where he gets them all from."

Finn had a pretty good idea where Cooper got them—from friends, neighbors, anyone who was foolish enough to leave a key lying around. He thanked her and hung up. He'd get a Moses Lake officer to verify that Cooper Trigg was not living at the Taylor residence, but it sounded like Dorothy was telling the truth.

He checked the latest arrest report again. The car Trigg had been driving for his DUIs was an old beater that was not registered to him, and there was no insurance. The police report noted that the car was likely a total loss after a collision with a tree. He'd have to check on the registered owner's name, but he was already willing to bet that Trigg had "borrowed" the car, or at best, paid a few hundred bucks in cash to the previous owner and then never bothered to record the transaction.

Cooper Trigg was in the wind. Finn would post a report to get all agencies to search for Trigg as soon as he got back to the office, but without a current vehicle description, he wasn't particularly hopeful. It was much easier to match a car than locate a young man who didn't want to be found.

The parents eagerly awaited the six o'clock news from Spokane in the administration trailer, but they seemed even more anxious and depressed after viewing the report. Seeing the girls' photos on the television screen drove home the reality that their daughters were "out there" somewhere, that anyone might have them, that anything could have happened to Mia and Darcy.

The day was quickly giving way to evening, so Finn filled in the parents on what he'd found, or more accurately, not found, and then told the Irelands and Valdezes to call it a night, go get something to eat and some sleep. Their faces were drawn; each of them looked twenty years older than when he'd first met them. He couldn't imagine what it felt like to have your child remain missing for another day.

After verifying that Deputy Wilder would stay overnight, he followed the parents to the exit. Deciding his next move was to locate other campers from the festival, he drove toward his office. It was going to be a long night, working his way through the list that Vaughn had given him.

He called Grace on the way to excuse himself yet again from another evening with her. "Did you have fun last night?"

"Definitely. Tony got his buddy Tom to come dancing with us after dinner. I hadn't danced for years!"

Finn was glad she couldn't see his expression. Tony Zyrnek was an interesting, charming guy and a painting buddy of Finn's, and Tony's son Jon Zyrnek, nicknamed Z, had been Grace's most dependable staff member for a couple of years. But Tony was also an ex-con, albeit currently on the straight and narrow. Was this Tom a parolee, too? He didn't like to think of Grace in this guy's arms, whoever he was. "I wish I could have been there."

"Me too, Matt. And now I have these bones for you."

"*Bones?* As in plural?"

"Kanoni gave me two. I've inspected the entire gorilla enclosure, and I can't find anywhere they've been digging. Neema says *up* and *bird*, so my best guess is that a crow brought these in. I'll try to find the time tomorrow to have a look around the forest nearby. Can you come and help?"

"I'm still tied up with these missing girls."

"Sorry to hear that. Their parents must be frantic."

The anguished faces of the Irelands and the Valdezes swam up through his thoughts. "Yeah."

"Want to come by tomorrow and get these bones?"

"I have to meet an FBI agent at nine a.m. in the office, but then I'll go back to the Gorge. Will you be around about ten a.m. or so?"

"I'm always around these days, Finn," she complained. "You know I've only got Z here part-time now, and I never know if any of the others will show up or not."

"I'll keep my feelers out to find you some volunteers. I'll drop by tomorrow morning and pick up those bones, okay?" The silence hung between them for a minute. Then he asked, "What have you been up to today?"

"The gorillas were bored, so I blew up a kiddie pool and filled it with water in the barn. You've got to see the video! All three of them were wary at first, but then Kanoni galloped over and gave it a good whack, and soon all of them were playing in it and dipping all their toys in. I worked at teaching them the sign for swimming. I think Neema has already got it, and Kanoni and Gumu will soon, too."

"Do they already know the sign for pool?"

"No. There's really no sign for pool, just finger spelling, and you know they can't do that. Neema called it a 'water spot,' which is pretty descriptive, I think."

"Smart gorilla." It always amazed him how that ape could put together signs to describe things she'd seen. "Tree candy" for lollipop. "Skin bracelet" had been one of Neema's more creative descriptions when she didn't have a sign for a wrist tattoo. When signing about Gumu, Neema called the silverback Big Big Gorilla.

"It's way past dinner, but do you have time for a glass of wine?"

"I wish." He sighed heavily. "I'm on my way to the station. More paperwork and phone calls."

There was a pause, then she said, "I guess we're both prisoners of our jobs right now."

"Seems like it. With luck, Agent Foster will help get this resolved sooner. As I recall, she's very efficient."

The hesitation on the other end of the connection told Finn that Grace had registered that the agent was female. Surely she wasn't jealous? He quickly added, "Sweetheart, I *will* stop at your place tomorrow before heading out again. I'll get those bones then."

"See you tomorrow, then. Night, Matt."

It was all so ... unsatisfactory. Especially since he wasn't even headed home to sleep, but just into the station to pull another long evening. He knew he'd be there for at least a couple of hours. His stomach growled to remind him that he hadn't eaten since the breakfast burrito.

He passed three more flyers on his way back to Evansburg. The Irelands and Valdezes must have been up all night posting them everywhere. The faces of those girls would be burned into his dreams tonight. Assuming he ever got to sleep at all.

As he walked toward his desk, he noticed his voicemail message light blinking. The mechanical voice told him he had seven messages. All of them were from reporters. As soon as he heard them mention their news stations, he quickly deleted the message.

Across the room, Detective Melendez said into her phone, "All right. Halt all the work. I'll be there in half an hour, maybe sooner." She put the receiver back into its cradle, puffed up her cheeks, and then blew out a slow breath. "Oh boy. Oh crap. Damn it! Why me? Shit!"

"What's up?" Finn asked.

She pushed a hand through her short chestnut hair, sweeping it back from her brow. "A crew was bulldozing the ruins of the Rodale barn, you know, the first one burned. The blade scraped up some of the dirt floor."

"And?"

"The blade crunched into a human skull." She reached for the jacket hanging from the back of her chair. "Shit. I was really hoping to get home at a reasonable hour tonight. My husband's going to shoot me, and pretty soon my kids won't even recognize me. And now I have to call Rodrigo back in."

"*He's* the one who's likely to shoot you." Finn's brain flashed on the two bones the gorillas had found. Was it a local habit to bury bodies in the dirt floor of a barn? Sooner or later he'd have to get a cadaver dog, or maybe ground penetrating radar out to Grace's area. Shit, indeed. "Any idea who the skull belongs to?"

Sara shook her head. "Nope. Could be from a long time ago, and—oh sweet Jesus—please don't make this a discovery of an Indian graveyard or something. You know what a can of worms that could open up." She groaned. "I'll see if Miki can put together a list of missing people from this area for the last twenty years."

"I'll get her on that," Finn volunteered.

She glanced at him, surprised.

"Might be useful to me, too."

"Thanks, Finn."

"Oh, and an FBI agent is coming here tomorrow. Just in case this is a kidnapping. Special Agent Alice Foster— remember her from the Ivy Morgan case?"

"Of course I remember her. Lucky you. Can Foster help with these arsons, too?" Melendez ran her fingers through her hair again, then shook her head. "I suppose not. She can use Kat's desk." She indicated Detective Larson's area with a jerk of her chin. Wearily, she pushed herself to her feet. "Guess I'll go check out this skull."

Sliding her arms into her jacket sleeves, she strode toward the door.

She was back in less than a minute. Sticking her head through the doorway, she said, "Reporters at the front door."

"Thanks for the warning," he said.

Melendez headed toward the back door of the station.

It was ten p.m. when Finn got to the last name on his list of festival attendees who had rented campsites immediately bordering the one occupied by Mia Valdez and Darcy Ireland.

The name on the rental list was Grant Dekoster. Finn apologized for calling so late and explained what he was after.

"Of course I remember those girls," Dekoster said. "They were *hot*. Especially the little blonde."

Finn winced at the guy's tone. "They are seventeen."

There was a long pause. "I didn't know teenagers could get in." Then, after a few seconds more of silence, "Shit. I heard someone talking about a news story of two women missing after the festival. *Those* girls are missing?"

"Afraid so." Finn pulled the phone away from his mouth as he yawned.

"I knew those girls were going to get into trouble. They could have partied with us in the campground. They never should have gone off with those motorcycle riders."

Finn's fatigue drained away like a plug had been pulled. "What motorcycle riders?" He picked up his pen, hovering it over his notepad.

"Two young guys in leather on bikes. Darcy and Mia went off with them."

Thinking of the young men in the video with the girls, Finn asked, "Did one of the guys have earplugs or an earring?"

"Wouldn't know, man. When I saw 'em, they both had helmets on."

"Can you describe their clothing? Their motorcycles?"

"Man, I don't know bikes. They were like, one red, one blue. And like I said," Dekoster reminded him, "they were wearing black leather jackets and leggings. The back of their jackets had a weird symbol: a possum, belly up."

Finn wrote it down.

"And there was a name, too. Roadkill Riders. Does that help?"

"You possibly just gave me the first real clue of the day, Mr.

Dekoster," Finn told him. "Thank you. You have my number if you think of anything else."

According to Google, Roadkill Riders was, unfortunately, a Meetup group. Which meant the members signed up online to meet up in person for—as the site advertised—*Adventures! On Wheels!* Each ride was posted, then people signed up to meet at the starting point. *We don't care who you are or where you come from. Pick a rider name for yourself, and let's go! We're all about having FUN.*

The organizer was listed as a woman with the email name Starling. In her photo, Starling was a bleached blonde with weathered skin, lots of wrinkles, and a big toothy smile. She was holding a motorcycle helmet under one arm. With no other way of contacting Starling for now, he emailed her.

He left instructions for Miki, asking her to come up ASAP with a list of missing females in this area that went back twenty years. And then, remembering how Deputy Wilder had mentioned Todd Sutter, he asked for information on that case, too.

The clock read 11:57 p.m. when he left the station. He hoped he would have a lead on Cooper Trigg and Roadkill Riders by the time Agent Foster showed up in the morning. And he fervently hoped he'd have something to report to the parents when he met them again tomorrow.

Lok and Kee and Cargo were at first resentful about his neglect of proper pet ownership duties, but after each was fed and stroked and apologized to, all three showed their forgiveness by using him as a heating pad for the rest of the night. Sleep was a long time coming, and when he finally slipped into it, he dreamed that a skeleton turned up in Grace's barn, and it belonged to Darcy Ireland.

In the dream, Grace's response was, "Well, what did you expect?" As if he should have been able to predict that.

He woke up in the morning with his jaws aching from grinding his teeth all night.

Chapter 15

Wednesday

Agent Alice Foster was more attractive than Finn remembered. His recall of her from three years ago was a polite but stiff woman in a gray pantsuit who was determined to do everything by the book. Today, her brown hair was not clipped back into her previous severe style but swung freely in a shining, chin-length bob. She wore a blue tailored blouse over white slacks and a tan jacket pulled over the pistol holstered at her waist.

She noticed his interest. Smiling, she put one hand on her hip and struck a pose. "I know. I look different."

"Yes." Finn was afraid to say anything else, lest it be regarded as sexual harassment.

"Chalk it up to being a newbie then, and having a starched shirt by my side at all times."

Her partner *had* been a two-piece-suit-and-crew-cut type of guy.

"I saw all the MISSING posters on my way into town." She rolled his visitor chair next to his seat, and then pulled out a notebook and pen from the leather satchel she carried. "What have we got, Detective?"

She might have changed her appearance, but Agent Foster

was still all business. He filled her in on everything he'd learned so far.

"I'll focus on finding this Cooper Tripp," she offered.

"That would be great."

"I see the press is already involved."

He grimaced. "Not my doing. The parents invited them in."

She shrugged. "News coverage could help."

"Yeah, but we've got limited personnel to monitor the tip line." Only Micaela, to be precise. But he knew the aide fancied herself a detective and would much rather listen to all those messages than perform her usual clerical duties.

"Did I understand correctly that you assigned the *parents* of the missing girls to review the tapes from the festival?" Foster raised a sleek eyebrow.

He waved his hands in the air. "I know, I know. Hardly proper procedure. But we're short-handed here. Detective Dawes is recuperating from knee surgery, and Detective Larson is away on her honeymoon. We need to proceed quickly, and the parents are most likely to recognize their girls."

"Understood. But I'd like to see those tapes, too. I might spot suspicious activity that civilians wouldn't be on the lookout for."

"We can arrange that onsite." He logged out of his computer, then noticed the paper file left on his desk. *Finn* was scrawled in black marker across the outside of the plain manila folder, and a Post-it note was pasted on the outside: *What you asked for. Copy on Melendez's desk.—Miki*

He flipped the file open.

Agent Foster leaned forward. "What's that?"

"A list of females reported missing from this area for the last twenty years." He shuffled the pages. "And a history of the Todd Sutter case. He was a serial rapist and murderer who was convicted and incarcerated here more than a decade ago."

Her brows came together. "Do you have reasons to be thinking copycat?"

The FBI agent was right; it made no sense, based on what he'd learned so far. But there had been just too many killings in his jurisdiction for his comfort. He felt like he was missing vital information that he should know.

Sara Melendez walked in. Staggered in, was more like it. The poor woman looked like he felt, as if she'd been up most of the night. She held a large travel mug in one hand and a windbreaker in the other, and as she came through the door she groaned. "There were more bones, Finn. Not too new, not too old—"

She stopped when she spotted Agent Foster sitting at Finn's desk. "Oh, hello." Sliding the jacket and coffee cup onto her desk, she walked over and held out a hand. "Detective Melendez. You're the FBI agent Finn mentioned. Foster, right?"

Foster stood up. "You remember."

"Of course." Melendez shook hands. "Not so many of us women that I'd forget."

"Absolutely correct on that. Call me Alice."

"Sara."

"What's this about bones?" The two women moved over to Melendez's desk.

Finn briefly wondered if he should feel rejected, but chose to review the printout of missing women as he listened to Melendez and Foster. Their discussion, along with this list, might seem even more relevant if either the detective or the FBI agent knew about the bones found in Grace's barn, but he wasn't ready to go there yet. He was still hoping the bones belonged to a bear or to an ancient pioneer or Native American buried a century ago.

The list of missing females was short, and for once Finn was grateful to be working in a farming area with sparse population. There were only seven names from his county and the surrounding area.

> **2002—Heidi Skouras, 20.** Missing from rural Kittitas county, last seen at a diner along I-90.
>
> **2002—Anna Moran, 18.** Missing from Evansburg, last seen at a high school football game.
>
> **2003—Magdalena Aguilar, 20.** Missing from Vantage. Last seen at a Gorge Amphitheatre concert.
>
> **2004—Angela Albro, 22.** Missing from a migrant farm camp near Othello, last seen hitchhiking to a friend's house. Discovered in the trunk of Todd Sutter's car. TODD SUTTER—CONVICTION 2006 was noted after that name.
>
> **2007—Cristina Disanto, 16**, missing from a migrant farm worker camp near Quincy.
>
> **2009—Sheryl Pratt, 19**. From Spokane, last seen at a Gorge Amphitheatre concert.
>
> **2016—Colleen Kelly, 16**, from Evansburg. Last seen hitchhiking east.

And if something didn't break soon, he would need to add "Darcy Ireland, 17," and "Mia Valdez, 17," to the list.

He quickly skimmed the Sutter file, noted that while the man had been convicted of killing Angela Albro, he had also been accused of kidnapping and raping Skouras, but she'd vanished before a trial could be held. A notation from the Moses Lake Police Department described the suspicion that Sutter was responsible for Aguilar and Moran, too.

But Sutter had been sent to prison in 2006, so the next three were mysteries. The Disanto and Pratt cases might be related, but with a seven year gap between the last two, Colleen Kelly's disappearance was probably not connected to the others. The fact that Aguilar and Pratt had both been seen last at the Gorge site was troubling. Maybe Agent Foster was right, concerts at the amphitheater provided hunting grounds for traffickers trolling for victims.

After the front-page list, Miki had copied the details of each case, and Finn thumbed through to the Pratt case to see if anything there might help find Darcy and Mia. Sheryl Pratt had hitchhiked to the concert, and her friends believed she'd also hitched out. But she never arrived home. No description of who might have picked her up. Not much to go on there.

He was gratified to see that dental records and likely sources for the young women's DNA—hairbrushes and toothbrushes—had been collected and logged into storage for all the cases. If the storage had been careful and remains of the missing were ever located, they stood a good chance of being identified.

"Didn't you say we needed to be at the venue at ten a.m.?"

Agent Foster stood by his elbow, her leather satchel tucked under her arm. "I'm ready when you are," she told him. "Carpool?"

He scooped up the copies to bring along.

After silently elbowing their way through a cluster of shouting reporters, they took Finn's car and drove east. As they neared Grace's compound, Finn remembered his promise to drop by and pick up the bones. He turned off on her road, explaining to Agent Foster, "I need to make a short stop."

When they rolled up into the center of the compound, all three gorillas were in their exterior pen, chasing one another up and down the rope net and making so much noise that a blind man could not have missed their presence. Grace was inside with the apes, but when she spotted Finn's car, she started for the gate.

Foster was entranced. "This is where Neema lives?" As soon as Finn parked, she reached for the door handle. "I've always wanted to meet the gorilla that solved a kidnapping case."

Finn clenched his jaw in frustration but knew it was useless to protest that *he'd* had something to do with that. Foster herself had assisted in capturing the perpetrator and closing the case. The gorilla was always the most memorable aspect of the Ivy Morgan case.

Grace and Alice Foster shook hands, and then, at Foster's request, Grace agreed to introduce the FBI agent to Neema and family. Before she led them into the enclosure, Grace stopped at the gate. "I need you to remove your weapon, Agent Foster."

Foster placed her hand protectively on the handle of her pistol.

"The gorillas are fast, and they sometimes like to grab things," Grace explained. "And they do have opposable thumbs."

Foster surveyed the compound.

"We are the only humans here," Grace promised. "Unfortunately, I have no volunteers helping today."

Finn pulled his pistol from his holster and left it on the ground, covering it with his jacket. After a slight hesitation, Alice Foster did the same.

Inside the enclosure, Gumu climbed to the top of the rope net and stayed there, his usual antisocial self. Grace called Neema, and the mother gorilla eagerly loped over to meet the newcomer, Kanoni romping by her side.

After giving Neema a hello sign, Foster asked if Grace could have the mother gorilla sign something.

"She is." Grace pointed to Neema's hand, which she was

twisting in the air. "She's saying your blouse is blue. In ASL, the sign is supposed to be made by forming the letter B and then twisting like that, but gorillas aren't good with spelling, so that's Neema's version."

Neema leaned forward, placing her huge head close to Foster, who looked a bit alarmed but didn't flinch. The gorilla's nostrils flared as she took in the agent's scent. Then she sat back on her haunches and fixed her eyes on Grace as she ground one hand into the other.

Foster asked, "What's she signing now?"

Grace laughed. "Cookie. Here." Taking a small cookie from a bag she had in her jacket pocket, Grace handed it to Alice Foster.

Neema transferred her intense gaze to Foster and repeated the sign. Foster handed the treat to Neema. The gorilla made a quick *thank you* sign with one hand as she stuffed the cookie into her mouth with the other.

Kanoni immediately leapt forward, signing *cookie cookie cookie* and then tugging on Agent Foster's jacket. Grace rolled her eyes but handed Foster another cookie, which the agent gave to the baby gorilla, laughing.

Grace bumped a hip into Finn. When he glanced her way, she slid her hand into his and transferred two small, hard bits to his palm. Oh yeah, the bones. He clutched his fingers around them as Grace withdrew her hand, then transferred them to his pants pocket.

Gumu barreled down the net, four hundred pounds of muscle-bound gorilla rocketing in their direction like a runaway locomotive. Foster took three quick steps backward and collided with the fence behind her, reflexively reaching a hand toward her holster. Finn was proud of himself for not flinching as the silverback rushed toward them.

Gumu stopped a couple of feet away. His nostrils flared, and his fierce brown-eyed gaze shifted from Grace to Agent Foster to Finn and then scanned back.

Grace held out another cookie to Agent Foster. "Want to?"

After a few seconds, the agent stepped forward and took the cookie. "Hell, yeah." She regarded the silverback warily. "He doesn't sign?"

"He knows a few signs," Grace said. "But Gumu cooperates only when he feels like it, don't you, Gumu?"

The silverback twisted one hand into the palm of the other, signing *cookie*, and then held out a massive black hand toward Agent Foster.

Grace's jaw dropped. "I'll be damned. Good, Gumu! Good gorilla!" She signed and nodded toward Foster, who gingerly held out the cookie.

Gumu snatched the treat and crammed it into his mouth. Kanoni grabbed handfuls of the fur on her father's arms, hoping for a share, but Gumu studiously ignored the baby. Then all the gorillas sat back on their rumps and stared at the three humans, waiting.

"All gone." Grace turned her bare palms outward. "Finished."

Foster held up her hands, too. And then reluctantly, Finn did the same.

Signaled by a grunt from Gumu, the gorillas climbed back into the net. Grace led the humans out of the enclosure, closing and locking the gate behind them, and Finn and Foster recovered their guns.

As they headed for their car, Grace abruptly said, "You nearly forgot what you came for, Matt." She dashed into her trailer and emerged with his sunglasses in hand. "Here you go."

He tucked them into his pocket, thinking, not for the first

time, that sometimes Dr. Grace McKenna might be a little faster on the uptake than he was. Of course Agent Foster would be curious about why they'd stopped, and Grace guessed he wouldn't have told her about the bones. "Thanks. Coffee next time, okay?"

Surprising him, Grace threw both arms around his neck and pulled him down into a fervent kiss. This was unusual behavior from his girlfriend. She rarely showed much affection in public. As a career police officer, he was not accustomed to such displays, either. It took him too long to put his arms around her.

Finally releasing him, Grace said, "See you later, Matt. Nice to meet you, Agent Foster. I hope you find those girls soon." She strode off toward the gorilla barn.

Finn rubbed his chin. What was *that* about?

Chapter 16

Wednesday

The Irelands and the Valdezes were tired, rumpled, and irritated that Finn arrived forty minutes later than he'd promised. He introduced Agent Foster and summarized everything he'd done since he'd seen them last evening. Although he'd made dozens of phone calls, he hadn't located Cooper Trigg, and he knew that none of his activities would satisfy the anxious parents. Still, he felt compelled to tell the parents about the girls riding off on motorcycles. They were understandably horrified.

Neither he nor Agent Foster mentioned the skeleton in Melendez's burned barn or the list of missing girls. They had no reason yet to believe any of those cases were related to the disappearance of Darcy and Mia.

Finn was describing how searchers were combing the area on horseback and that the Civil Air Patrol was using their drone club to search the area from the air, when a loud rap on the trailer door startled them all.

The door opened. It was the deputy who had been manning the entrance this morning.

"Knew you'd want to see this." He glanced back over his shoulder. A dark-haired girl in dirt-stained jeans and a ripped denim jacket ducked under his arm and slunk into the trailer. Her demeanor reminded Finn of Cargo's posture after the dog ate Finn's best leather belt.

Andrea Ireland stood up so fast that her chair tipped over, hitting the floor with a bang. She rushed to the girl. "Darcy! Oh my God, Darcy!" She enfolded her daughter in her arms.

"I'm sorry, Mom," the girl mumbled into her mother's neck. Her face was red from sunburn or exposure, her lips were chapped, and she was missing an earring from her left ear. Peering over Andrea's shoulder, the teen added, "Sorry, Dad."

Paul Ireland walked to them and wrapped his arms around the two women. The three of them rocked in a huddle for a long moment, as Darcy and Andrea sobbed and Paul sighed, "Thank God. Thank you, Jesus."

The Valdezes were also on their feet, frozen in position, breathless as they stared at the door. The deputy stepped back out, closed the door behind him. When the latch clicked into place, Robin's face collapsed, and she and Keith surged toward the other family. The wave of emotion that preceded them crashed over Finn as they demanded, "Where's Mia?"

Darcy struggled in her parents' arms, and Paul and Andrea released her. The teen stared at the Valdezes. "What do you—?" Her eyes glistened with sudden tears. "Oh shit, you mean Mia's not here?"

Finn gestured at the table. "Let's all sit down."

The teen eyed the furnishings. "Can we go someplace with food? I'm starving. I haven't eaten since Sunday night."

Agent Foster asked, "This is Wednesday. Do you mean you left here on Sunday evening?"

"That's what I said. Jeez! I need food!" Darcy staggered forward, and her father grabbed her arms to steady her.

"I brought lunch," Andrea told Finn. "I'll go get it." She

headed out the door toward the parking lot.

Finn and Paul Ireland maneuvered the girl into a seat at the table. Agent Foster poured her a glass of water, which Darcy drank thirstily while Finn fixed her a cup of coffee thick with cream and sugar. She sipped it and then clutched her hands around the Styrofoam cup, staring into it.

Finn slid into his seat. "Where have you been, Darcy?"

She shook her head, then squeezed her eyes shut. "I don't know exactly. I woke up in this field. Some kind of grain field, as far as you could see. No, I think it was hay. Anyhow, it went on forever. The bastard just dumped me there."

"What bastard?"

"And I was so sick, so dizzy I could hardly stand up. I practically had to crawl to the road. And there was a rattlesnake."

Robin gasped and raised a hand to her face. "A rattlesnake?"

Darcy waved off the woman's concern. "I handled it. The snake didn't bite me. But then I didn't know where I was and I didn't know what time it was, and there were just gravel roads and I didn't even know which direction I was walking because I didn't have my cell phone!"

She burst into tears again. "And then there was a pickup full of these shithead boys. They tried to grab me. I barely got away. And then the sun went down, and I had to stay out there, all by myself, all night. I was sort of afraid to walk by the road when the sun came up again. But I kept going and I finally found a paved road, but the cars still kept passing me like I wasn't even there. Like I was invisible or something! One woman actually gave me the finger!"

"And then it got dark again before I got anywhere, so I just sat against this old shed all night. At least it had a water faucet outside. Then, this morning, finally, this old man stopped. He said his son was a highway patrolman and he'd seen the posters of these missing girls from the Gorge, and was I one? I was afraid to get in because he was, like, kinda creepy with ear hairs and eyebrows like white caterpillars, and I was afraid he might kill me."

She swiped at a tear, leaving a dark streak of dirt across her cheek. "I couldn't believe that nobody else would pick me up!"

Paul laid a hand on his daughter's forearm. "You're here now. You're okay, Darcy."

Across the table, Robin Valdez made a squeaking sound, and she pressed a fist against her lips. Finn knew the woman was wondering where *her* daughter was, if *Mia* was okay.

"What bastard, Darcy?" Finn asked again.

The girl flicked a hand in the air as if he was an annoyance. "The bastard who gave me a ride on his bike. And I thought he was cute." She slapped her palm against her forehead. "Majorly stupid."

"The bastard's name?" He held his pen above his notebook. "Cooper Trigg?"

"Cooper?" The teenager blinked at him. "Why would you think that? I don't know any Cooper."

"We saw a boy that Robin knew on a security video, Darcy," her mother told her. "Cooper Trigg. He was standing behind you and Mia in line at the concession stand. There were two other boys there with you and Mia, too."

"Oh." The teen swiped at her eyes. "No, those two guys left early, the creeps, said they had to go pick up their girlfriends. I went for a ride with another guy."

"Name?" Finn asked again.

She glanced at him from beneath lowered lashes. Mascara was smeared in rings around her eyes, giving her a bruised appearance. No wonder nobody had picked her up. Darcy looked like a homeless druggie who had been sleeping rough.

Finally she said, "Comet."

"Seriously?" Agent Foster asked as she wrote down the word.

"We were just having fun. We were pretending it was like the Sixties and everyone had these silly nicknames. He said Comet, so I said I was Blackbird." Darcy tugged at a lock of black hair to demonstrate why.

"And Mia?" Keith Valdez prompted, leaning forward.

"Uh." She flattened her hands on the table for a moment, thinking. "Sunshine. Mia was Sunshine."

Keith was fidgeting, his hands clenching and loosening as if he wanted to shake the girl. "Where's Mia, Darcy?"

Darcy's eyes darted around the room. "You honestly don't know where Mia is? You haven't heard from her? Omigod . . ."

"So you were with Comet, on a motorcycle?" Finn asked.

Darcy nodded. "Omigod, Mia's really not back?"

"You were with Comet, and Mia was with—?" prompted Agent Foster.

Andrea burst through the door with paper bags in hand. Putting them on the table, she pulled out a sandwich, unwrapped it, and handed it to her daughter. Darcy mashed her dirty fingers into it and tore off a huge chunk, chewing with her mouth open. The motion made her chapped lip bleed, and she touched a fingertip to the split. Then she took a sip of coffee. When she put down the cup, Andrea slid the cup away and replaced it with a bottle of vitamin water.

Finn tapped Darcy gently on the arm. "And Mia was with—?"

The girl thought for another long minute as she chewed. After swallowing, she looked up. "Rusty?"

"Did Rusty have red hair?" Foster asked.

"No. Dusty, that was it." She took another bite. "Blond."

Finn thought the tuna salad sandwich smelled pretty good. "Last names?"

Darcy shook her head. "No, that was part of the fun. We just all used made-up names, like we were hippies or something."

Finn made a conscious effort to relax his jaw. "And Mia was riding with Dusty on his motorcycle?"

Darcy nodded, then pushed the last of the sandwich into her mouth and chewed. Placing her hand on another sandwich, she glanced at her mother. Andrea nodded and Darcy unwrapped it.

Finn slid the printout of the foursome at the concession stand from the envelope and showed the teen. "Is this Dusty and Comet?"

"Jeez, no." She giggled. "That's um ... Daniel and"— she trained her attention on the ceiling as she tried to remember— "Brandon. No, Brendan, that was it. They said they were staying in the campground, too, but I don't know where, because like I said, they left early."

Which reminded Finn that he still needed to talk to the rest of the festival attendees who were camping in the area. Maybe one of them was more observant than Darcy or Grant Dekoster. Had this Daniel and Brendan really been staying in the campground, or had they just dropped in to troll the attendees?

"And this guy?" Finn pointed to Cooper Trigg's face in the photo between Mia and Darcy.

"What about him?" Darcy asked.

"That's Cooper Trigg." Andrea touched her daughter's arm. "He's kind of a bad guy. Did he seem like he knew Mia?"

Confusion twisted Darcy's features. "No. Why would he? I don't think he ever even talked to us. This is a really lame photo. He does look sorta like Dusty, but ..." She shook her head. "No, I'm sure Dusty didn't have an earring. I would have noticed that. But why do you care about this guy?" She tapped the photo.

"Well . . ." Robin Valdez began.

"Never mind." Finn chopped a hand through the air to cut off the discussion of Cooper Trigg's past history. Trigg still might be involved somehow, but it was clear that Darcy believed he wasn't one of the boys she and Mia rode off with.

"But maybe he was C," Darcy suggested.

"What?" her father asked.

"Like the letter *C*." The teen drew the letter in the air with a finger. "Someone left a note on the car and signed it 'C.'" She rolled her eyes. "Like we were supposed to know who *that* was."

"What did the note say?" Finn asked.

She took a bite of the second sandwich—another tuna salad, according to Finn's nose—and chewed for a few seconds. "Well, it was for Mia, actually, and it said something like 'I knew that was you. What were you doing with that other guy? Here's my number, let's hook up.' And then it just said 'C.'"

Agent Foster stopped scribbling on her notepad. "Did you keep the note?"

Darcy shook her head. "No. Mia didn't have clue who 'C' was, so she threw the note away."

Now Finn wanted to strangle the teenager. But of course she couldn't have known what was coming.

Agent Foster refocused. "Darcy, please describe Comet and Dusty."

The teen twisted the cap off the water bottle. "Hmm. They both looked like farm boys, I guess."

Finn raised an eyebrow. "What do you mean by that?"

"Their hair was, like, pretty short, and they were both really tan, and their hair was, like, bleached by the sun. Comet had the bluest eyes." Darcy sounded dreamy about that for a minute, then frowned, probably at the memory of being dumped by Mr. Blue Eyes. "And they didn't have beards or mustaches or anything."

"Earrings? Studs? Jewelry?" Foster asked.

"Umm." The girl studied the ceiling. "No earrings or studs."

"Tattoos?"

"None that I saw. I think Dusty had a watch, which is a little weird."

Finn glanced at his own watch. Was it really only 12:55?

"The kids mostly use their cell phones to tell time now," Andrea explained.

Robin Valdez clutched the sleeve of the girl's jacket. "Darcy, where's Mia?"

The girl shook her head. "I don't know. She was on the bike with Dusty, and after we had this picnic, they were bringing us back to the concert and—"

A tear spilled down her cheek. She wiped it away with the back of her hand, leaving another trail of dirt across her face. "And that's the last thing I remember, being on the bike with Comet, and Mia riding with Dusty. Then I woke up in that damn field. And I couldn't find my cell. It must have fallen out of my pocket. Or Comet stole it, along with my backpack."

Robin removed the hand she had clamped across her mouth. "They drugged you."

Foster nodded. "Sounds like maybe Rohypnol."

"They roofied us?" Darcy glanced at her parents. "I'm so sorry. And I'm so stupid."

"Oh, Dar," Andrea began. "Did they—"

Her daughter slashed her hand through the air between them to cut off her mother's question. "I didn't get raped. At least, I don't think so."

Robin bit down on a knuckle, her eyes shining with tears.

Finn wanted to ask why Darcy seemed unsure, but he felt like Foster needed to do that. Or maybe he could broach the subject later with Andrea Ireland. "Back to describing the boys," he urged. "Tall, short? Skinny, fat? Moles, tattoos? Hair color? Eye color?"

"They were, like, nondescript," the teen told him. "Comet was the tallest—that's why he was mine. Maybe five ten or so. Blue eyes, like I said. Dusty was a couple of inches shorter, and I don't have a clue what color his eyes were. They weren't fat or skinny, and like I already said, they both had tan skin and bleached-out hair—you know, brown underneath but almost white on top. And they had muscles—you know, like farm boys. But they weren't exactly boys." She flashed a worried glance at her parents. "They were probably more like twenty-five."

"Oh, Darcy," Paul Ireland groaned. "What—"

Finn held up a hand to halt the fatherly criticism. "What were they wearing?"

"Blue jeans. Black boots. T-shirts—Comet's was blue and Dusty's was orange. Helmets, of course. And they had helmets for us, too," she quickly added, glancing at her parents before turning back to Finn. "They both had these cool black leather jackets with a dead possum on the back."

That confirmed what Dekoster had told him. Roadkill Riders.

Andrea made a face. "A dead possum?"

"Or maybe it was an armadillo, but on its back, legs in the air, like it was dead." The girl threw back her head, stuck out her tongue, and lifted her arms up to demonstrate. She seemed to be recovering quickly from her trauma.

"Any words or letters on their clothes?" Finn asked.

Darcy shook her head. "I don't think so."

"Did their jackets say Roadkill Riders?" Finn asked.

Foster glared at him. He was leading the witness, so to speak. But this was all going way too slowly.

"Oh." Darcy picked up the water bottle. "Maybe they did. I was distracted by the dead possum."

"Roadkill Riders was the Meetup site I mentioned," Finn told Agent Foster. "I'm waiting for email from the owner."

Foster nodded at him, then leaned close and touched the girl's arm. "Can you describe the motorcycles?"

"Um." Darcy took a swallow of water. "The one I was on was red. I think Mia's was blue." She shook her head. "Omigod, Mia!"

"The motorcycles," Foster pressed.

Darcy sniffed and swallowed. "They had black leather seats and silver trim. And they both had these upright things in back to keep the passengers on or tie stuff to or something."

Finn made notes, but had to work hard to keep his expression impassive at the generally useless information. "Do you remember any brand names, like Honda or Harley Davidson or Kawasaki or—? Do you remember any words or numbers or letters on the bikes?"

Darcy pressed her lips together for a moment, then said, "Uh, no. I don't really know motorcycles."

"Do you think you'd recognize photos of those motorcycle types if you saw them?" Agent Foster asked.

Darcy blinked, gave the agent a slight smile. "Maybe."

She studied the tabletop for a moment, and then said, "Dad, the car door got scratched somehow in the campground."

"I saw," Paul said. "Don't worry about it. The important thing is that you're safe."

"But what about Mia?" Darcy swiveled to face Robin Valdez. "I'm so sorry, Mrs. Valdez."

Robin clapped a hand over her mouth, but still burst into loud sobs. Keith said nothing as he put his arms around his wife, but his cheeks were wet, too.

Chapter 17

Wednesday

"I just want to go home!" Darcy whined. She turned to her mother. "Mom, can't we just go home? I'm so tired. And I'm so dirty, I'm disgusting. And I'm still hungry and thirsty. Dad?" She twisted around to her father. "We could just go home, couldn't we?"

Finn hated to be the bad guy, but someone needed to be. "I'm sorry, Darcy, but I need you to tell me everything you remember. We need to know everything so we can find Mia."

"I'm so tired." The teenager crossed her arms on the table in front of her and then pressed her forehead down on them. "And I already told you everything," she mumbled through her crossed arms.

Robin leaned close to the girl. "There's got to be something you remember, Darcy, that could help Mia. Please, Darcy."

Agent Foster raised her gaze from her notes and said in a no-nonsense voice, "Darcy. Sit up."

The teen reluctantly did as she was told, scowling at the FBI agent.

Foster put her hand on top of Darcy's. "I realize we've been at this for hours. I know you've been through hell, I know you're exhausted, and I think you're a hero to find your way back. You've been incredibly brave. But now, we really need your help, Darcy. I know you want to help Mia."

Darcy nodded, the tears in her eyes threatening to spill over at any moment.

Agent Foster turned to Finn. "You said you knew the caretakers here, Detective Finn? Do you think you could get them to open up the concession stand, maybe come up with a cold soda or two—" She looked toward Darcy.

"Dr. Pepper, please," Darcy said. "And maybe some chips?"

Agent Foster continued. "And Mom"—she glanced at Andrea—"do you think you could come up with some clean clothes for Darcy? Maybe there are some in her car? We need to take the clothes she has on."

Finn pulled out his cell and stood up to step outside and call the Bradys. As Andrea preceded him through the door, he heard Alice Foster say, "When everything's arranged, we'll take a little break, but until then, we'll just keep talking, okay?"

He made the call as short as possible and then ducked back in before he missed much.

"How did you first meet Comet and Dusty?" Foster was asking.

"They rode their motorcycles up to us in the campground and asked us if we wanted to go for a ride." Darcy shot a glance at her father. "I didn't think that was a good idea, but Mia was, like, 'Oh yeah, that'll be an adventure!'" The girl's eyes flicked briefly toward Robin and Keith Valdez and then back to Agent Foster.

"You said they took you on a picnic? How long did you ride before you stopped?"

"Ummm—maybe forty minutes? I didn't look at my cell."

Finn rubbed a finger across his chin. The kid's reliance on her cell phone for every shred of information was grating on his nerves. Could teenagers not know what day it was or not add two plus two without a cell phone now? When the electromagnetic burst took out the electrical network, would everyone under thirty just stagger around like zombies with blank expressions on their faces, completely clueless? It was an unsettling image.

He struggled to bring his thoughts back to the present.

" . . . all twisty and loopy and up and down, and we finally ended up on top of this hill where you could see, like, forever." Darcy held her hands wide to demonstrate vast distances. "Well, for miles, anyway."

This description might be useful to pinpoint an area. He leaned in toward the girl. "Sounds like a cool place, Darcy. What could you see?"

"All these fields. All different colors, like a patchwork quilt."

"Any buildings? Houses, barns?"

Darcy thought for a moment. "I guess there could have been one or two, but I don't remember."

Finn thought longingly of Neema, who would probably have noticed a barn or least some sort of pattern. His thoughts flashed back to the purple swoosh the gorilla had noticed that helped to crack the Ivy Morgan case. "Were there any special shapes?"

The teen's dark eyebrows knit together. "Shapes?"

All heads turned to focus on him. Finn waved a hand in the air. "You know, how sometimes roads make S-shapes, or the plowing of a field is a spiral, or a patch of trees is a triangle?"

Darcy shook her head. "No, I don't remember anything like that. It was just squares, brown, gold, and green. But there was one tree I remember, because it was the only one, and it was right in the middle of this gold square."

"That's good, Darcy." He made a note. Maybe the drone

club could do aerial photography that would help. Maybe Google Earth would show the gold square and the tree. Otherwise, he might have to drive to the top of every hill within fifty miles of the Columbia Gorge.

Foster took over, asking about what the boys had brought to the picnic, whether the containers had any markings, if they had a cooler for the beer. She was good, realizing that any small detail might be helpful. But Darcy had clearly been more focused on Comet's blue eyes than on anything else.

Then Brynne Brady arrived with keys to the concession stand, Andrea Ireland trailing her, bearing a stack of clothes she'd rummaged from the Ford Edge.

"You're doing great, Darcy," Agent Foster praised. She stood up from her chair and stretched. "Take a break, wash up, change your clothes, have a cold drink."

Darcy stood up and walked toward the restroom door, following her mother.

"I'm coming, too," Alice Foster announced, trailing the mother and daughter into the tiny restroom.

Finn knew it was a good idea to stay with the witness. If anything significant happened, if the girl had visible bruises, or if any words of importance passed between Darcy and her mother, the FBI agent wanted to be there. Before she vanished through the door, Foster tossed a look at Finn and said, "And then we'll start all over again."

Finn stood up and stretched his arms over his head. The Valdezes were watching him expectantly, so he suppressed the groan that nearly escaped his lips. Their daughter was still out there somewhere. It was going to be another long, long evening.

"We're making progress here," he told them.

He hoped it was true.

Chapter 18

Thursday

At ten-thirty a.m. the next day, Grace watched Matthew Finn drive into her compound. She was glad to see him, but again, he wasn't alone. He had a different woman with him, a blonde this time. Grace groaned inwardly. Her stomach felt queasy; Kanoni was developing a cold, with both a runny nose and diarrhea. Company was the last thing she needed. First, the attractive FBI agent, and now, another pretty woman?

Grace felt like a grimy dishrag that had been wadded up and left to mildew on the kitchen counter. Had she even brushed her hair this morning? Her teeth? She ran her tongue around her mouth.

When Finn introduced the woman as Robin Valdez, the mother of the missing girl, Grace's attitude did an about-face.

"I called you this morning," he said. "I left you a voicemail message?"

"Sorry, I must have left my phone in the house," Grace apologized, patting her pockets for her cell phone. "I've been a little distracted."

The Irelands, he explained, parents of the luckier girl, had driven back to Bellingham this morning.

"I saw the news last night," Grace told the two of them.

"That's great that the other girl made it back."

Finn's lips twisted in exasperation, and she touched his sleeve. "You handled it well, Matt."

The press conference had been like a celebration, with reporters cheering like the case was successfully resolved. Everyone wanted to talk to Darcy Ireland and her parents. Finn had abruptly ended the barrage of shouted questions from reporters by stepping up to the microphone and saying, "We are pleased that Darcy Ireland survived her abduction, but we must all remember that another girl, seventeen-year-old Mia Valdez, remains missing." Then he shepherded the Irelands away.

"Thank God Detective Finn was there," Robin Valdez said. She was petite, and when she gazed up, Grace noted that beneath her carefully colored blond bangs, worry lines were carved into her forehead. She looked older than Grace would have expected the mother of a teen to be.

Focusing on Grace, Robin said, "My husband Keith needed to go home. I know that seems cold, but we own a mail-order company, business cards and stationery and all that, and we have no staff. If we're not filling orders, well, there's no money coming in, and it's been three days." Her voice cracked on the last few words, and she forced a brief smile that ended up seeming apologetic. "So my husband is driving back today."

She clutched her hands together. "But I just can't. I've got to stay close until they find her." Robin's blue eyes beseeched Grace. "You understand, don't you?"

"Of course." What Grace didn't understand was why Matt had brought Robin here.

"Detective Finn"—Robin glanced briefly in his direction— "said you might be able to help me with a place to stay. I mean, we don't know how long it will take before"—a shadow passed over her face, and her voice caught for a second—"Mia comes back. I can help you. I can cook and clean. I'm good with a hammer, and I'm even better with a computer. I can't afford to pay much, but I'd be glad to help you however I can."

Help. Now there was a magical word. "You're welcome here, Robin, for as long as you need. You don't need to pay at all," Grace told her. "As long as you're willing to sleep in a bunk in that trailer." She pointed toward the trailer that held her staff quarters. "Most of the time you'll be alone in there."

"A bunk is fine. A bunk is great. Thank you so much." Robin reached out to take Grace's hand in hers. "But I need to *do* something, too. I can't just sit around. Please, put me to work."

Grace shot Finn a look. Really? His lips formed a silent *anything.*

She turned back to Robin. "How do you feel about gorillas?"

Robin blinked. "Gorillas?"

"I have three. They're part of a psychology project. I teach them sign language and observe their communication."

The blonde's chin jerked up. "Really? I know some sign language." Then her expression sagged. "I learned it from my daughter Mia, when she was studying ASL as a second language last year."

Grace brightened. Sign language was a bonus. "So you're not afraid of gorillas?"

Robin touched Grace's arm. "Hon, I volunteer with special needs kids, and some of them have a lot of 'issues' controlling themselves." She enclosed the word 'issues' in air quotes, curling her fingers in the air. "Those kids seem like primitive species some days. How bad could actual gorillas be?"

"You might be surprised."

"I'll pay for my meals and anything else I can, and I'll help you any way you need." Robin turned to Finn. Bending to the small travel bag at her feet, she pulled out a sheaf of flyers. MISSING ~ MIA VALDEZ, with Mia's smiling face and description on them. "But the first thing I'd like to do is put these up everywhere. Is there Uber or Lyft or some taxi service I can call to take me to a car rental place?"

Grace's heart twisted at the photo of the missing teen. What could that poor girl be going through right now? "You can borrow my van, Robin, for as long as you want."

"That would be wonderful, thank you." Robin flashed a tired smile at Grace before turning to Finn. "And Detective Finn, you will let me know about each new development, right?"

Grace saw a twinge of anxiety flash through Finn's eyes before he replied, "I'll be in contact whenever I have anything to report, Mrs. Valdez."

"Call me Robin, please. And thank you, Detective." Robin picked up her small travel bag and held it front of her as she faced Grace. "And thank you, Grace. Any unoccupied bunk, right?" She headed toward the staff trailer.

They watched her walk away.

Finn rubbed his neck. "She's holding up well, given what she's going through. I'm so glad I'll never have to worry about where my child is."

Grace flinched. Now he was glad he didn't have children? She turned to him, rested her hands gently on his biceps. She always felt like it was wrong to hug Finn while he was wearing his gun. "You look like you didn't sleep last night, Matt. Can you sit down, stay for a while?"

"Afraid not." He watched Robin Valdez open the door of the trailer across the yard.

Turning to Grace, he gently pushed a strand of hair from her forehead. "Thank you for taking her in. Let me know if she's a burden."

"Are you kidding? Of course I'd let anyone in that circumstance stay here. It's the least I can do. The staff trailer is hardly the Ritz. And I *can* use any help I can get."

"Wish *I* could give you some." Leaning in, he gave her a quick kiss. The rasp of his whiskers told her he needed a shave. "But I've got to run." He hesitated a second before asking, "Any more bones?"

"Not as far as I know." She shook her head and was immediately sorry as a wave of dizziness sloshed over her.

Clasping both her shoulders, he studied her face. "You okay, sweetheart? You're a little green around the gills."

Grace grimaced. "I'm fine. Just tired."

"You do look exhausted." He traced a finger down her cheek.

She swallowed the saliva pooling in her mouth. Exhaustion was only half of her problem. "You're one to talk. You're working too hard."

"Not a lot of choice right now." His gaze bore into hers. "Robin really does need something to do with her time while she's here; please let her help."

"I will." The nausea rose again, and Grace pressed a hand against her stomach.

Finn kissed her forehead. "I'll make it up to you, Grace, after this is over." His jaw muscles clenched for a moment, and she knew that he was thinking about how long a missing persons case could take, and that there would always be yet another case to occupy his time. "We'll take a vacation, get away together for a couple of weeks. We both deserve it."

Like that would ever happen. "Sounds good."

"It's a date." Turning, he headed for his car.

Grace bolted for the toilet and threw up.

* * * * *

Robin turned out to be a huge help. After she returned from stapling up her new flyers, Grace introduced her to the gorillas. Robin volunteered to chop and prepare meals for them and help with enrichment and entertainment activities. She was understandably nervous around the adult gorillas, but she showed Kanoni how to stack plastic rings on a peg and wear the largest rings as bracelets. Because the baby gorilla was subdued today, and she had an assistant to help, in the afternoon Grace decided that it might be a good time for painting.

The two women set up the painting supplies on a low table in the outdoor enclosure, uncapping jars of bright acrylic paints and laying out canvasses and large brushes and a roll of paper towels. Grace placed the brushes inside the paint jars. Even Gumu came to watch.

Robin anxiously observed the silverback's approach until Gumu sat down a few yards away. She turned sideways to keep an eye on the huge male and the painting setup. "They really like to paint?"

"They do. The hard part is to keep them focused so they don't start hitting one another with canvasses or drinking the paint."

The gorillas edged closer to the table to inspect the supplies.

"Why is the table so low?" Robin stepped back to stand closer to the fence.

"You'll see." Grace handed Gumu a canvas. He sat on his haunches by the edge of the table, grasped the canvas with both of his hand-like feet, and then reached for a large brush in a jar of bright fuchsia and made a brilliant half circle on his canvas.

Robin clasped her hands together. "I can't believe it."

"I almost forgot." Grace pulled out her cell phone. "I make

videos of them creating the paintings, or at least part of each painting, so the buyer will know they're getting artworks by real apes."

Kanoni grabbed a dry brush from the table top and put it into her mouth, and then spun in a circle. She tried to touch her brush to Gumu's painting but the silverback elbowed her away. Grace, still focused on filming Gumu, grabbed the baby gorilla's arm and, walking backward, tugged her to the other side of the table, then put the smallest canvas onto the ground in front of her. The little ape immediately chose a brush already dunked into bright yellow paint and jabbed it at her canvas. Robin pulled out her own cell phone and began to videotape Kanoni.

Neema grabbed the remaining canvas, slid it down the table, and leaned over it. She seemed to carefully consider the possibilities, pushed the canvas into a vertical position against the table, then selected a large brush soaked in purple paint. As Grace switched position to record her actions, Neema brushed on a wide zigzag of purple.

Kanoni scampered over and tried to steal the purple brush from her mother.

Grace tolerantly pushed her away, led Kanoni back to her own canvas, set the yellow brush down on the table, dipped a new paintbrush in purple and handed it to the baby. Kanoni chirped with delight and made an oval shape on her canvas, partially obscuring the yellow jabs.

Gumu picked up the discarded yellow brush and painted big swoops across his canvas.

"It's remarkable," Robin remarked. "They each have their own styles."

Grace chuckled. "Well, they all paint abstracts. But they do have their favorite colors and shapes." She turned from

Kanoni's painting to study Neema's. "How about adding some blue or green, Neema?" She signed as she spoke.

The mother gorilla placed her purple brush horizontally into her mouth, holding it with her teeth as she solemnly regarded Grace. Then she picked up a blue-dipped brush and made blue splotches on her canvas.

"I do make color suggestions," Grace explained, "but they make the paintings. You obviously have to monitor them, or these artists can get into a paint fight, and believe me, paint is not easy to get out of gorilla fur."

Gumu had switched to black, and Kanoni was trying to grab his brush again. Grace gave the baby a smaller brush filled with black paint. "I try to keep the paintings individual, one per gorilla," she explained. "That way people are more likely to buy two or three paintings, whereas I'd only sell one if all three gorillas did one canvas."

"Fundraising?"

"Exactly."

"I wondered who was paying for all this." Robin held out her arms to indicate the compound. "It's got to cost a lot to care for three huge animals."

Grace sighed. "It does. When Neema and Gumu were owned by a university, I had grants and paid staff, but since I purchased the gorillas, I have to rely on volunteers and donations. And internet sales of ape artwork." She handed Gumu a green brush and stood back to film him some more.

"You have a website?"

"Yep. That's how I sell the paintings."

"Mind if I take a look at your website?" Robin asked. "I am a wizard at online sales."

"We could definitely use some wizardry, couldn't we, Gumu?" The silverback regarded Grace with his usual haughty expression, as if she were a servant who dared to speak to him. He handed her his paintbrush and then strolled back to the rope net.

Robin picked up the painting he'd left on the ground. Black streaks slashed vertically through splotches of fuchsia, yellow, and green. "Bold use of darks to add drama, with brilliant touches of color. I'd name it Summer Storm."

Grace laughed. "You're hired. Neema, what do you call your painting?"

The two women regarded the results produced by the mother gorilla. Bright purple, yellow, blue, and green splotches, bunched together.

"Neema never uses black," Grace explained. "She's an optimistic gorilla. Aren't you, sweetie?" She patted Neema on the shoulder.

Robin slumped and her face stiffened, and Grace knew she was thinking about her daughter. Maybe Robin and Mia had painted together. She was afraid to ask.

Neema motioned with her arms. Grace translated as she copied the motions. "Yes, you're a good gorilla." Then she pointed to Neema's painting. "What do you call this painting?"

Neema pinched her fingers together and held them to her nose.

"Flower?" Robin guessed.

"Yes. She calls almost all her paintings flowers." She regarded the mother gorilla. "Are you finished?"

Neema twisted her arms in the air.

"Finished," Robin pronounced.

Tree candy me, Neema signed.

Robin's brow wrinkled. "I didn't catch that."

"She's asking for a lollipop, that's her favorite treat. No tree candy," Grace signed as she spoke.

Juice.

Robin said, "I did understand that. Juice, right?"

Grace nodded. "Juice, in a minute." She picked up Neema's painting.

"You finished, Kanoni?" Robin asked the baby gorilla, signing the word for "done."

The little ape regarded her solemnly as she chewed the end of the yellow paintbrush. Snot ran from her wide nostrils down over her upper lip. Robin wiped it off with a paper towel. After a few seconds, Kanoni signed *juice juice juice.*

When Robin held out her hand for the paintbrush, the baby gorilla placed it into her hand, bristles first.

"You're a natural," Grace observed.

Robin wiped her hand on a paper towel, and then picked up Kanoni's painting and brushed the dirt from the edges. "They may be big and strong and hairy, but they're children, aren't they? I'm used to dealing with children. I had . . . four of my own, you know."

Grace put a hand on the other woman's shoulder.

"Thank you for sharing *your* family with me," Robin said softly.

"Thank *you* for understanding they are family." Grace brushed her hand across her belly for a second, then busied herself putting the paintings in the drying rack and helping Robin wash out brushes and cap the paint jars. "You'll want to wash your hands. Kanoni seems to be getting a cold."

"Can I use your computer for a couple of hours?" Robin asked hesitantly. "I want to check the Facebook feeds on Mia's page; it's so hard to do on a cell phone. And if it's okay, I'll post a couple of photos on Instagram and Snapchat and Twitter." She swallowed hard. "To remind everyone to keep looking. To keep thinking about her."

"Of course." A lump formed in Grace's own throat. Why hadn't she thought to offer Robin the use of her computer? "Anytime. You don't even need to ask."

"And I can look at your website. And if you lend me your cell phone, I'll put these painting videos together for you." She held out her hand.

Grace handed Robin her cell. "That would be fantastic, but you don't need to do all that."

"I do. It helps me; keeps me from thinking too much."

While Robin used the computer, Grace dared to take a nap. When she got up, she found the older woman sitting on the porch steps of the staff trailer, sipping a glass of water and silently crying.

As Grace approached, Robin hastily wiped the tears from her cheeks on her shirt sleeve. Her cell phone buzzed. She glanced at it and tapped in a message. "Darcy again," she explained. She stood up, squeegeed the moisture from her eyes with her fingers this time. "Excuse the tears. Just thinking about Mia and feeling sorry for myself."

"You've got a right."

"Mia's the only one left," Robin murmured. "If I lose her, too, I don't think I can stand it."

Grace studied the other woman's face, afraid to ask.

"Detective Finn didn't tell you?"

Grace shook her head.

Robin volunteered, "Keith and I lost our three older children in a car crash."

"My God." Grace dropped to the steps beside Robin and put an arm around her shoulders. "I'm so sorry. I can't wrap my brain around that kind of tragedy."

Robin took a deep breath. With her gaze focused on the ground, she said, "Jared had just turned eighteen. He was driving. And he had his brother and sisters with him. Justin and Julie were sixteen and fifteen. And Mia was in the back, too. She was only five, and she was strapped into a child seat."

The enormity of the loss rendered Grace speechless. And now this poor woman's remaining child might be gone, too. Mia. Matt had shown her the first photo he'd received of the blond girl. The picture depicted Mia staring at the camera, one hand on her hip and a sly smile on her face, a petite teenager who appeared delicate but somehow vivacious and daring at the same time.

Grace wanted to ask more about Mia, but it didn't seem right to press for details now.

"It was a long time ago. Twelve years." Robin took another deep breath and wiped her eyes again. "And now, this. I feel cursed."

She sat up straighter. "The Irelands think Keith and I smother Mia." She sighed. "Mia hates being only five feet tall; did I tell you that? The other kids took after Keith, taller, with dark hair. Mia apparently got my genes. She once told me that there are no short leaders in history except for Napoleon, and everyone makes fun of him." She moved her sorrowful gaze to the trees at the edge of the yard. "I hope I never made her feel small."

"I'm sure you didn't," Grace said. "I'm sure you made her feel loved."

Robin didn't appear convinced. "Some people are even suggesting that she might have run away. I can't believe she'd do that to us." Taking a tissue from her pocket, she blew her nose. "But it's pointless to whine, isn't it? I'm sure you have problems, too."

"Teensy ones, by comparison. Can I ask how old you were when Mia was born?"

"Forty-two, nearly forty-three."

"You must have gotten pregnant a long time after . . . the others." It seemed almost sacrilegious to mention the dead children. "How did you feel about that?"

Robin's blue eyes met hers. "At first, I was shocked, and frankly, a bit resentful."

Grace swallowed. "I can understand that."

"But then I realized what a blessing a new baby could be at that stage of my life."

Grace turned away to focus on the horizon. A blessing? When she got pregnant at forty-two, Robin had a steady husband and had already been a mother three times over. She had wanted children, she understood children, she planned for children. Robin wasn't treading water in a rising tide of fear and dread.

How could Grace explain her emotional turmoil to this mother who had so loved and so tragically lost her children?

As far as Grace knew, every major problem on earth could be traced back to *homo sapiens*. People were the reason that the oceans were filling with plastic, that there was no longer room for orangutans and tigers in Asia, for gorillas in Africa. People were the reason that orcas were starving in the sea. Human greed and ignorance murdered elephants for ivory and rhinos for their horns, and drowned dolphins and turtles in drift nets.

She had always felt righteous for not adding another destructive human to the overloaded planetary ecosystem.

Even if she could get over that feeling—a monumental *if*—how could she have a child now? She lived in a single-wide trailer, for heaven's sake. She'd have to change her tiny office into a nursery to keep a baby there.

No upwardly mobile career path stretched out in front of

her, not even a trail that promised a comfortable life and a secure retirement. Just an endless calendar of gorilla care and struggles for money.

Her next birthday cake would have forty-one candles. It would be a conflagration; she'd need to keep a fire extinguisher close by. When this child was ready for college, she'd be in her sixties. She already felt old.

But maybe a child would change that feeling. This was not just any baby. It was her baby, and Matthew Finn's. She knew Matt had moved from Chicago to Evansburg to raise a family with his wife. He was still bitter that Wendy had divorced him to have a baby with her former lover.

Grace flattened a hand against her abdomen. The embryo, if there really was an embryo in there, wouldn't be bigger than a peanut. She couldn't feel anything inside yet, but she could envision this child. A girl with Finn's piercing blue eyes and the dark hair they shared. Black Irish coloring.

Or a boy. Didn't most men want a boy? Just one child to add to the world, to the human gene pool. She and Matt had good genes. She often felt like a lesser woman in the company of mothers, and she knew she was missing out on the loving bonds they felt with their children.

Nobody else seemed to feel this burden of environmental guilt; why should she? She could teach this child to love nature and appreciate the amazing skills and intelligence of all animals, wild and domestic. She could teach her—or him—to understand the complexity of ecosystems, to respect and preserve the environment.

But Matt had said he was *glad* that he wasn't a parent. When had that changed?

She wanted Matt in her life. He was an honorable man, a kind man, a considerate lover. This could be a way of snaring him. She knew that he would ask her to move in with him, even to marry him. And the child could be a playmate for Kanoni for years to come.

She caught her lower lip between her teeth. She didn't really want to *snare* Matt, did she? And as for a playmate for Kanoni, *that* thought proved how insane the whole notion was—what sort of unnatural human mother considered the welfare of an ape before her own child?

She could still be wrong. Maybe she should hope this was early menopause.

Grace felt Robin's gaze on her face. Her voice low, the other woman quietly asked, "Are you . . .?"

She nodded, swallowed hard. "I think I might be."

"You *think*?"

Grace grimaced. "Evansburg is a small town. A gossipy town. I can't march into the drugstore and waltz out with a pregnancy test. The news that Gorilla Woman might be pregnant would be all over town within a couple of hours. There'd be jokes that I was having a baby gorilla. And Finn can't know."

Sliding her hand under Grace's where it rested on her abdomen, Robin interwove their fingers and then gave Grace's hand a squeeze. "It will be our secret."

Fine lines pulled at the corners of Robin's eyes and mouth. Purple shadows smudged her cheeks. How could this sad woman be comforting *her* now? This was the fourth night her daughter was missing. Tiny Mia, of the shining blond tresses and Cupid's bow smile.

Grace leaned forward to give Robin a hug.

Chapter 19

Thursday

Finn stared at a yellow rectangle in the Google Earth window. Probably a wheat field, with a single tree in the middle of it. That field seemed likely to be the place that Darcy had described, about eighteen miles east and slightly south of Vantage, sandwiched between farm roads. He wrote down the GPS coordinates and the names of the roads that bordered it. The information would at least confirm where Comet had dumped Darcy Ireland, and that might be a starting point for finding Mia. He checked his watch. Nearly four p.m. already. He'd have to see if Grant County deputies could search the area, make sure the body of a teenage girl wasn't somewhere close by. His imagination conjured up the awful image of a young blond corpse under that waving wheat.

His desk phone rang again, and he wearily picked it up. "Detective Finn."

"My name is Felicia Morris, and I'm a reporter with—"

"I have no comment at this time." He tapped the phone back into its cradle. Why did the desk clerk keep putting reporters through to his extension? He called her to ask.

"I'm sorry. Most don't tell me they're reporters," she said.

He hung up. Of course they wouldn't.

"My skeleton is Magdalena Aguilar," Sara Melendez startled Finn by saying from her desk across the room. "Confirmed by dental records." She swiveled in her chair to face his desk.

Finn found it a little creepy that the other detective had said "*my* skeleton." "You got a whole skeleton?"

"Not a single bone missing. We borrowed a Ground-Penetrating Radar device from the utility company. That barn hadn't been used for anything but storing hay for decades, so anyone could have swung by to bury a body, but Magdalena was on Todd Sutter's list of probables." She put a hand to her forehead. "The press is gonna love this."

"Good," he said. "Get 'em off my back."

"Unfortunately, Magdalena's only a skeleton now, and after the fire, there's nothing left to link Sutter to her."

"At least the Aguilar family will know for sure. And it could come in useful when Sutter's up for parole."

Melendez's eyes narrowed. "If there's any justice, Sutter will *never* be up for parole."

Finn agreed, but they both knew that wasn't the way the system always worked. "Where's that GPR unit now?"

"Locked in the evidence room. Someone's coming to get it day after tomorrow. Why?"

He briefly considered telling her about the bones in Grace's barn, but he'd promised Grace. Once the news was out, it would be all over Evansburg in a flash. He settled for saying, "Grace McKenna's gorillas live in an old barn. I just want to make sure there's not another body buried under there."

"Ugh." After wincing at the idea, she then said, "Maybe we should check all the barns in the county."

"Maybe all the barns in the state. Sutter picked up victims from several counties, didn't he?" He made a mental note to read the entire Sutter file. "Any leads on your arsonist?"

Melendez frowned. "We know he's using gasoline and he's targeting abandoned buildings, and we've found tire tracks." Shaking her head, she added, "Unfortunately, they're from really common tires. Half the pickups in the county are rolling on 'em right now."

"The fact that he—or she—is targeting abandoned buildings means he—or she—is a local."

"She? How many arsonists are women?"

Finn shrugged. "Something like fifteen percent."

"And their motive is usually revenge. What sort of a kick would this one get from burning down abandoned buildings?"

"Just trying to give women equal opportunity."

"Well, stop it. Trust me, it will turn out to be a guy. Probably multiple guys. Probably multiple guys under the age of twenty-five. I have a few delinquents in mind." She swiveled back to her computer.

Hours later, Finn was eager to finish his GPR scan of Grace's barn floor. When he arrived, he'd been relieved to find Robin Valdez was out on an errand. He had no news for her, and he didn't want to explain that he was searching for human bones under the dirt floor of the barn. It was bad enough to have a missing daughter, but it would be even worse to imagine she might be the latest victim of a serial killer.

Finn noticed Kanoni was wearing a diaper.

"Diarrhea," Grace explained. "It's easier to change her than to constantly wash her and Neema."

Slowly rolling the wheeled radar device forward, he watched the screen on the attached laptop, while Grace stood by with a shovel to dig as needed. They found a couple of metal pieces from some ancient farm implement, two broken bricks, a bit from a horse bridle, and an ancient spur that some cowboy had lost over the years. The only troubling discovery was another bone, buried only a few inches below the surface. This was the shortest yet, maybe the end bone of a finger or one of the smallest bones in a foot.

Could someone have scattered a skeleton over the entire compound? Should he walk the machine over the courtyard between Grace's trailers?

Grace queried the gorillas about the latest bone. None of the apes showed any recognition of what she was talking about, which shouldn't have been surprising, since the bone had been buried.

Never one to pass up an opportunity to ask for food, Neema asked for *apple*. When Grace refused, Neema signed *chase*.

Grace raised her hands and stomped her foot, and then her questions gave way to a wild, ear-splitting game of ape tag. Kanoni lagged behind the adult gorillas for a change.

Grace pursued the apes outside into the rope net. Sliding the newest bone fragment into his pants pocket, Finn continued with his scan.

When he was on his last pass, Robin Valdez slipped into the barn. Grace joined her, and both women leaned side-by-side against the far wall as they discussed something in voices too low to hear. Finn was hyperaware of Robin's eyes following his every move, probably wondering why he wasn't out chasing down leads to find her daughter.

"This will only take a few minutes more," he apologized. "The machine is on loan."

"What are you looking for with that thing?" Robin asked.

Finn hesitated. No way was he going to admit to this anxious mother that he was searching for a skeleton. "Construction debris," he finally said. "This barn was remodeled, and we suspect the crew simply buried the scraps instead of carting them away like they should have."

Grace shot him a querying look, but when Robin turned her way, Grace added, "I don't want the gorillas digging up anything dangerous."

Robin must have wondered at the timing.

The apes, tired of chasing one another up and down the netting outside, returned to the barn to observe the humans. Neema wanted to push the GPR unit like Finn had, and although it made him feel like an idiot, he let the mother gorilla have a go for a few yards. Then Kanoni wanted a try, but she couldn't roll it far and ended up swinging on the handle by a hand and a foot until Finn pulled her off.

Then Gumu, who had been watching from the doorway, lumbered toward the machine, eyeing it warily.

He heard Robin mutter, "Oh, this should be good."

"No way." Finn held out his hand in a "stop" motion. He was having visions of the silverback swinging the expensive GPR device around his head like a lariat. "This is a valuable machine. Not a toy for gorillas."

Gumu rocked forward on his knuckles and glared at Finn for a few seconds. Then he rose up to his full height and pounded with cupped hands on the black leather of his chest, bared his huge canine teeth, and grunted to add menace to his threat display.

Finn glanced nervously at Grace. She seemed to be more interested in her cell phone than in keeping her gorillas under control.

He squared his body between the machine and the silverback. "No!" he shouted, snapping the hand sign at the gigantic ape.

Gumu sank back down to his knuckles, then reached around Finn and slapped the handle of the GPR machine as if to prove he could touch it if he really wanted to. Snorting, the silverback strutted stiff-legged to the doorway as though he'd won the contest.

Grace held her cell phone in front of her with both hands, filming.

Finn threw a hand up in front of his face. "Stop that!"

After poking the screen with her index finger, Grace lowered her phone. "That was very interesting. A meeting of two alpha males."

Robin Valdez covered her mouth with her hand, trying to hide a smile.

Finn fumed. "Gumu could have ripped out my throat."

"But you prevailed," Grace said. "He respects you."

A scoffing noise escaped his throat. He aimed an index finger at her. "Do *not* post that video anywhere."

"Detective Finn!" A voice hailed him from outside the barn. Agent Alice Foster. He welcomed the interruption.

The FBI agent stood on the other side of the enclosure. "I have information to share."

Finn pushed the GPR init outside, detached the laptop, and with the help of Agent Foster, loaded the device into his car trunk. He was grateful Foster had not seen his argument with Gumu. He needed to preserve *some* dignity in his work relationships.

"Cooper Trigg is rumored to be in Spokane, so I put some feelers out there, but we haven't scooped him up yet," she told him.

Finn envied the FBI's resources. "Okay."

"We got email back from the organizer of the Roadkill Riders Meetup website," she told him. "Get this: she doesn't even attend most of the rides."

"Great."

"But she knew Comet. He's Kane Metrios, lives just outside of Evansburg, works at the local SpeediLube. Want to go grill him with me?"

"You betcha."

Robin Valdez was watching both of them, her expression hopeful.

"We may have found one of the boys who took Darcy and Mia," he told her. "It might not lead to anything right away, but every clue helps."

The woman pressed her hands together in front of her chest as if praying.

Kane Metrios was as Darcy had described him, a clean-cut type with buzz-cut hair and startling blue eyes. He was an oil change technician at SpeediLube and nervous as hell that a police detective and an FBI agent had surprised him at work. They interviewed him at a picnic table set up outside the shop for employee breaks.

According to his driver's license, Metrios was twenty years old. When they showed him their badges, he immediately blurted, "I didn't rape that girl."

"Interesting way to start a conversation," Agent Foster observed.

"Well, I didn't." He crossed his arms. "So you can't pin that on me."

Finn leaned in. "We're more interested in your friend. What is Dusty's full name?"

Metrios seemed relieved. He clasped his hands on the table in front of him. "I'd like to help you guys. But see, I don't really know Dusty. See, that's the thing about the club. Roadkill Riders. It's just all for fun, right? We all use these nicknames, and it's not like we hang out all the time. We just ride together sometimes."

"And kidnap girls," Agent Foster added.

Metrios blanched and moved his hands to his lap. "Not true. That was the first time."

"So you admit you abducted Darcy and Mia?" she pressed.

A perplexed expression crossed his face. "They said Sunshine and Blackbird. You know, more nicknames. They wanted to join in the fun."

"Where'd you get the idea to cruise the Sasquatch Festival?" Finn wanted to know. It nagged him that Melendez's skeleton had been a girl picked up at the Gorge Amphitheatre. Could there be a connection between Sutter's previous crimes and this current case?

"Ah, you know." Metrios grinned. "Concerts. Lotsa pretty girls. Girls who are looking for fun. They like to go for rides."

Finn supposed it was logical, in a perverted way. "Did you have tickets to the festival?"

The list of ticket buyers might contain a clue, but he cringed inwardly at the idea of having to sort through hundreds of names.

Metrios stared at him as though Finn were especially dense. "Just rode into the campgrounds. People go in and out that gate all day long."

Finn's neck muscles tightened at all the possibilities that provided.

"You started off together," Agent Foster stated. "Why'd you and Dusty split up?"

Metrios glanced over Finn's shoulder at the SpeediLube building window.

Finn turned. Two of Metrios's colleagues watched through the glass. Finn assessed their ages as late teens or maybe early twenties. One young man was a redhead, but they turned away so quickly that the only other detail Finn caught was the smudge of a tattoo on the back of the dark boy's neck. Was Metrios lying? Could one of them be Dusty? Did they know about the kidnapping?

"Kane, why did you and Dusty split up?" Agent Foster repeated.

Metrios turned back to her. "Dusty wanted to." He shrugged. "I mean, we each had one, so why not?"

Finn pulled out the grainy photo from the video at the concession stand. He pointed to the young man Robin had identified as Cooper Trigg. "Is this Dusty?"

Metrios leaned forward to squint at the photo. "Could be."

Finn wondered if slugging Metrios might improve his memory.

The kid recognized the threat in Finn's expression. "Like I said, I don't really know the dude, and you have to admit, this pic is crap."

Finn narrowed his eyes. "Where are Dusty and Mia—I mean Sunshine—now?"

At that question, Metrios abruptly seemed to realize how serious this situation could be. He pushed himself up out of his slouch. "Hell, I don't know. I told you, I don't know that Dusty dude. Don't know where he lives, don't know where he works, don't know what his real name is. All I can tell you is that he rides an old Harley Sportster. A blue one."

"License plate?" Foster's pen was poised over her writing pad.

Metrios rolled his eyes. Finn had a sinking feeling that Metrios knew no more than the Meetup organizer had.

What kind of club didn't know who its members were? They'd have to track down the email addresses and then possibly even the computers they'd come from . . . It was giving him a headache to think about how long that might take.

Robin Valdez's prayerful gesture flashed onto the screen of his memory.

Foster looked up from her notes. "Where'd you get the Roadkill jackets?"

"Online," Metrios told her. "There's a website. $89.95. Plus tax. Free shipping."

Finn was starting to hate the internet, that font of boundless and so often useless information that took forever to sort through. He levered himself up from the bench and gestured with his left hand while reaching for his handcuffs with his right. "Kane Metrios, stand up and turn around."

The kid grabbed onto the edge of the table top with both hands. "But I cooperated. I helped, didn't I? And I didn't rape that girl. If she says I did, she's lying."

"Maybe you didn't rape her." Agent Foster put one hand on the kid's upper arm and one on the back of his neck. "But you did kidnap Darcy Ireland, drug her, and dump her in the middle of nowhere, didn't you, Kane?"

"She said her name was Blackbird," he protested, as if that was an excuse. "She *wanted* to come with us. They both did."

"Then why did you drug her?"

He stared at the tabletop. "That was all Dusty's idea. I didn't know he was going to slip that shit into the beer like that. But then . . . hell, my girl was unconscious. I could barely keep her on the back of the bike. So it just didn't seem right." He looked up at them, his eyes begging. "I wouldn't do that. I didn't rape her."

"Put him in the back of my car," Finn told Alice Foster after cuffing Metrios. "I want to talk to the other employees."

"I'll be back." She steered the kid around and marched him toward the parking lot.

The two boys who had been watching through the

window, redhead Becker Symes and tattooed Joe Greco, seemed overly nervous during questioning. But then, both were only nineteen, and teenage boys often had something to hide, if only illegal purchases of cigarettes and alcohol, reckless driving, and underage drinking. When shown photos of the girls, each shook his head. The blurry still from the video produced no sign of recognition of the three men in the photo, either.

Neither Symes nor Greco owned a motorcycle, and both claimed they were working on Sunday when the girls had ridden off into danger. The SpeediLube manager verified that, and showed Finn the timecards. For the moment, Finn and Foster dismissed them as unimportant, but he took photos of all the licenses in the parking lot just for good measure.

"I have a feeling those two know more than they're saying," Alice Foster said as they exited the SpeediLube office.

Finn agreed. "But *what* do they know more about?"

"Good question." She shrugged. "You take Metrios and check out the home, and I'll check out the Roadkill Riders and the jacket purchases online. I'll see what else I can pick up about Cooper Trigg, too." She pulled open her car door.

"Thank you," he said sincerely, nearly wanting to kiss her in gratitude. He hated computer searches.

By the time he'd booked Metrios into jail and secured a warrant to search the kid's home, it was growing dark. Finn was on his way out to the Metrios home to inform Kane's parents that their son was in jail, and to make sure that no girl was being held prisoner on the premises, when his phone chimed. He pressed the hands-free button on the steering wheel to answer.

"Detective Finn," the desk sergeant began. "You might be

interested in this. A good Samaritan just delivered a backpack and cell phone that he found in a field about twenty miles east of Evansburg."

"Yeah?" An orange glow backlighting a hill in the distance caught Finn's attention.

"They belong to Mia Valdez, or at least the cell does. There's a little sticker on the back of it."

"Fingerprints?"

"We recovered only the victim's."

"Is the phone functional?"

"The screen is cracked, but when I plugged it in, I was able to turn it on. But it's password-protected."

"Her mother might know the password. Save it for me. I'll be back to pick it up"—he checked his watch and frowned—"tomorrow morning."

Maybe, just maybe, there'd be a clue of some kind on it. Maybe even a GPS history? Assuming they could get in and the girl had left the GPS function turned on.

He crested the hill. The glow was from a barn, fully engulfed in flames. *His* barn, the one he'd photographed, the one he was painting. Black figures silhouetted against the conflagration showed that the volunteer fire department was present, but they seemed to be mostly standing back, waiting for the structure to collapse.

He pulled to the side of the road to watch the spectacle. Probably another arson of an unoccupied barn. Was one of the silhouettes Sara Melendez? Would either of them ever come to the end of their respective cases?

As half the barn collapsed, the black figures swept back like a wave receding from the shore. Bright sparks leapt in the night air like dancing fireflies. The scene was actually quite beautiful in a hellish sort of way.

"Damn vandals," he muttered to himself. He had planned a traditional pastoral painting with wildflowers in the foreground, but now he could envision creating a more dramatic artwork with the scarlet and ultramarine and cobalt black and cadmium yellows of an active fire. He pulled out his phone and snapped a photo for future reference.

After punching in Robin Valdez's number, he gave her the report of the sparse info they'd gleaned from Kane Metrios. Then he told her about Mia's backpack and cell, asked if she knew the password.

"I might be able to guess it," she responded.

"I'll call you when I have it in hand tomorrow morning. Robin, I know there's nothing definitive yet, but when we have enough of these puzzle pieces, we'll be able to put together the whole picture and find Mia."

There was a long silence before Robin answered in a solemn tone, "Thank you, Detective."

His watch read 9:37 p.m. "I should talk to Grace. Is she around?"

"She's already in bed."

"Is she sick?"

Again, a hesitation, then, "No, I don't think so. Just really tired."

He could identify with fatigue.

"Kanoni is the one who is sick."

"Oh, no." He had a vision of Grace carrying the baby gorilla around all day long. She'd done it before, when Neema and Gumu were missing and Kanoni was temporarily an orphan. Grace was as much a mother to that little ape as Neema was. "I'm sorry to hear that. I hope it's not serious."

"Me too."

"Well, if there's anything I can do . . ." He let the sentence trail off.

Robin said nothing, but Finn knew she was thinking that what he should be doing was looking for *her* child, not worrying about Grace or a gorilla.

"I hope I'll get back to you with good news soon, Robin," he said in a lame attempt to recover. "I'm working on finding Mia. Agent Foster is, too."

"Thank you," she said again in a nearly inaudible voice.

He said goodnight and then pulled back onto the highway, feeling as though he had let Robin down. Grace, too; it was another long evening he couldn't share with her. And when he finally got home, Cargo and Lok and Kee would tell him once again how disappointed they were in him.

Chapter 20

Thursday

Mia wrestled with the legs of the table until she felt faint from hunger and thirst. Although she couldn't see what she was doing in the darkness, she could feel how wobbly the table leg was, that it was barely screwed on, but the last inch of screw refused to separate from the table top. She'd saved the fruit pie for hours, but finally had to eat it, dry-swallowing it in tiny pieces, making it last. Maybe she'd just go crazy in here, trapped without light, without food or water. Insanity would be better than being so lost in her own head.

She couldn't stop thinking about her parents. After her sibs died, her mother and father had been ghosts, drifting around the house, forgetting to make dinner or even breakfast, forgetting that there was no milk in the fridge, forgetting that Mia was still there. She'd once overheard her mother say to her Aunt Jo that she didn't see much point in living anymore. Mia could understand that attitude now.

"But what about Miracle?" Jo had asked.

Then, as if they'd suddenly come to a joint decision, her parents glommed onto her like gum sticking to the bottom of a shoe. *You're our precious jewel, Miracle girl. You're all we think about. You have all our hopes and dreams. You're all we live for. You're the only one left.*

What would Mom and Dad do when *she* was gone? They couldn't even tell good stories about her. Her sibs were heroes. She was an idiot. She squeezed her eyes shut, but she was too dehydrated to cry.

The room stank. She stank. The sheets on the bed had stiff patches of dried semen and blood; she couldn't stand to lie on them. The bucket was half full, and she couldn't take hovering over it any more. Last time she peed in the far corner, where a whisper of air came through the crack in the wall.

Think, Mia, think. She had to come up with a plan, something between simply giving up and dying and getting that damn table leg off and killing Dusty with it. There had to be a Plan B. Or was it Plan C, if dying was first?

The door rattled. Mia leapt from the bed, righted the table. It sagged now, its wobbly leg splayed out to the side. She nudged the leg back into vertical with her toe, but the table still looked pretty bad. She set the empty Coke can on top and was still standing next to the table when the door opened and Dusty blinded her with the flashlight beam.

"There you are, darlin'," he said, as if pleased to discover her here.

"As if I could be anywhere else, honey," she sneered.

"Don't be that way, Mia." He set the flashlight on end on the ground. He was dressed, as usual, in khaki pants and a blue shirt, a tidily combed vision of an upright working citizen. He pulled the stun gun from his pocket. In the other hand, he clutched two sacks this time, one from Burger Hut, and the other a pretty pink bag. When he set the burger bag down on the table, she held her breath, praying it wouldn't collapse.

"Whew!" He wrinkled his nose. "It really stinks in here."

"No shit," she snarled. "Or actually, a whole lot of shit. What did you expect, Dusty? A girl's gotta go, you know."

He frowned.

"But you're right, it stinks in here. *I* stink in here. If I were you, I'd just leave."

"That's not gonna happen." But then he turned and went out the door, locking it behind him.

Mia focused on the door for a few seconds, confused. But he'd left the food bag. Halleluiah! She fell on it, gulping down Coke from the cup inside and ripping off huge mouthfuls of cheeseburger.

Then the door opened again, and he stood there, framed by the darkness of the building beyond. She had a huge mouthful of burger and was frantically chewing before he could take it away. The stun gun was in his pocket. Could she rush him in time to get past him?

Then he raised his right hand, and she could see he held a water hose, his thumb on the sprayer. He let loose a jet that hit her smack in the middle of her left breast, as if he were aiming for her heart. The water was cold, the jet was a painful needle of force, stabbing her chest. She turned sideways, gasping, and tried to hunch over but kept cramming the food and drink into her mouth, even as the jet bruised her shoulders.

Dusty laughed. "We've got to get that stink off you." The stream hit her in the back of the head. It felt like she'd been whacked with a two-by-four, and she began to choke on the burger. "Turn around," he ordered.

She glanced over her shoulder, and the spray hit her forehead. She quickly turned back around and ducked.

"I said, turn around!" he shouted. "Do it now, unless you want *this*."

She glanced back again, and sure enough, he was holding

out the stun gun. She wondered briefly if he'd get electrocuted if he used it with all this water around, but she wasn't ready to die, with or without him, so she turned. He hit her in the face with the jet and then worked his way down to her toes. She closed her eyes and tried to stay standing directly in front of the food sack to preserve whatever was left to eat. God, that jet hurt. She'd be covered in bruises.

Finally the cold spray mercifully stopped. "Take your clothes off."

"No."

He stepped forward, the stun gun held out.

"Okay, okay. I'm doing it." Blinking streams of water out of her eyes, she pulled off her top, then sat down on the soaked bed to unzip her dripping jeans. He waited until she had them bunched around her ankles, then he stepped forward and snagged the reeking toilet bucket and slung it outside the door, quickly closing it behind him. She balled up her wet clothes, tossed them between the mattress and the wall, and stood up.

"Bra and panties, too."

Ashamed of her cowardice, she shucked them off.

"Now, that's not so bad, is it, darlin'?" he crooned. "Everything smells a lot better now, doesn't it?"

"Yes." He was right about that.

"I got something for you." He bent at the knees to grab the pink sack, which he had set down just inside the door.

She took advantage of his motion to grab another bite of burger. The paper wrapping was soaked, and the bun came apart in her fingers, but it still tasted good.

He tossed the pink sack. She made no move to catch it. The bag landed on the mattress, and she picked it up. Inside was a rose-colored negligee.

"Put it on." He gestured with the stun gun toward her. "And don't get hamburger grease all over it."

Hell, at least the negligee was mostly dry. She shimmied into it. It was way too long, and pooled in the dirt around her feet. "I need petite," she said.

Then he was on her, his hands clutching her shoulders. "You should be grateful! Why aren't you grateful?"

"What for?" she asked.

He zapped her with the stun gun. "Because you're alive," he snarled, his face close to hers.

She was incapable of saying anything more as he tossed her onto the wet bed and raped her again. Every time she felt movement returning to her limbs, he jolted her.

She had her answer about whether the stun gun would electrocute him in the wet room.

Chapter 21

Friday

Robin Valdez had not been able to guess her daughter's password. After ten tries, she slumped in defeat. "I'm learning that Mia had a lot of secrets she didn't share with me."

Agent Foster took the phone to the FBI office in Spokane in hopes of unlocking it. She had also obtained an address where Cooper Trigg might be holding a young girl captive. Finn was more optimistic about focusing on the location where Mia's phone and backpack had been found, off I-90 nearly twenty miles east of Evansburg, on a county line road. At least it was somewhere to start. But he had no idea if the backpack and cell phone had been dumped before or after Mia had been taken somewhere. He went to the office to use Google Earth on a large screen, see if he could glean a clue from the bird's-eye view.

Before he got started, the Grant County Sheriff called to report that they'd knocked on every door within a ten-mile radius of the wheat field Darcy had described. Nobody in that area knew anything about a missing girl. Deputies had found and photographed the hillside where the foursome had picnicked and later, the track left by Metrios's motorcycle in the hayfield, and the mashed grass where Darcy had lain for hours. But that was it. The second motorcycle track vanished on I-90 not far from the picnic site, direction undetermined.

"I'll send you the reports. Those posters of her are everywhere. We're keeping an eye out for your girl."

That sounded like a dismissal. "She disappeared in *your* county," Finn reminded him.

"Well, yeah, we'll help where we can, but you've been assigned. I hear you've got the FBI on it, too. Hope you find her alive, like the other one," the sheriff told him. "I saw the news. Your department found one of Todd Sutter's old victims?"

"Magdalena Aguilar," Finn confirmed. "Buried in the latest arson-burned barn."

"Interesting," the sheriff commented. "Over here, we expect that one of these days we'll run across a skeleton or two from Sutter's collection. But so far, we've been lucky."

Todd Sutter. The name kept coming up, and with the discovery of Magdalena Aguilar's remains, the local media's interest in Sutter's past crimes had been revived. The similarity of Magdalena's disappearance and Mia's troubled Finn. Sutter had lived and worked within two adjacent counties. It was possible, even probable, that others in the area knew about his activities and associates. Pulling out the paper file again, Finn thumbed through it, searching for background information. There was little beyond Sutter's address at the time of his arrest in Moses Lake, his wife's name, Deanna Morris Sutter, and the fact that he had worked as a mechanic for a farm equipment manufacturer outside of town.

Firing up his computer, Finn located and skimmed the transcript from Sutter's trial for the murder of Angela Albro. The file contained little about Sutter's life, just the facts of the crime. Since Sutter had been caught with Albro's body in his

car and his DNA all over her corpse, the case was pretty cut
and dried. Sutter was clearly a scumbag of the first order. A
charge of kidnapping and rape against Sutter had been
dismissed eighteen months previous to his murder charge
because the victim, Heidi Skouras, had vanished. Odds were
good that Skouras's body was buried somewhere within
Sutter's territory.

"What are you doing?"

Sara Melendez was leaning over his shoulder, staring at the
paper file on his desk. She'd obviously showered and changed
her clothes, but she still smelled vaguely of smoke.

"I saw your fire last night." He picked up his mug of coffee
and took a sip of the lukewarm brew.

She straightened, let out an exasperated snort, and waved a
sheet of paper in the air. "The tips that have come in are
useless—Mister Smith burns illegal garbage, Grandma twice
set the house on fire with a candle, my neighbor hates my dog
so I'm sure he's an arsonist, et cetera, et cetera. I want to
round up every male in two counties, age sixteen to thirty, and
grill them. Somebody—more than one somebody, too—knows
who is setting these fires."

"Any skeletons in this latest one?"

She shrugged. "It was too hot to check last night. I'm going
back with the GPR unit this afternoon." She lifted her chin
toward his computer screen. "Didn't you say Grace's barn came
up clean? Why are you checking out Sutter?"

"His name keeps cropping up," he said. "I figured I should
educate myself about the creep."

"Old news," she said. "Sutter's been in lockup since 2006.
We might stumble across one of his victims now and then, but
how could he have a connection to your missing girl?"

"He probably doesn't," Finn acknowledged. "But there are

coincidences—the Gorge concerts, young girls . . ."

"You think you might be chasing a copycat?"

The thought had occurred to him, even while he suspected he was grasping at straws. And Agent Foster had suggested the possibility, too. It seemed unlikely that Cooper Trigg had a relationship with Todd Sutter, but there was always that "six degrees of separation" theory . . .

Finn considered trekking over to Walla Walla to interview Sutter in the state penitentiary, but odds were good that the scumbag wouldn't tell him the truth, since Finn had nothing to bargain with. Better to talk to someone who knew Sutter but wouldn't necessarily feel loyal to him.

His desk phone buzzed. He didn't pick it up. Probably another reporter. The calls had lessened as Mia Valdez became old news, but they still came in now and then. Let them leave voicemail messages.

Melendez sat down in her chair and turned on her computer. As soon as her email came up, she swore. "Damn it! Sarge just dumped another case in my lap. Drug theft, veterinarian office. Seems more like your kind of thing, Finn."

"Nope." He was grateful the assignment had ended up in her inbox instead of his. "It's all yours. Do you know what happened to Sutter's wife?" Finn checked the file again. "Deanna Morris Sutter?"

"I remember she filed for divorce as soon as he was convicted. Smart woman." Melendez hesitated. "Well, maybe not so smart. She married the pervert, after all."

His cell phone buzzed.

"I've got Cooper Trigg," Agent Foster announced.

"Where are you?"

"Spokane Municipal Jail, for now," she told him. "Of course, Trigg claims he's innocent, doesn't have a motorcycle, was never at the Gorge Concert, doesn't know who Mia Valdez is. But get this: he had a pair of women's panties in his jacket pocket."

"Mia's?"

"No way to know. They're clean, so I don't know if any DNA will show up. I'll send you a photo that you can have Robin look at."

Finn wasn't sure he should do that yet.

There was a rustle of paper on her end of the conversation. "And I checked the names of the ticket buyers that you got from Boylan. Trigg's name is not on the list. But he did have a credit card in his pocket that's stolen from one Sharon Waverly, so we can hold him for that as well as his bench warrant."

"I remember a few ticket purchases were flagged as invalid."

"These checked ones, I'd guess."

"Yeah. Boylan's scarily efficient."

"I see where you're going," she murmured, then, "Yes! Sharon Waverly's name is flagged on the purchase list. With Robin Valdez's recognition of him on the video, this is definitely corroborating evidence that Trigg *was* there. I'll keep holding this dirtbag's feet to the fire."

"Be sure to find out if he has any connection to Todd Sutter."

"You're still thinking copycat?"

"The Gorge connection," he reminded her. "I'm still pursuing that angle. Even if Trigg didn't kidnap Mia Valdez, he might still be involved."

"Agreed. I'm on it." She hung up.

Finn turned back to his computer, feeling that his team might finally be making progress. He switched to the departmental database used for general background information, and typed in *Deanna Morris Sutter*. Since he didn't have a date of birth or social for her, he typed in the qualifier of the Moses Lake address to be sure the correct record would be returned.

And there it was, only now she was Deanna Hansen, age fifty-two, married to Jeff Hansen and half owner of Hansen's Feed & Farm Store in Quincy, Washington. Less than two hours away.

He perused the long list of her previous addresses and bank information. It didn't appear as though Todd and Deanna Sutter had ever purchased property. They'd probably always rented. Many of the addresses were only post office boxes: Vantage, Moses Lake, Othello, and one from 2001 to 2006, in Evansburg.

He decided to drive to Quincy and talk to Sutter's ex-wife. It would be faster just to call her, but a detective always gleaned more from in-person interviews. He shut down his computer, swiveled in his chair. "I'm off to Quincy to interview Sutter's ex."

"Going to tell Sarge?" Melendez asked.

They both knew the sergeant was unlikely to approve of a trip that right now seemed like a wild goose chase.

"No," Finn said. "And you're not telling him, either."

"Course not." She pressed a final key combination and then shut down her computer. She sighed as she stood up. "I'm off to the old barn and then to see a vet about some missing drugs. Do we really still have ten days until Kat and Perry get back?"

"Eight days for Kat, but Perry's got medical leave for another two weeks. And then he'll probably ride a desk for another month."

"Yeesh," she said. "Makes me want to get married or blow out a knee, too."

"Aren't you already married?"

"Oh, yeah." She tucked a strand of brown hair behind her ear. "So that's who the old man and those rug rats were this morning. They seemed vaguely familiar." She pulled her service weapon from her desk drawer, slid it into the holster at her waist.

"Good luck catching the bad guys, Sara."

She snorted. "You too, Finn."

As Finn entered Hansen's Feed & Farm store in Quincy ninety-five minutes later, the balding man behind the cash register looked up. The place smelled like grain dust. Finn swallowed a sneeze. Baldy wore a nametag that proclaimed him to be Jeff, so Finn guessed that he was Jeff Hansen.

"Howdy," Hansen said. "What can I do for you?"

"Is Deanna around?"

"I think she's in the storeroom." He jerked a thumb toward the rear of the building.

An elderly man approached the counter with a shovel in his hand.

Jeff slid out from behind the counter. "Can I tell Dee who's asking for her?"

Finn turned away from the customer, flashed his badge, and quietly said, "Detective Finn. I just want to talk to her."

Jeff's forehead creased and his mouth opened as if to ask something, but he apparently thought better of it. "Wait here," he told Finn. "Be right back to ring you up, Fred," he said over his shoulder as he headed for the back of the store.

He returned with a woman in tow. Deanna Hansen wore a canvas apron over a T-shirt and jeans. She was in good shape for fifty-two, with a trim build and muscular arms that probably came from hefting bags of livestock feed.

Her husband slid back behind the counter as she placed

herself in front of Finn, her cheeks pink from exertion or anxiety. "What's this about?"

"I want to talk to you about Todd Sutter."

She immediately grabbed his arm and hauled him away from the counter. "Let's chat in the break room." After pulling him a few steps, she flashed an apologetic look at Finn and let go of him. "Sorry. But please . . ." She gestured toward a door in the far wall, and then preceded him and opened it.

"Sorry," she apologized again, shutting the door. "Hardly anybody here knows about Todd, and I want to keep it that way." She pulled a chair out from the small table.

"I suspected that." He sat down. "I don't blame you."

Once Deanna started talking, she couldn't stop. She told him how revolted she'd been at discovering what her former husband, Todd Sutter, had been up to when he was out of the house. "I believed he was just riding around the countryside, enjoying the fresh air and sunshine."

Finn straightened. "Riding?"

She waved a hand in the air. "He had an old motorcycle he loved a lot more than me. I made him keep it at work, though. I didn't want it around the house."

Neither the file nor the court transcript had mentioned a motorcycle. Finn made a note.

"Do you know a young man by the name of Cooper Trigg?" he asked. He patted his pocket for the photo and then realized he'd left it in his jacket at the station.

Deanna's brow wrinkled. "I don't think so."

"He'd be about twenty-two. Blond. Earring in one ear."

"No, I don't know him. But Trevor or Sienna might."

"Trevor? Sienna?"

"Our kids."

"Kids?" The database files indicated the Sutters had no

children.

"Foster kids. But of course, we—I—lost them after the arrest. The poor things. They had to live with other families until they aged out at eighteen. They just toss them out into the world; isn't that horrible?"

"It's a cruel system," he agreed.

"But they turned out all right, amazingly enough."

"You're still in contact?"

"Well, with Sienna, anyway. She's married, has two children, lives in Boise."

Finn dismissed Sienna as irrelevant for his purpose. "And Trevor? How old was he when you lost custody?"

"Seventeen, and halfway through his senior year." She gave a shake of her head. "When Todd was arrested, Trevor was crushed. Of course, we all were shocked and horrified, but especially Trevor. He *worshipped* Todd. Todd was the only male role model Trevor ever knew. Lord!" She put her head into her hands for a moment.

"Did Trevor believe Todd was innocent?"

Deanne raised her head. "How could anyone believe that? There was a corpse in Todd's car." She shuddered. "Trevor was a lost soul for a long time after that."

Finn nodded, trying hard to suppress his growing excitement. He had to talk to this kid. Odds were good that Trevor would know a lot of Sutter's former associates. Trevor could very well provide the key that would unlock this case.

"You'd think the state would have let Trevor stay until he graduated, wouldn't you? But no . . ." Deanna scowled. "All because of Todd. I hope that filthy asshole dies in prison. That goddamn lying pervert, pardon my language."

"No problem," he said mildly. "You said Trevor turned out okay?"

"Trevor went into the military after he graduated high school."

Finn's enthusiasm dimmed a little. "Is he still a soldier?"

"No, he's out now. He runs a rock shop in Vantage and has a little apartment in the back, does a variety of things around Evansburg. I think he has a new job with the county there. I'm sure he'd talk to you." Her expression clouded. "But I'd really rather you didn't look him up. None of us want to be reminded of Todd."

"I get it. Do you have a photo of Trevor?"

She shook her head. "Not here."

"What's Trevor's last name?"

"Vollmar." She spelled it. "Trevor Lee Vollmar. Everyone likes Trevor; ask anyone. I just wish he could find a nice young girl and settle down like Sienna did."

Finn was tempted to leap up and gallop out the door to research Trevor Lee Vollmar, but he made himself focus on the list of questions he'd brought with him. "I see you and Todd had a post office box in Evansburg for a while," he remarked. "So you lived in that area?"

Deanna nodded. "On Old Forest Road."

Finn's pulse sped up. Old Forest Road ran behind Grace's compound. Even if this didn't lead to Mia, he might be close to tracking down the bones Grace had found. "That's a farm area, right?"

"Yeah. We rented a small farm there, about forty acres, kept a few cattle and sheep and a horse. The kids loved it. *I* loved it. But then Todd got a job in Moses Lake. He only came home on weekends."

Trevor. Old Forest Road. Clues? He hoped so. He closed his notebook and stood up. "Thank you for talking with me, Mrs. Hansen."

She slid back her chair and stood up, too. "You're welcome. But I still don't understand what this is about. Todd, may he rot in hell, is in prison for good."

"We found a skeleton in an old barn," he told her. "We think it's one of Todd's victims."

She raised a hand to her throat. "Dear God. May she rest in peace." She swallowed, took a deep breath. "I'll walk you out, Detective."

As they passed through the store to the front door, she asked, "Have they found out anything more about that girl missing from the Gorge concert?"

Finn was grateful that she didn't know he was the "they" she was asking about. "Nothing more, for now."

As soon as he was in the car, he called Miki at the station and asked her to research Trevor Lee Vollmar, age thirty.

"Where the heck have you been?" she asked. "Sarge is having a fit. The media keeps asking about the Mia Valdez case, and you're not even around to make a statement."

"Research 41 Old Forest Road, too."

"What does that mean, research?"

"Get me a map of the property, and sales records."

"But where have you been? Plus, Sarge has a suspected livestock poisoning case for you."

That's all he needed, dead cows to worry about on top of a missing teenager. "I'm working, Miki. And you should be, too. I'll expect that research on my desk by the time I get there in"—he checked his watch—"ninety minutes."

On his way back to Evansburg, he stopped in the tiny hamlet of Vantage. The rock shop had a big red CLOSED sign on the front door, but he knocked anyway, then walked around the building. The blinds were all pulled. Nobody seemed to be inside. Where was Trevor Lee Vollmar right now?

Chapter 22

Friday

Seated on a bench in the barn, Grace held Kanoni in her arms, trying to get the baby gorilla to take a bottle filled with a mix of juice, cough syrup, and Tylenol. The vet had confirmed that the little ape had a fever, and the discharge that streamed from her flat nostrils was ample evidence of a bad cold. Grace's shirt and pants were streaked with greenish snot. Kanoni still wore a diaper, and both Grace and Robin were tired of changing her.

Nothing was worse than when one of her gorillas was sick. They were sullen and uncooperative, and there was no way to explain the problem to them or tell them it would get better, and there was always the danger of violence from a miserable, frustrated ape.

Neema hovered next to Grace, worried about her baby. *Kanoni cry*, she signed. *Give.*

The mother gorilla repeatedly pulled on Grace's wrist, trying to take the bottle. Grace knew that if she got it, Neema was likely to drink it herself.

"Medicine for Kanoni," Grace told the big gorilla, but doubted Neema understood the concept.

After signing *Baby sad give me,* Neema tugged on Kanoni's leg. The baby gorilla whimpered. Her little ape fingers tightened, clinging to Grace's arms, but Kanoni's hot body seemed limp.

"Please, Brittany, distract Neema," Grace begged the young volunteer, who was overseeing her daughter Ivy as the three-year-old picked up toys from the sawdust floor.

"Can I use F-O-O-D?" Brittany spelled the last word.

Food, Neema signed. *Give me eat.* Then she tugged on Grace's arm again, yanking the bottle away from Kanoni's face. Not that it mattered. The baby gorilla was still refusing to suck from the rubber nipple.

"Yes. Neema, you want some watermelon?" Grace's hands were full, but the mother gorilla understood a lot of words even without the signs.

Juice fruit, Neema signed, using the signs she'd combined to describe a watermelon. *Me give hurry hurry.*

"Me too!" Ivy chirped, making the same *juice fruit* signs. "Watermelon!"

"Back in a couple of minutes. Wait here for Mama, Ivy." Brittany strode though the barn door and used the staff key to let herself out of the gate. Ivy turned to Grace, an uncertain expression on her baby face, and hooked a finger in her mouth.

"Stay over there, Ivy," Grace told her. "Kanoni has a bad cold, and I don't want you to catch it."

The little girl, dragging a bedraggled stuffed cat, traced her mother's path as far as the gate.

Grace was grateful when Neema followed Ivy to the outside enclosure. "Kanoni," she murmured. The baby gorilla looked up at Grace. The little ape's eyes were red, inflamed. "You need to drink this, baby," Grace told her. "It will make you feel better."

Kanoni's body spasmed with several bark-like coughs. She licked the snot from her upper lip. Grace had never witnessed a cold this bad in any of her gorillas. She prayed it wouldn't spread. So far Neema and Gumu had shown no symptoms.

"Please, Kanoni, drink." Grace rubbed the nipple over the gorilla's lips. "It's juice. Plus, if you don't drink it, I'm afraid we're going to have to sedate you and plug a couple of IVs into you. I guarantee you won't like that. Your mama won't, either."

When Kanoni finally accepted the nipple between her lips and took a couple of sucks, Grace wanted to sing. "Good gorilla, Kanoni. Drink it all."

Brittany came back into the barn, carrying pieces of cut-up watermelon in a plastic bin.

"That was fast," Grace remarked.

"Robin already had it all cut up. I really like her. I understand what she's going through."

Grace guessed the young woman would. Both Brittany and Robin had their daughters vanish. Thanks to Finn, Ivy had been recovered as an infant. Grace hoped Robin would be as lucky.

Brittany doled out pieces of melon to Neema and to Gumu, who had followed the young woman into the barn, and then handed one to her daughter Ivy. Grace was dismayed when Kanoni didn't seem to even register the presence of one of her favorite treats.

"No babysitting Sophia today?" she asked Brittany.

"No, just Ivy. Sophia was really sick last week, but now she's finally well again." Bending over her daughter, Brittany tugged playfully on her strawberry blond ponytail. "We went to see her yesterday, didn't we, Ivy?"

She's finally well again? Alarm bells clanged in Grace's head. "What was wrong with Sophia?"

"Oh, I think it was measles. But she's over it now."

Grace went cold with horror. "Measles?"

Realizing what she'd just said, Brittany straightened and briefly clapped a hand over her mouth. When she slid her hand away, she said, "I didn't know. Honestly. When I brought her, Sophia was fine."

"Measles." Blood roared in Grace's head. "Sophia wasn't vaccinated?"

"Uh, no. Kara doesn't believe in vaccinations because of, you know, the autism thing." Brittany's eyes were huge. "But I do, of course," she hastened to add, flattening a hand against her chest. "Ivy's had all her vaccinations. Me too. Of course."

Grace studied the sick baby gorilla in her arms. Kanoni had released the nipple after drinking less than half the mixture and lay listlessly, staring up at Grace with dull eyes.

How could she have let this happen? "Brittany, you do know measles can kill apes? Especially baby apes?"

Brittany twisted her hands together. "Yes, you told us that. But I didn't know about Sophia, really I didn't."

Grace closed her eyes, tried to regain her equanimity. The damage was done; she needed her volunteers, and usually Britt was one of the better ones. Opening her eyes, she said, "Please, don't bring anyone else here unless you know for sure they've been vaccinated, Brittany."

The girl nodded eagerly. "Of course, Grace. I'm so sorry." She took a step forward. "Can I help with Kanoni?"

A huge black hand closed around Grace's elbow. *Cry you Kanoni sad*, Neema signed.

"Yes, I'm sad because Kanoni is sick," Grace said aloud, unable to sign with her arms full.

Me sad give me. Neema tugged on Kanoni's foot.

Gumu had wandered close, and now sat to the side of Grace. She could feel the silverback's warm breath on her knee as he leaned in to peer at his daughter. Grace had no idea what was going through his head or what he might do next. If the huge male grabbed Kanoni or Grace, he could easily injure them.

Brittany stood a few yards away, a chastened expression on her pretty young face. "Britt, can you go play with Neema?"

Neema perked up at the mention of her name.

"Maybe a game of chase and tickle?" Grace suggested.

Chase, Neema signed. *Tickle tickle good gorilla me.*

Gumu thumped his chest once and signed *chase*.

"Me too!" Ivy chirped. "Chase me! Tickle me!"

Brittany raised her arms in a fake threatening gesture. "I'm going to get all of you! I'm going to tickle you to death!"

Amid excited ape hoots and shrieks from Ivy, gorillas and human playmates rushed through the door to the outside area.

. . . to death. An unfortunate choice of words. Grace hugged the baby gorilla close to her shoulder with one hand, wiping more snot across her shirt, as she pulled her cell phone from her pants pocket to call the vet. As she listened to the rings on the other end, she whispered to Kanoni, "Please don't die."

The vet never answered. Grace left a voicemail message.

Robin Valdez came through the barn door. "It's pandemonium out there." She pointed to the sunlight behind her. "I got everything you wanted from the grocery store and put it all away." She laid a gentle hand on the crown of the baby gorilla's head. "She's not getting better?"

Grace shook her head miserably. "I'm pretty sure she has measles. From Ivy's unvaccinated little friend, about two weeks ago."

"Oh, no! I didn't know that could happen. Poor baby." She took the little gorilla's foot in one hand.

"You've been vaccinated, right?" Grace asked.

"Of course."

"Me, too. And Neema and Gumu. But not Kanoni. I was

waiting until she was a little older."

The baby gorilla barked her cough. Grace stroked her little black face, then lifted her up to her shoulder again and patted her back.

Robin glanced at the door and then back to Grace. "I hate to add to your worries, but there are two men outside. Agricultural inspectors?"

Grace's heart sank. "Oh, please, not now."

Robin did a half turn, hesitating, her hands fluttering uncertainly in the air. "Should I tell them to leave?"

Who knew what they'd write if she did that? Surprise inspections were designed to find out what happened on a daily basis. How Grace cared for her *wildlife*. Whether her gorillas were safely contained. They might suspect she was hiding something.

"I'm coming." She stood up and held out Kanoni. "Could you?"

"Of course." Robin took the baby gorilla. "I'll go out the back, take her to the staff trailer?"

"Thank you."

Collecting a handful of tree leaves from the floor, Grace used them to brush the snot from her clothes as best she could, and then let herself out of the gorilla enclosure to meet the two men. She introduced herself, but held up her hands instead of shaking. "My baby gorilla has a bad cold. I don't want to share any germs."

"We appreciate that." The older man sported a silver mustache and introduced himself as Jay Barder. She remembered him from last year. He tilted his head toward his younger companion. "And this is Trevor Vollmar, my new assistant. He's learning the job."

After verifying that all the information on their county forms was still correct, Grace led them on a tour of the compound, showing them first her own trailer, computer, and filing system. She let them look around her office while she excused herself to wash her hands. Then she took them to the gorilla enclosure. Grace was glad that Brittany had the adult gorillas settled down by then. Gumu watched from the top of the rope net, a hulking presence sitting in the farthest corner.

Grace explained to the men that the apes had both indoor and outdoor areas to enjoy, space to exercise, and a warm, heated barn to sleep in and get out of bad weather. She demonstrated the lock system on the exterior gate before she led them through it.

"Is it safe?" Vollmar asked, nervously eyeing the silverback. "In here with him?"

"As long as you're with me," Grace responded. She had never revealed her suspicion that Gumu had killed a man last year. Even gorillas had a right to self-defense. "Mr. Barder has survived the last two years," she told the younger inspector.

"No problem," Barder told his colleague. "You'll get used to going into pens with all sorts of stock, Vollmar." He double-checked the keyed lock on the exterior of the enclosure, swung the gate closed, tested it.

The gate held with a gentle pull on the handle, but when he depressed the latch, it easily swung open.

"All staff members lock the gate as soon as we come through." Grace demonstrated, pulling a key on a retractable steel cord from her belt and twisting it in the double-sided lock.

"You use keys to get in *and* out?" Vollmar asked Grace. "Isn't that dangerous? How would you get out in a hurry?"

Grace returned the key to the ring attached to her belt. "If I couldn't reach a key, I guess I *wouldn't* get out. But better that I be locked in here than the gorillas escape, right?" She glanced toward the older inspector, who nodded in agreement.

"There's really no other system," she told Vollmar. "Gorillas have opposable thumbs and they can unlatch doors just like we can."

"Couldn't you use a computerized lock?" he asked.

"They'd learn the combination pretty fast."

"Really?" Vollmar eyed Gumu suspiciously.

"Really," Grace assured him and motioned them forward. They stepped inside the barn.

"Whoa!" Barder remarked, stroking his mustache. "You've done a fair bit of remodeling in here since last year. And I see you're bringing the outdoors in." Picking up a twig from the sawdust floor, he twirled it in his fingers.

"I try to provide a natural habitat, as much as possible, so it's always evolving," she told him.

"Evolving," Barder chuckled.

"My two-year-old gorilla does a lot of remodeling for me," Grace remarked. "And so do her parents. That was Gumu outside, and there's Neema." She pointed at the mother gorilla, who had climbed halfway up the "tree" to the third platform.

On hearing her name, Neema leaned forward to study them. She signed *baby give me.* Grace signed back *wait.*

Vollmar's brow wrinkled in confusion, but he said nothing.

Neema was often suspicious of men, for which Grace was now grateful. She was also thankful that Brittany had left with Ivy. Although Ivy had known these apes since she was an infant, Grace wasn't sure what the inspectors would make of a three-year-old locked inside an enclosure with adult gorillas.

Vollmar was drawn to the climbing pole with its spiraling platforms. Shielding his eyes, he studied the structure and the roof overhead. "Have you been up there?" He pointed to the peak.

"Never." Grace waved a hand at the stout pole from which the platforms radiated. "The gorillas can't reach the roof, either. These support poles were part of the original structure. I just had workmen add the platforms to this one. The highest platform is about twelve feet below the peak. There was a hay loft on the second floor, but we took that down."

Barder strode to the back door and was inspecting the door and the lock there, but Vollmar stayed in the center of the building, seeming more interested in the structures overhead. She couldn't tell what he was thinking.

"Did you find anything unusual during your remodel?" he asked.

Grace was unprepared for that odd question. What was he concerned about? Sharp metal pieces? Animal corpses? Hantavirus? The three small bones abruptly bobbed to the surface of her thoughts, but she kept her face impassive. "We never found anything dangerous. Just pieces of old farm machinery, leather straps from harnesses, things like that. And all the debris was removed."

Vollmar continued to gaze upward.

"I've been assured the framework is all very sound," she told him.

"I'm sure it is. They built barns to last in the old days."

A swallow flitted in through the louvered vent at the top of the building.

"You have birds nesting up there," Vollmar said.

"Just swallows." Was he a birder? "Bigger birds like owls can't get in, and as you can see, the swallows can easily come in and go out."

A flash of white caught her eye. A tail? A *cat* tail? Snow?

Of course. *Snow. Up. Bird.* A heavy gorilla might not be able to shimmy up the support post, but a cat could. If Vollmar was a birder, he probably wouldn't take kindly to the idea of bird-hunting cats. She quickly diverted her gaze to Vollmar's face. "I don't think swallows are anything worth worrying about. Do you?"

"No," Vollmar said quickly, dropping his head. "No, not at all." Finding his partner near the back door, he joined Barder to review the checklist on the man's clipboard.

"You still have three gorillas?" Barder asked.

Of course they wanted to see Kanoni. Grace hesitated, but she couldn't refuse. "The baby gorilla is sick," she told them. "My volunteer is taking care of her."

"I understand," Barder said. "I just need to see her, to account for her presence here."

Grace made a big show of double-checking all the locks as they left the enclosure and then reluctantly led the two men to the staff trailer. Opening the door, she was relieved to find that the interior was in order. When her college-age volunteers had been present, the waste bins had often been stuffed with old pizza boxes and the countertops lined with beer and soda bottles, but now the table and countertops were gleaming. Clearly, Robin Valdez had spent her spare time cleaning. Grace led the men toward the bunk room.

Robin held up a finger in front of her lips when they entered, then pointed to the mass of blankets on the bed. "I made her a nest. She's asleep."

Both men briefly leaned over the snuffling little gorilla curled into the covers, but then tiptoed out. Grace was grateful that Barder asked only if Kanoni had been seen by a veterinarian.

"Of course," she answered. "Dr. Black is keeping track of her condition."

After signing off on Barder's form, she said goodbye to the

inspectors, hoping their investigation of her apes would not extend to speaking with the veterinarian. She didn't want to lie about Kanoni's illness, but she worried that if she reported measles to the inspector, the county council might be bombarded with local protests over gorillas spreading communicable human diseases.

Her cell buzzed as a text came in from Dr. Black. *Will visit you 3 p.m.* Grace walked back to the staff trailer to check on Robin and Kanoni.

"While you were in your trailer, I told Brittany she could take off," Robin told her.

"Good thinking."

"Did the inspection go okay?"

"I think so. The guy in training seemed worried about the locks and the platform structure, but I assured him everything could securely contain three gorillas. And the good news is that I've located Snow, our white cat. He's bird hunting up in the rafters." Grace sat down on the bunk beside the sleeping gorilla. "How is she?"

Robin sighed. "No better."

Placing a gentle hand on Kanoni's brow, Grace felt the fever burning through the little body. She'd read about measles devastating entire gorilla families in Africa. She told Robin about the vet coming. "Dr. Black will likely want to put Kanoni on an IV."

"Good idea," Robin said. "She must be getting dehydrated. I'll watch her. How are *you*?"

Grace felt a lump forming in her throat. She swallowed before answering. "Okay, I guess."

The other woman lifted her chin, a question on her face. "Did you—?"

Moving her focus back to the baby gorilla, Grace brushed

her hand softly over Kanoni's fuzzy head. "Yes, I did that test you brought. Peed on the stick. Thank you."

Robin waited.

Grace inhaled a deep breath, blew it back out, then raised her face to meet Robin's gaze. "It's official now. I'm pregnant."

"Congratulations?" Robin said uncertainly.

Grace burst into tears.

Chapter 23

Friday

Finn discovered that Grace's compound had been part of the original farm at 41 Old Forest Road. According to the online property records, Grace's barn had been there at the time the Sutters were renting the place. The old farmhouse was on the other section of land that had been subdivided into two parcels. The address of the farmhouse was still on Old Forest Road, while Grace's property had been assigned a new address on the county road that bordered it.

Finn suddenly had a suspicion that the bones in Grace's barn were not from some pioneer settler's grave.

Bird.

Up.

Fly.

The gorillas might not be fabricating stories after all; they could be providing the only clues they had to offer.

Unlike most of the dilapidated barns in the area, the structural beams of Grace's barn were huge. He'd wondered at them before, astounded that the original builders could lever the massive beams into place. The building was the primary reason Grace had chosen that location to house the gorillas. According to the old photos, the building originally had hay storage on the second floor and probably a block-and-tackle system to lift and lower bales.

He remembered to call Grace, ask her how her day was going. She told him about Kanoni, who was in critical condition. Measles. He couldn't believe that some parents didn't vaccinate their kids, and it was news to him that apes could get the disease, too. Grace made him promise not to spread that news around.

"The vet sedated her, and she's strapped down to a bunk in the staff trailer with an IV in each arm." Grace sounded as if she might burst into tears. "Neema's agitated. And Gumu's acting up, too."

"I'm sorry you're going through all this and I can't be there, Grace. How are *you* feeling?"

"I'm a little under the weather, but I'll live. How are you, Matt?"

"I'll live, too."

"To top off my day," Grace added, "the damned inspectors showed up."

He tried to make appropriate sympathetic noises. She told him about how Barder had been pretty easygoing, but Vollmar seemed overly worried about the construction of the posts and beams and the man-made tree, as well as the lock system.

"But guess what? Neema was telling the truth about up and birds and Snow. That darn cat climbed all the way up to the main beam. He's hunting those swallows up there."

Finn suspected there might be more than swallows and a cat up in the rafters. "Uh-huh," he said, distracted by his own thoughts. He reached for his pen and notepad. "Those inspectors, what did you say their names were?"

"Barder, he's the same one as last year. And Vollmar, he's a trainee, I guess."

Vollmar. His pulse sped up. Deanna Hansen told him Trevor had a new job with the county. Of course Trevor Vollmar was interested in that barn. He would remember it from when he lived on the property with Todd Sutter. "When did they leave?"

"About two hours ago."

It was nearly six p.m. "Sounds like you've had a hard day, sweetheart," he said. "I hope Kanoni gets better soon. I have to go. Take care of yourself. I'll talk to you soon."

He called the county agricultural department, got a message saying they'd closed for the day. After pressing zero, he connected with an operator who gave him Trevor Vollmar's cell phone number. Nobody answered his call there. Not wanting to spook the guy, Finn left a message saying he wanted to talk to him regarding an agricultural inspection. Next, he tried the rock shop in Vantage. No answer there, either.

He paced for a minute, trying to think of a way to locate Vollmar. He didn't have enough evidence to put out an APB. Finally, he called Grace back. "Hon, I'm going to come out in an hour or so, okay? I'll have one or two other folks with me."

"What's going on, Matt?"

"It's about . . ." He almost said "the bones," but Miki was stacking papers on Melendez's desk, and the young aide was an incorrigible eavesdropper. "I'll explain when I get there. See you soon." Ending the call, he searched for the number of a local construction rental company.

Two hours later, he stood inside Grace's barn with the equipment operator. Grace had sequestered Neema and Gumu in the exterior enclosure, then gone back to confer with the vet, who had returned to check on Kanoni. She was distraught, her face streaked with tears, clearly fearful that the baby gorilla might die. Finn wished he had time to help her, or at least to comfort her, but he knew his time would be better spent here.

Robin Valdez had wanted to know if this had something to do with finding Mia. The question made him feel vaguely guilty, since he wasn't at all sure. "I hope so," he told her.

"This is unusual construction, must have been built by a first-timer," the operator hollered from his position in the bucket lift up near the roof.

"Why do you say that?" Finn peered up into the shafts of dusty sunlight. He'd sent the guy up to recover the cat while he tried to psych himself up to go next.

The operator peered down at Finn, the headlamp on his helmet a bright spot in the gloom above. "This beam is so massive—must be half a tree trunk up here. A whole herd of gorillas could swing from this thing. It will last forever." He snapped a tape measure from his belt and extended it. "The beam is twenty-two inches across. Probably weighs at least a ton."

"How did anyone get it up there?" Finn wondered aloud.

"I'd guess block-and-tackle, pulleys. And maybe a draft-horse team or two. I've seen old-timey photos of barn raisings like that. Pretty interesting." His tape measure retracted with a snap. "Anyhoo, the rafters just rest on the beam, and then they meet up above at the peak. There's plenty of space for birds' nests, for sure. No wonder that cat's up here."

"At least these birds are swallows," the operator said, moving his headlamp along the beam. "Not starlings; you definitely don't want starlings. I can fix that vent so swallows can't get in, but you might want to wait until they leave for the season because they're nesting right now. Swallows are nice birds; they eat mosquitoes. That cat probably ate all the chicks,

but I can still see a nest with eggs. Come here, you white devil."
The bucket shifted sideways a few feet. "Gotcha!" A shower of
dust drifted down from the side of the main beam. "I got him."
Then the operator yelped, "Oh, shit!"

Finn shielded his eyes. "What?"

The operator pushed a control and the bucket hummed
sideways for several feet. "Oh shit," he repeated. Finn could see
a bundle of white fur struggling in the man's arms. "You'd
better come up here, Detective. You need to see this. You'll
want your camera." Pressing the controls, he shakily
maneuvered the bucket back to the ground, and dumped the
cat out onto the ground.

Snow ran to a bench along the far wall and perched there,
insulted, licking his fur back into place.

The operator unsnapped his harness and stepped out,
gesturing for Finn to take his place. Removing his helmet, he
swiped his fingers through his hair. "Christ, I didn't want to
see that."

A twinge of guilt cramped Finn's gut. He'd suspected what
the operator might find up there but had hoped he was wrong.

The last thing Finn wanted to do was to climb into that
boom lift bucket. The contraption looked as if it could
topple over at any second. Suck it up, he told himself;
detectives couldn't afford to have acrophobia. If he didn't
go up there, that tale would be all over town in a flash.
He'd no longer be the ape detective or the sap whose wife
left him, but the chicken-shit ape detective or the cowardly
sap whose wife left him.

"You're gonna need this." The operator handed Finn his
helmet with the headlamp still illuminated.

Finn stepped into the bucket. The control was basically a
joystick, with the directions clearly labeled: UP, DOWN, RIGHT,

LEFT. There was also a LOCK lever and a POWER button. And a safety harness that clipped to the bar at the top of the bucket. That seemed ominous.

"Always a good idea to attach the harness," the operator told him. "The bucket's not supposed to tilt much, but I've seen it happen."

Well, that's great news. Finn shrugged his way into the harness and tugged on the short line to be sure it was securely attached. Then he took a deep breath and shoved the joystick toward UP. The bucket leapt up from the ground with a jolt. Finn took his hand off the stick and grabbed the rail as the bucket bounced in the air like a rodeo bronc.

"Steady there," the operator told him, failing to completely stifle a laugh. "A gentle pressure is best."

"No shit." Finn pressed his thumb gingerly against the stick, nudging it toward UP. The contraption rose in a slightly less terrifying way, the articulating arm unfolding beneath him with a whine. Glancing up, he realized he was going to smash his head into the beam, so he nudged the stick toward RIGHT until he'd cleared, and then pressed back toward UP, finally bringing the bucket up just below and beside the beam. His head cleared the roof by only a couple of inches.

A swallow swooped by, nearly taking off his nose, and he startled, rocking the bucket. Grabbing onto the safety bar, he took a breath. *Focus.*

He studied the space on top of the main beam. The roof trusses were not nailed into the side of the beam as they would have been in more modern construction. Instead, the trusses rose above the beam and met overhead in a peak, leaving a triangular space about a foot high above the beam. He adjusted his helmet and headlamp to shine into that space.

"At the far end," the operator told him from below.

Finn pressed the stick toward RIGHT, and the bucket slid sideways toward the end of the beam. Wedged into the triangular space was a wad of clothing. Although the fabric was gray with dust and riddled with holes, he could tell that it was denim. Jeans. And a long-sleeved flannel shirt that at one time had been some shade of red. The clothing lay in clumps, held up by the skeleton's kneecaps and pelvic bones and ribcage.

Most horrific of all was the skull. Strands of long black hair straggled from scraps of leathery skin still attached to the crown. The lower jaw was detached and lay tilted off the side of the vertebrae, along with a tiny crucifix on a delicate chain. In the space between the lower and upper teeth was a swallow nest, with three eggs. One was cracking and as he watched, a scrawny chick emerged, all huge eyes and beak, downy feathers plastered against its head. The chick trembled with the effort of escaping the shell. It was a macabre and strangely beautiful scene, new life cradled by death.

He pulled out his cell phone, made sure the setting was right, and took a series of photos. Rodrigo would do a better job, but he wanted to be sure he documented this in case something got rearranged before the tech got here. Sure enough, a couple of finger bones were missing, and a toe, too, dislodged by birds or the cat. He wondered what had happened to her shoes.

Crucifix. Black hair. Finn guessed the woman may have been Hispanic. Although the evangelical religions were growing faster now, most Hispanic immigrants in the area were still Catholic. He was expecting Heidi Skouras or Anna Moran, Todd Sutter's suspected-but-so-far-unfound victims. But according to their descriptions, they were both fair-haired. Finn was reasonably sure he'd found Cristina Disanto.

If he remembered correctly, Disanto had been reported missing in 2007, a year *after* Sutter had been imprisoned. A year after Deanna had lost the foster kids and moved away. The barn would likely have been empty then.

His heartbeat leapt into overdrive. He needed to catch up with Trevor Lee Vollmar as soon as he could.

A swallow, tired of waiting for Finn to leave, flitted in and stuffed a still-thrashing moth into the chick's mouth, then swooped off again. Finn lowered the bucket to the ground, slightly more sure-fingered than he had been on the way up.

The operator had been pacing across the floor, but now he had folded his arms around himself as if he had a chill. Dipping his head, he said, "That's something, huh?" He blew out a long slow breath. "I'm gonna have a hard time getting that vision out of my head."

"You and me both," Finn agreed. "Looks like we'll need to keep this boom lift for another day."

"Roger that," the guy said. "I'll tell the boss." Taking back his safety helmet, he tucked it under one arm. "If you're done with me, I'll take the truck and get out of your hair."

Finn nodded, and the operator left through the sliding back door of the barn. Pulling out his cell phone again, Finn called Rodrigo to tell him about another crime scene he needed to process.

As he listened to the rings on the other end, Grace opened the door to the exterior enclosure. "I saw the truck leave," she told him. "Now, what's up, Matt?"

Behind her was Robin Valdez. And then Neema and Gumu trailed in as well, and Finn rushed to close the back door before a gorilla escaped.

"You're going to need to keep the gorillas outside," Finn told them. "Crime Scene will need access to the interior."

"This is about those bones, right?" Grace wanted to know. Violet shadows underscored her eyes, and her cheeks were gaunt. Her hair was dull. He was pretty sure she was wearing the same clothes as she had yesterday.

"Bones?" Robin asked.

There was no longer any point in being cagey about the situation. "There's a body up there," Finn said.

Robin gasped, put a hand to her cheek.

"Sorry," he said. "Not a recent body. A skeleton. From years ago."

"What?" Rodrigo yelled in his ear.

"I'll explain in a minute," Finn told the two women, turning his back on them to speak to his crime scene technician.

Rodrigo complained, "It's already getting dark. I'd have to bring in major lights. And I've never used a lift gizmo before. I'd need help. And what about those gorillas? Who's gonna keep them away? I mean, really, how many years has that skeleton been up there? Can't this wait until morning?"

Finn considered. "I suppose it can. Put it on your schedule for tomorrow."

He was already tapping in his second call, to Miki at the station. "I need everything you've got on Trevor Lee Vollmar. Send it to my cell *now*."

When he hung up, Grace asked, "Did you say Vollmar? The inspector?" When she looked back at him, her eyes seemed to lose focus. She held a hand to her forehead, then moved it to her abdomen.

"Grace, honey, are you all right?" He touched her arm. "You're not getting sick, too, are you?"

She swallowed. "I don't think so."

"You've got to get some rest. Robin can watch Kanoni; you know she'll take good care of her."

"I will," Robin promised. "And the vet is checking in every few hours."

Wavering a bit on her feet, Grace shut her eyes and nodded. "Okay."

"Does this," Robin began, waving her arm to encompass the boom lift, the barn roof, and him, "any of this, have anything to do with Mia?"

Should he tell her his suspicions? No, it was too soon. And he didn't yet have all the pieces to put the puzzle together. Still, the desperate mother needed hope.

"Maybe," he admitted.

Grace collapsed onto the sawdust floor.

Chapter 24

Friday

Dusty hadn't brought back the bucket, so Mia was forced to use the far corner of her room as the toilet. But he'd left the food bag and her clothes, so as soon as she could move again, she ripped off the negligee and dressed in her clothes, which were a bit cleaner now. It didn't matter that her jeans and T-shirt were wet. Everything in the room was soaked.

She ate every scrap of food from the bag even though she had to lick the soggy messes off the papers they were wrapped in.

As her prison grew pitch black again, she worked feverishly at the table leg, and almost broke into a cheer when the thing finally snapped off.

"Yes!" She brandished it over her head and then took a few practice swings. One hit the wall with a satisfying thunk.

She felt her way to the door and got into striking position, the table leg over her shoulder like a baseball bat. The cold wetness of her clothing helped to keep her awake. She didn't know how many hours passed while she crouched there, envisioning smashing Dusty's head. When the door opened and the flashlight beamed in, she tensed her muscles and blinked as fast as she could to adjust her eyes. Dusty had only begun to say something when she smacked the table leg into his face.

He staggered backward through the open door, falling on his back. She leapt over him, tossing away the table leg as she ran, racing for the opening she could see at the far end of the cavernous barn.

Once through that doorway, she would find a road, other people, woods, anything. She kicked out, she pumped her arms. She was doing it.

She was escaping.

She was going to be free.

Mia was within a yard of the opening when she was hit from behind and slammed facedown in the dirt. She bit her tongue.

Dusty clamped his hands around one ankle. Mia kicked and screamed, but he dragged her by her leg, banging her head across the uneven ground, grinding dirt into her hair and skin, scooping it up under her shirt.

He dragged her back across the threshold of her prison. Instead of shocking her this time or even throwing her on the bed, he jerked her up from the ground and grabbed her around the throat, holding her against the wall.

"Why don't you beg?" he snarled. Blood ran down his face from a gash over his eye, and his nose was pushed to the side. "You're supposed to beg!"

She couldn't breathe. She tried to knock his hands away like Toshi had taught her, but that required leverage, and Dusty was holding her off the ground.

She couldn't breathe.

She kicked and flailed her arms, but she was a butterfly nailed to the wall. The hands tightened. Why had she thrown away the table leg? How stupid could she get? She deserved to die.

Black spots danced in her vision. The roar in her head grew louder. This was it. She was going to die, and the face of her rapist would be the last thing she'd ever see. She shut her eyes.

Sorry, Mom.

Sorry, Dad.

I'm so sorry I was the only one left.

Chapter 25

Friday

"Grace!" Finn dropped his cell phone and dove to his knees beside her unconscious figure. Turning her over gently, he brushed the sawdust from her face. "Grace!"

Robin knelt beside her, took her friend's hand in hers.

"What's wrong with her?" Finn demanded.

Robin just shook her head.

Finn recovered his cell phone, pressed 9-1-1, asked for an EMT response. By the time he'd finished the call, Neema and Gumu were looming over them. Neema whimpered and rocked from side to side. Gumu reached for Grace's ankle, latched onto it, and tugged. Grace slid a few inches, a rag doll in the dirt.

"Stop, Gumu!" Finn yelled. Pocketing the cell phone, he slid an arm under Grace's shoulders, then snaked the other arm beneath her knees and struggled to lift her from the floor.

A violent thump on the back of his head made him see stars.

"No!" Robin yelped.

Fighting the blackness that swarmed in front of his eyes, Finn gently released Grace to the ground again, and then sat, stunned for a few seconds, until his vision returned to normal. Less than two yards away, Gumu rose to his back legs and pounded his chest, baring his fierce canine teeth and roaring at Finn.

Robin scuttled backward on her hands and feet, taking refuge near the wall. Neema hooted and huddled into a ball a short distance away.

"Stop!" Finn yelled, rising to his feet. He staggered a few steps, but remained upright, trying to blink away the black spots he saw.

Gumu pounded his chest again, then rushed at Finn and smacked him hard on the shoulder. Finn landed his own blow on the ape's massive back as the silverback passed. When Gumu turned and displayed his teeth again, Finn bellowed "Stop!" at the top of his lungs, making the sign as well. "Stop!"

Gumu roared and pounded his chest again. Finn was painfully aware that he was facing the same gorilla who had killed an intruder last year. Gumu glared, balancing on his fists, ready to charge again.

Grace was part of Gumu's family. Finn was pretty sure that *he* was not included in the silverback's idea of clan. He held out both hands. "Stop!"

When Gumu rocked forward, Finn pounded his own chest and roared as best he could.

Gumu's gaze stayed fixed on Finn. The silverback's nostrils flared, and he grunted uncertainly.

Finn lowered his voice and used the few signs he knew. "I love Grace. Grace comes with me. I love Grace. Good Gumu. Good gorilla."

He turned toward Neema. She crouched near the wall, near Robin. No help there. The mother gorilla was clearly not going to come to his rescue.

Red-and-blue flickers of light on the barn wall indicated the aid truck had arrived. "Hello?" someone shouted. "Fire

Department! EMTs!"

"Coming!" Finn knelt to lift Grace. Gumu rocked forward and flashed his canines again, snapping his jaws together as he rose to his feet and slapped his leathery chest in a loud drumbeat.

"Stop!" Finn thrust out his hand in the sign. "I love Grace."

The massive silverback watched, grunting, as Finn picked up Grace's limp form and then staggered to the door of the barn. "C'mon, Robin," he told the cowering woman.

She quickly preceded him out of the gorilla barn.

"Take Grace's keys from her belt. Let us out."

Robin did as he asked. They both turned their backs to the gate, watching Gumu and Neema, who had followed them into the exterior enclosure. After handing Grace over to the EMTs, Finn turned back to observe Robin locking the gate behind them, her hands shaking so hard she could barely slide the key into the lock.

On the other side of the fence, Neema signed.

"Is Neema talking about Grace?" Finn asked.

"No, Kanoni. Baby give my baby," Robin told him. "Kanoni's in the staff quarters. She's restrained and sedated so she won't pull out her IVs."

"Can you stay here?"

Robin nodded.

Neema signed again.

"Grace sad me baby give," Robin translated. She rubbed a hand against the side of her face. "Now Neema's worried about Grace, too."

"She's not the only one," Finn said.

The EMTs loaded the gurney. The man climbed into the driver's seat, and the woman climbed in the back and started to close the door.

"I'm going with her," he told the female EMT, climbing in.

Robin Valdez watched as the door closed, her face anxious. "I'll call you as soon as I can," he shouted at her.

As they rocketed down the road, the EMT wrapped a blood pressure cuff around Grace's arm, listened to her heart, shined a penlight into her eyes. She groaned. Her face was pale and shiny with perspiration, and her jeans were dark and clingy as if she'd wet herself.

Finn tried to answer the EMT's questions as best he could. Not diabetic, no. No history of epilepsy or heart disease. Her parents had seemed healthy enough the last time he'd seen them, so her genes were good, as far as he knew.

Grace groaned again, opened her eyes, shut them. "I can't go to the hospital."

"Yes," he told her. "You can. And you are. Robin stayed behind."

"The gorillas . . ." she started.

The female EMT's eye rounded in surprise.

"I managed," he said. It might take a while to get the image of a threatening silverback out of his head.

It was nearly ten p.m. when they arrived at the hospital. The staff wouldn't let Finn into the exam area with Grace because he wasn't family. After taking down the basic information, they left him in the waiting area.

He paced. He couldn't lose Grace. They'd barely begun their relationship. They were just getting to finally understand each other, accept each other's lifestyle. Gorillas and detective work were a unique mix. He couldn't lose her.

His cell phone chimed several times as he paced, and he finally thought to check it. Miki had sent him information on Trevor Lee Vollmar. As his foster mother Deanna had told Finn, Trevor was fifteen in 2004 when Sutter was arrested with Angela Albro in his trunk, seventeen in 2006 when Sutter was sent to prison and Trevor was forced to change families. That was after Deanna had lost custody of her foster teens and had to move away from the farm on Old Forest Road.

Trevor had lived with the Sutters from age twelve through seventeen and a half. He would have been living with Todd Sutter when Heidi Skouras, Anna Moran, and Magdalena Aguilar had gone missing. He hadn't been with Sutter when the scumbag was caught with Albro, but what were the odds that Trevor knew what his foster father had been up to? What were the odds that he'd helped? What were the odds that he'd learned about the Gorge concerts as a prime hunting ground and discovered a perverted pleasure in torturing women?

There was a gap of three years between Albro and Disanto. Maybe Trevor was just screwing up his courage to try on his own? Perfecting his techniques? He would have been twenty when Disanto went missing. And he would have known that Sutter had hidden corpses in abandoned barns, would have known the barn on Old Forest Road was empty. He would have been twenty-two when he went for Sheryl Pratt in 2009.

The gap between Pratt, missing in 2009, and Kelly, missing in 2016, bothered Finn. Was he on the wrong track?

He checked Vollmar's history again. 2010 through 2015, Trevor Vollmar had been a soldier doing multiple tours in Iraq and Afghanistan.

He impatiently scanned Vollmar's multiple addresses, scrolled through his vehicle history. There! Vollmar was the registered owner of a motorcycle, an older Harley Roadster model.

Vollmar had been especially interested in the beams holding up the roof of the gorilla barn, had even asked Grace if anything had been found during the remodel.

It all fit. Finn called the station, asked for an APB on Trevor Lee Vollmar as a person of interest in the abduction of Mia Valdez.

He was reviewing the map where Mia's cell and backpack had been found, scrolling and scrolling on the damn tiny cell phone screen, when Grace's doctor, a woman who seemed impossibly young, walked into the waiting room.

He introduced himself as Grace's fiancé in the hopes that would convince her to tell him all the pertinent details. "How is she?"

"She was very dehydrated, had low blood sugar, and is running a bit of a fever."

"Could that happen if she was exposed to measles?"

The doctor shrugged. "If she's been vaccinated, a reaction would be rare, but it has happened. I'll put a note in the file that she's been exposed. She seems to be exhausted, and in her condition, it's little wonder she passed out."

"Is Grace going to be okay?"

The doctor eyed him. "*She'll* recover just fine."

The woman was covering up some detail. "But?" he asked.

"You're not family yet, Detective Finn. Where *is* her family, by the way?

His thoughts flashed to Neema and Gumu and Kanoni, then, angrily, to himself, and finally to her parents. "Her mother and father are in California."

"Can you call them?"

"Of course." He nodded, all the while thinking, *like hell I will*. Grace wouldn't want her folks to know anything about this unless she had a terminal condition. "Can I see her?"

"Dr. McKenna will have to give permission. And she's sleeping right now. I suggest you leave her alone to rest, for at least a few hours."

He couldn't stay at the hospital a few hours. He couldn't stay ten more minutes, not while there was still a chance for Mia Valdez. "Can you give Grace a note?"

"Leave it with the admitting nurse," the doctor told him. "He'll see she gets it."

He tore a sheet of paper out of his pocket notepad, then hesitated for the span of several heartbeats, his pen hovering over the paper. Finally, he settled on writing, *I love you. I'll be back. I'll always be back. —Matt.*

After hitching a ride in a patrol car back to Grace's to collect his own vehicle, Finn drove to the station where he could use a decent-size computer screen to review local maps. Centering the location where Mia's belongings had been found, he scanned outward using an overhead view on Google Earth. He had to start somewhere, so he settled on a ten-mile radius. There were three dilapidated structures within ten miles of where the backpack had been found, two old barns and a building that looked like it had once been part of a chicken farm. Scribbling down the addresses, he dashed for his car and plugged them into the GPS system.

He thought about calling for backup. But he was making a lot of assumptions; he still could be wrong. He didn't need police cruisers with flashing lights following him around the county as he found nothing. No. He'd call in when he found something definitive.

The county roads were dark. There were no streetlights outside of downtown Evansburg. Clicking on his brights, he raced down the road to the first location on his list.

Chapter 26

Friday

When she struggled to consciousness, Mia was not completely sure she was still alive. The darkness in the room was so complete that she saw nothing. But her throat couldn't possibly hurt this bad if she were dead. And her pants wouldn't be down around her ankles, either. She pulled them up, glad she hadn't been conscious for the assault this time. The mattress beneath her was still wet, and she was shivering with cold. Dusty had taken away what was left of the bedside table, so now the only remaining items were the two stacked mattresses and the sodden bedding. The shithead had even taken her shoes.

No light filtered in through the crack or knothole in the exterior wall. Evening? Or the middle of the night? She felt her way around the room, sniffing for the aroma of food, but he'd left her nothing. The air in the room stank, but this time it wasn't the smell of her own excrement. Instead, she got a vague whiff of something like gasoline.

She'd made her way to the door, feeling along the wall with her hand and the floor with her toes, when she heard a faint voice from the other side of the room. "This will be the biggest one yet."

A voice outside? Hallucination? Dusty? She couldn't decide.

"Light it up."

A different voice? Tailing her hand along the rough boards, she moved back to the exterior wall.

"Let me."

"No, all together. One, two, three!"

Definitely multiple voices. Her heart in her throat, she pounded on the wall. "Hey! Help! Help! I'm locked in here!" Her throat was so swollen she could barely get the words out.

A loud whooshing sound drowned out her feeble cries, and then, through the knothole, she saw light dancing outside. Flashlights?

"Did you hear that?" one of the voices asked.

"Fuck, didn't you check inside?"

"Help!" she screeched. "Help me!"

"What the fuck?"

"Shit, someone's coming. Run!"

"No! Don't go!" She kicked the wall, pounded again, shouting as loudly as she could. "Help me! I'm locked in here! Help!"

"Leave the truck. Go! Just go!"

An engine approached. She heard the slam of a car door. Another voice. "You fuckheads! Fuck! Goddamn fuckheads!"

The last sounded a little like Dusty. But it couldn't be Dusty. He only came once a day, in the evening, and he'd already tortured her today.

The light outside grew brighter, and the beam streaming from the knothole revealed wisps of smoke snaking in between the boards in the exterior wall.

The barn was on fire.

"Help!" she screamed.

A horrific groan came from somewhere overhead, as if the

building was in terrible pain. The smoke was pouring in, now so thick she could taste it. Her throat started to close up, and then she started coughing, so hard she couldn't get her breath to shout. It hurt so bad. She pounded on the wall, using both her hands and feet.

A loud snapping sound was followed by a crash. Was that the roof giving way?

The whooshing and crackling and groaning grew louder. The smoke trailing across the room overhead seemed to snag on the light fixture. She watched it swirl and crawl, and realized that any second the ceiling would catch fire.

Someone had to see the fire, didn't they?

Please God I'm not ready to die!

She took a deep breath, screeched "Help me!" again, but her cry was thin and hoarse. Then her throat clenched and she choked, retching, gasping for breath.

The ceiling flamed, a brilliant streak of light and heat overhead, and she started to scream again, but the sound caught in her throat, gagging her. *Down, get down out of the smoke.* She fell to her hands and knees. Embers rained on her from the ceiling. More of the exterior wall was ablaze now, and for a second she imagined she could crawl through the flames to the outside, but her eyes streamed, making everything a blur, and she couldn't see an opening anywhere.

God, she was so hot, so hot, her skin was going to bubble into blisters like zombies in the horror movies.

No way could she break through the metal door. No window to climb out.

She banged on the wall. The wood scorched her fists. She tried to yell again, but her throat was closing up.

She was going to burn to death.

Chapter 27

Friday

The old chicken factory was every bit as empty as the first barn had been. As Finn swept up the next rise to the third location on his list, he wondered if his assumptions about Trevor Vollmar had been completely off track. But after he crested the hill, a glow of flames greeted him. Leaning forward in his seat, he pressed his foot harder on the gas pedal.

No! He couldn't be too late.

Pressing the button on his steering wheel, he called 9-1-1, identified himself, reported the fire. Then he asked to be connected with Detective Melendez.

"I heard the call go out," she said on answering. "I'm on my way."

"I'm almost there." He screeched around a curve.

"What are *you* doing there?"

He missed the turnoff to the barn, identifying the gravel lane out of the corner of his eye as he passed. "Later, Sara." He punched END.

He stomped on the brake, his tires squealing as he wrestled the car around. A loud crash sounded somewhere near the fire.

Then he was tearing down the gravel road, trees whipping past, and then he slammed his car into PARK ten yards back from the flaming structure. The barn was fully engulfed, the roof already falling in. He was too late.

Although there were no other buildings in sight, two pickups were parked nearby, a white one back near the trees, a black one far too close. He watched as a chunk of flaming debris from the barn roof tumbled onto the cab of that one.

The sirens neared. The fire department volunteers were on their way. But once again, they'd be too late to save anything.

He grabbed his flashlight, stepped out of his car, and quickly inspected both vehicles. Empty. Then he heard what sounded like pounding.

Was that a shout? He raced toward the front of the barn where the doorway revealed that the barn was completely ablaze. Flames licked up the walls and crawled across the roof above, and everything below was obscured by dense black smoke. The structure groaned as a wall shifted, and Finn had no doubt that the building was within minutes of collapsing.

Then he noticed that a long water hose stretched from the shadowy woods across the dirt and then snaked into the flaming interior.

"Mia!" he yelled. "Mia Valdez! Is anyone inside?"

Chapter 28

Friday

The door of her prison burst open, and flames leapt across the ceiling to race toward the opening. A jet of water hit her in the shoulder, spurting into her face and over her back. Now she welcomed its cold wetness. But water wasn't air. She needed *air*. On her hands and knees, Mia crawled in the direction of the door, water dripping into her eyes. Something clamped viciously onto her arm.

Dusty dragged her to her feet, sprayed water over her again. A bandage covered most of his forehead, and his nose and mouth were hidden under a wet kerchief. She was choking so hard she could barely straighten up, but she pulled against his grip, straining to precede him out of her prison. *Air*.

He held tight to her arm, hissing in a hoarse voice, "You want to live, you tell them I saved you. Got it? I saved you!" He coughed then, his fingers crushing her arm.

She struggled to get free, to get through that door. An ember fell from above, burning into her scalp. She wanted to slap it away, but he held both her arms in a viselike grip.

"Got it?" he growled between coughs.

Her face was burning. Smoke was rising from her clothes. She could feel the soles of her feet melting, sticking to the dirt.

"Got it," she managed to choke out.

Then he was dragging her out the door. Like demons circling them, flames cackled against a background roar of thumps and creaks, warning that the worst was yet to come. The smoke was so dense, she was eating it. No, it was eating her. Overhead, the roof of the barn was on fire. Walls of flame danced around them. Black caustic fog swirled, replacing all the air. Her eyes were flooded with tears. The whole world was a blur, too bright, too hot. Dusty dragged her first one way and then the other, like a kid manhandling a rag doll.

"Mia Valdez!" Through the roar of the fire, she heard a stranger's voice over her left shoulder. "Run this way! Run this way!"

She turned toward the voice. Through leaping flames, she could barely make out the darker rectangle of the barn door. Who stood there?

"Run this way!"

"Remember," Dusty growled, nearly crushing her arms. "I didn't have to come back. I could have let you burn. You owe me. Remember."

With an ominous creak and then a loud snap, a rafter crashed down behind them. A new wall of flame erupted from the pile. Dusty glanced over his shoulder in that direction.

"I'll remember forever, darlin'." Twisting her arm to pull it from his grip, Mia bent at the waist, and head-butted him.

It wasn't an elegant move. It wasn't even karate.

Dusty grabbed a fistful of her hair, pulling her with him as he fell backward onto the flaming rafter.

Chapter 29

Friday

Finn watched in horror as parts of the roof fell in. Flames dropped to the ground, and a new volcano of fire erupted in the center of the building. He knew that the sane thing to do would be to wait for the volunteer firefighters to arrive.

But then he heard the screams. He couldn't have come so close to the solution, only to let Mia Valdez die when he was standing only a few yards away.

He ran inside the burning barn, waving his arms in a useless attempt to clear away the dense smoke so that he could see. "Mia? Mia Valdez? Are you in here?"

Flames crawled along the rafters overhead, and as the far end of the barn fell, a gale of superheated air rushed through the building. The building groaned and shrieked like a live creature. Any second now, the whole structure would come down.

Chapter 30

Friday

It hurt like hell, but Mia managed to rip her hair from Dusty's fists. Her head was burning. Her feet were burning. Dusty's screams followed her as she leapt through the flames and ran through the raining debris toward the front of the barn, where, through streaming eyes, she thought she could make out a blurry black square that had to be the doorway.

A large man clamped an arm around her. "Mia? Mia Valdez?" Then he started slapping her head with his free hand.

"No!" she screamed, struggling against his grip. "Let me go!"

He pulled her toward the opening. "I'm Detective Finn, Mia. I've got you."

Her legs collapsed. He swept her up into his arms and jogged outside. "We've been looking for you for so long," he said softly. Kindly. She started sobbing.

Cradling her awkwardly in his arms, he still managed to brush embers from her hair, another away from the back of her neck. Mia used her fingers to comb a glowing particle from his hair. The sleeve of his jacket was smoking, and she slapped her hand against the fabric until it stopped. He opened his mouth, then broke into a fit of coughing, and hefted her higher against his chest.

She choked and cried into his shoulder as he carried her away from the fire, out of the smoke, into the cool night air. She gripped his shirt sleeve in her fist, and couldn't stop crying and coughing.

Still holding her in his arms, the man leaned against a car and watched the fire as a wall gave way and the entire roof crashed down into the flames below. He started to say something, then choked, swallowed, took a deep breath, and finally, in a hoarse voice, managed to ask, "Anyone else in there?"

"No," she croaked.

Chapter 31

Friday

Finn held Mia Valdez in his arms as a fire engine and aid truck pulled onto the site, followed by two police cruisers and a dark sedan. The girl was soaking wet and couldn't stop coughing, her eyes and nostrils streaming, her face black with soot. Half her hair had burned away, a blister on her scalp was raw-looking, and she no doubt had many more injuries he couldn't see. He waited until the EMTs had a gurney ready before he handed her over. She held tight to his shirt until he told her it was okay to let go. "You're safe now, Mia."

"Darcy?" she croaked, and then her hacking began again.

"She's okay. She's back home."

Mia's blistered lips formed the word *good* but the sound wouldn't come out. Then she made the sign for "thank you."

Shaking his head, an EMT placed an oxygen mask over her face and then the aid truck took her away.

Finn didn't feel worthy of thanks. It had taken him too long to figure it all out. Mia Valdez had nearly died. And, based on the screams he'd heard after he had Mia in his arms, someone else *had* died in there.

His right hand hurt, and in the flickering light, he saw blisters on his palm. A spot on his neck felt as if it was still smoldering, and when he touched it gingerly with his left hand, he felt a large bubble of skin there.

"Lucky you." Standing by his side, Detective Melendez tapped a metal flashlight against her thigh as she regarded the burning barn with disgust. She handed him a bottle of water.

"Lucky? Have mercy." He tucked the bottle under his arm. After coughing a few times, he spit black phlegm into the dirt before adding, "I'm wounded." He pulled down his collar to show her the red welts on the side of his neck, and he turned his hands palms up to show her the blisters.

"Oh, jeez, now you'll get a Purple Heart, too." Melendez rolled her eyes. "You save the girl while I get yet another arson case."

She took the bottle from him, unscrewed the cap, and handed it back.

"What's with this?" she asked, staring at the water hose lying at her feet.

"I don't know. It was here when I arrived. I suspect there was at least one more person inside." He gestured toward the mountain of flaming lumber that used to be a barn.

Melendez grimaced. "Oh, goody. Crispy critters, something to look forward to. But probably not my arsonists. Who sets a fire and then tries to put it out?"

Finn inhaled. It hurt, as if his lungs had forgotten how to expand and contract. A long swallow from the water bottle made his throat ache. "Those pickups"—he nodded in the direction of the white pickup parked near the trees, and then the black one parked close to the building—"were here when I drove up." He paused to cough and spit again. "I think you'll find the white one belongs to one of two boys who work at the SpeediLube. Names are Greco and Symes."

Melendez raised an eyebrow.

"Coincidence," he said. "I'll explain later."

"And that one?" She tilted her head toward the black truck that the fire department was hosing down in hopes of preventing it from bursting into flames.

"I suspect it might be registered to Trevor Vollmar. Foster son of Todd Sutter."

"Interesting." After staring at him for a long moment, blinking, she surveyed the vehicles, and then peered into the dark woods.

His coughing started again, burning up his throat from his scratchy lungs.

"Go to the hospital, Finn," she told him. "Johnson! Magruder!" she yelled at the uniformed officers. "Grab your flashlights. We're going hunting."

Chapter 32

Friday

"It's Detective Finn, Mrs. Valdez," Finn began when Robin Valdez answered her cell phone. He was using one of the hospital landlines, heeding the warning posted on the wall about no cell phone usage in the zone.

"Robin," she said immediately. "You sound awful. I can barely hear you. How's Grace?"

He had to clear his throat and swallow before he could respond. "Robin, I'm at the hospital now. The docs say Grace will be fine. I'll bring her back tomorrow."

"Thank God."

"Thank you for holding down the fort in Gorillaville. But I'm calling to give you an update on Mia. We had a major breakthrough tonight."

Her brief silence radiated tension, and he knew Robin was steeling herself for bad news. Finally she said, "Go ahead, Detective."

He handed the receiver to the girl on the bed beside him, using his unbandaged left hand. Mia hadn't let the staff chase Finn away from her side for a minute after he arrived at the hospital, but they'd insisted on inspecting his wounds.

Slipping down her oxygen mask, Mia said, "Mom." Her

voice was hoarse from smoke and emotion. "I'm okay."

Finn could hear Robin's exclamations from where he stood. Mia sobbed nonstop as she listened to her mother's voice, and Finn bet that Robin was crying, too. Mia wasn't exactly okay, he knew, and it might be some time before she was okay again. She'd been drugged, raped, choked, and burned. But the girl was a fighter.

He retrieved the phone long enough to tell Robin that he had sent a police cruiser out to pick her up. "You shouldn't be driving," he told her.

"Thank you, thank you, thank you," she said. "I can't thank you enough."

"You just did. I'm sending a veterinary tech to stay with Kanoni. I'll talk to you tomorrow. Here's Mia again."

Finn's joy at finding Mia overcame the pain of the burns on his hands and neck. It was nearly one a.m. The hospital was quiet as he strolled down the hallway, found a door with Grace McKenna's name in the slot outside. The nurses would have tossed him out if they'd known he had snuck into her room. He was surprised to see the gleam of her eyes in the dim light of her room. Touching her arm with his unburned left hand, he quietly told her the news about Mia.

"Oh, Matt, that's wonderful news." She seemed somber. Or maybe just sleepy. He promised to come back for her tomorrow as soon as she was released.

"Sounds good," she said, closing her eyes. "Kanoni?"

"Holding her own." He hoped that was true.

"You need a shower, Matt. You smell like smoke."

"I love you, Grace," he whispered. But she'd already fallen asleep.

Finn knew that Cargo and the cats were counting the minutes until he returned, so he drove straight home. The noise from the fire still echoed in his brain, contrasting with the silence of his house. Cargo's munching and the purring of the tabbies as they rubbed against him seemed overly loud. His bandaged right hand began to throb. He would need to wrap a plastic bag around it to take a shower.

Then his doorbell rang. Envisioning one of his neighbors complaining about Cargo howling about his abandonment until five minutes ago, he considered not answering it.

Fists pounded on the front door. "Police! Answer the damn door or we'll break it down!"

He rushed to open it before the neighbors heard *that*. In spilled Sara Melendez, Officers Rick Johnson and Marc Magruder, and at least half the volunteer fire department, carrying six-packs of beer and bottles of wine and bags of chips. Everyone still stank of smoke and sweat.

"Sara?" He questioned his colleague, "What about the hubby and kids?"

"They'll keep." Handing him a beer, she raised one to clink with his. "They're asleep right now. And they're not cops. Or firefighters." She pointed the neck of her beer bottle toward him. "You're single. So tonight, your house is party central! Two cases successfully closed, all fires out, scumbags in custody or in the morgue."

Finn briefly considered the mountain of reports he was going to have to fill out tomorrow to actually close the case. He suspected that Mia Valdez had saved the state of Washington major time and expense by exacting her own punishment on Trevor Vollmar. He was glad he had no way of proving whether Vollmar's death had been an accident. Now that they had good reason to believe that Sutter and Vollmar had disposed of their corpses in abandoned farm buildings, there would be weeks of work ahead to inspect all the likely properties and search for more victims.

"Lighten up, Finn." Sara gave him a gentle slap on the arm. "Tonight, you're a hero. Hell, I'm a hero. Hell, we are all heroes!"

The party went on until almost three in the morning. Cargo ate an entire bag of chips, then upchucked them on the bathroom rug. Lok and Kee were hiding under Finn's bed when he finally fell into it.

Chapter 33

Saturday

It was eleven a.m. before Finn dragged himself into the station the next morning. The media was already there en masse, but the captain was happily answering all their questions, so Finn managed to sneak past the crowd without their notice.

As he strolled into the shared detectives' office, he was surprised to see Detective Perry Dawes at his desk. A pair of crutches leaned on the wall behind him.

"Didn't you have a couple more weeks of leave?" Finn asked.

Dawes looked up from his email. "One more day at home, my wife and daughters were gonna make me take up knitting. Do you know what it's like to be surrounded by women?"

"I have a fair idea."

"I was going berserk. Besides, I hear you've been hogging the good cases and getting all the glory."

"Not *all* the glory." Sara Melendez walked through the door. "I got some, too." Sliding her purse into a drawer, she clanged it shut and winced at the noise. Her head probably throbbed as much as his did this morning.

Miki came in, carrying several sheets of paper in her hands and several rolled-up maps tucked under one arm. Heading for

Finn's desk, she dumped her load there. "Here are all the addresses I could come up with for old farm buildings in Kittitas and Grant counties. And you'll want these maps. And the captain says that you need to join a press briefing in the roll call room"—she dramatically checked her watch—"ten minutes ago." The aide turned toward Sara Melendez's desk. "You too, Melendez." She left.

"Oh, the glory of it all," Sara complained, rubbing her forehead.

Dawes pointed at the heap of materials Miki had left on Finn's desk. "Bring all that stuff over here."

"Really?" Finn gladly gathered up all the papers and transported them across the room.

"I may not be able to chase perps right now," Dawes said, "But I can detect from behind my computer. Maybe I can turn up a few old victims and resolve some cold cases, take the load off you, Finn. Then I can score some points, too, wrap up Sutter *and* Vollmar."

Melendez crossed her arms. "What about me?"

They both ignored her as Special Agent Alice Foster entered. Halfway to Finn's desk, she stopped and fisted her hands on her hips, a wry smile on her lips. "I can't believe you solved it without me, Finn."

"Sorry. I couldn't wait for you to get back from Spokane."

"Here's the unlocked cell phone." Pulling it from her jacket pocket, she clapped it down on his desk. "Not that you need it now. And by the way, Cooper Trigg will be transported tomorrow to Grant County for prosecution for the stolen credit cards. You might want to ask the Irelands if they want to add vandalism, too, for keying Darcy's car."

"Thank you."

She folded her arms, echoing Melendez's posture. "I'm glad

it wasn't human trafficking. Well, sort of. Now I have no reason to stick around. Congratulations, Detective." She faced Melendez. "And congrats to you, too, Sara, on nailing your arsonists."

"Thanks for your help." Finn extended his unbandaged left hand to Foster. "Your assistance expedited the case. Had we been one day later, Mia Valdez would be dead."

"Matthew Finn," she said, taking his hand. "I hope our paths cross again someday." Then she winked at him. "You could always *make* that happen."

"Uh." He couldn't think of an appropriate response.

"That's what I thought," Agent Foster said. "Have fun with Grace and the gorillas."

Chapter 34

Monday

Two days later, Finn flipped burgers left-handed on the grill as the evening transitioned into a purple twilight. Grace lounged nearby in a lawn chair, watching the gorillas in their enclosure across the yard. Finn had brought Cargo with him, and the big mutt reclined beside Grace, licking her hand whenever she stopped scratching his head.

The gorillas were climbing the rope net. Neema had Kanoni on her back, and Gumu carried the white cat Snow under one arm like a football.

Robin, Keith, and Mia Valdez watched from the ground next to the fence. Mia had been released from the hospital only hours ago and sat in a wheelchair to relieve her blistered feet.

Tonight, the family was staying in Grace's staff trailer, but they'd leave in the morning for Bellingham. Instead of the revealing clothing Mia had worn in her photos, the teen was now dressed in camouflage cargo pants and a loose T-shirt, and her blond hair was short and spiky. She was subdued and still croaking from smoke inhalation but seemed remarkably resilient, given what she'd been through.

When the gorillas reached the top of the rope net, Gumu cradled the cat, and Neema pulled Kanoni into her lap to nurse. *Baby happy me*, she signed to herself, or perhaps to the baby gorilla. Even Finn could understand those signs.

Grace smiled. "Kanoni's going to be okay. She's still weak, but her fever is gone and she's eating again. And now I have plenty of money to pay the vet."

He waited for the explanation of her sudden windfall.

"Get this: Robin set up this system on my website where people can order customized cards featuring their names and a painting by a gorilla. I couldn't believe it! It's automatic. People just fill in a form, choose the gorilla and the painting, pay the fee, and the order goes off to the printer, just like that." She snapped her fingers.

"Sounds magical." He mashed the spatula into a burger, checking for doneness.

"There have already been four hundred and thirty-two orders, and it's just getting started." She shook her head in amazement. "Money in the bank! Robin told me she was a wiz at online sales, but I had no idea. If it keeps up, I'll bring in enough money to actually hire staff again."

"That's fantastic, Grace. But even better: the cabin in the San Juan Islands."

The Valdezes had offered Finn and Grace the use of their vacation home on Lopez Island for two weeks in July, in gratitude for Finn saving their daughter.

"It's not luxurious," Keith had warned. "No television. Solar power, wood stove, composting toilet. But the location is beautiful. You might even see orcas."

"Sounds like heaven," Finn told him.

"Mia and I will come to Evansburg to watch over the gorillas while you're gone," Robin volunteered. Mother-daughter bonding, Robin had called it, saying she needed to get to know her daughter better.

While Finn felt slightly guilty about taking their offer for merely doing his job, he wasn't about to look this particular gift horse in the mouth. He and Grace rarely had whole days to themselves, let alone two weeks. He'd have time to finish his painting. Wildflowers were going to make up the foreground of the barn picture. He'd had enough of fire for a while.

Turning toward him, Grace said, "I can't believe you beat your chest and faced down Gumu."

"Robin told you about that?" He felt his cheeks flush. "I can't believe it, either."

"You are now the chief silverback in the troop."

"That's always been my secret ambition." Finn poured two glasses of red wine. Handing one to her, he sat down with the other on the lawn chair next to hers. "Grace, just for the record, I would have been okay with it."

She looked at him, her lips parted, a quizzical expression on her face.

"I would have been happy about the baby."

"How'd you know?"

It had taken him a while to clue in. The hospital had steadfastly refused to tell him anything, but Grace's recent behavior, the signs on the day she collapsed, and the doctor's odd inflection when she'd said, "*She'll* be okay," had led him to the conclusion that Grace had suffered a miscarriage.

He shrugged. "I'm a detective."

She studied his face. "How do you feel about it now?"

He reached for her hand. "I'm okay with it. How about you?"

"I'm a little sad. Neema signed *me cry sad you*, like she knew, too."

"She pays attention to your moods."

Grace sighed. "I have to admit, I'm also a little relieved. And *that* makes me feel guilty."

Across the yard, Neema lifted her head and gazed in their direction. Maybe she'd heard Grace say her name.

As the gorilla signed, Grace translated for Finn. "Gorilla good love baby."

Robin Valdez, watching from below, turned to face Finn and Grace, and then she also signed *my baby good love my baby*. She touched Mia on the shoulder, and then, meeting Finn's gaze, finished with the hand gesture that meant *thank you*.

He was getting pretty good at reading sign language, but the world didn't need to know that. Finn simply waved at her, and Robin turned her back again.

"It's been a hell of a week." He took a sip of wine. "I'm glad that everything turned out okay for that family."

"I'll be okay, too." Grace squeezed Finn's fingers. "And we already have our family." Lifting her chin, she indicated the gorillas, then patted Cargo. The dog moaned with pleasure.

"Our family is a little hairy," Finn commented.

"I know you never planned to take care of two cats and a dog," she murmured.

"But I can't imagine my house without the menagerie now." He took another sip of wine. "You probably never imagined you were living with a skeleton in your barn."

"Or that I'd become involved in kidnapping cases," she reminded him of their shared past.

He snorted. "I never thought I'd need clues from gorillas."

She laughed. "Matt, just so you know, I don't intend to be a gorilla keeper for the rest of my life. I want to find a sanctuary for Gumu and Neema and Kanoni, where they can be part of a bigger gorilla family like they would be in the wild. But until I can make that happen . . ."

She smiled at him over her wine glass. "Most people's lives are not nearly as interesting as ours, are they?"

Finn held up his wine glass in a toast. "Here's to interesting lives."

~ END ~

If you enjoyed *The Only One Left*, please consider
writing a review on any online book site.
Reviews help authors sell books.
Thank you!

Discussion Questions for Reading Groups

1. Dr. Grace McKenna clearly loves her gorillas, but has mixed feelings about keeping them. How do you feel about exotic animals kept in zoos or as pets?

2. On a whim, Darcy and Mia rode off with two strange boys on motorcycles. Did you ever do anything similarly risky in your life that could have ended in disaster? Do you feel that boys do not have to be as cautious as young girls do?

3. At times, Detective Matthew Finn feels defensive around smart women. Do you believe he has a right to?

4. Kanoni contracts measles from an unvaccinated human playmate. Did you know that humans and animals share some diseases? Do you think all humans should be vaccinated against common communicable diseases?

5. Grace is conflicted about her pregnancy so late in life. Did you sympathize with her reasoning?

6. How would you feel about living next door to Grace and Neema, Gumu, and Kanoni?

Are you familiar with Pamela Beason's
Sam Westin wilderness mysteries?
If you haven't read any, you'll probably want to start
with *Endangered*, the first novel in the series.
On the following pages you can read the beginning of
Backcountry, number four in the series.

Preview of
BACKCOUNTRY
Chapter 1

Sam Westin stared at the photo on her cell phone. The jagged granite mountains, ivory-barked alders, and cloudless azure sky were so perfectly mirrored in Pinnacle Lake that she couldn't tell the difference between the reflection in the water and the reality of peaks and vegetation above the shoreline.

This picture would make a perfect enlargement to replace the faded print of Table Mountain above her fireplace.

Except that every time she looked at the image, she might cry.

She thumbed the screen back to the selfie that had arrived in her e-mail three weeks ago. Kimberly Quintana, her curly brown hair frizzed around her head, her petite blond daughter Kyla Quintana-Johnson posed in front of her, the lake sparkling behind them.

Kim and Kyla died here.

"They probably sat right in this spot," Sam said aloud, touching her fingers to the rock ledge beneath her. Biting her lip, she turned away from the lake. Behind her, Chase was inspecting a small clearing in the shrubbery. "Who comes to such a beautiful place to commit murder?"

He folded his arms across his chest, his gaze fixed on the ground. "Whoever he or she was, the killer—or killers—didn't leave behind many clues. I can't even tell where it happened."

The word "it" wafted over Sam like a cold breeze. There was no blood. No outline where the bodies had lain, no yellow crime scene tape. Rain showers had drenched the site since the murders. Dozens of boot and shoe prints were etched into the mud near the lake shore, but they were smudged by weather and trampling; it was impossible to tell when they had been laid down. Sam recognized the tread patterns left by several brands of hiking boots and athletic shoes, but those might have been worn by the law enforcement personnel who had visited the site over the last several weeks.

The trees and bushes were myriad shades of green, only starting to change colors for the coming autumn. The ground cover was the usual mix of grass, lichens, and ferns. There were even a few blossoms left late in the alpine season; fuchsia monkeyflowers and violet penstemons and one lonely white trillium.

The lushness of the surroundings felt almost shameful. Violent death should not go unmarked. But wasn't this what she loved about nature? If left to her own devices, nature could heal all the wounds inflicted by humans. Wasn't that what Kim and Kyla loved, too? Sam hoped they'd had a chance to enjoy the beauty of this place before...

She didn't want to finish the sentence, even in her mind.

Chase lowered himself onto the rock ledge beside her, extending his long legs out to rest his heels in a patch of moss. He wrapped his arm around her shoulders. "I'm sorry I didn't make it to the memorial service."

"You didn't know them. I met them less than a year ago." She'd instantly bonded with the mother and daughter on a trail maintenance crew last November.

Chase studied her face. "Are you glad we came?"

"Glad" was a poor word choice, too. Sometimes human language was simply inadequate. She swallowed around the lump that partially blocked her throat. "I had to see it. Thanks for coming with me."

She and Chase had the place to themselves. They were not supposed to be here at all. The Forest Service trail was officially closed. But years of experience with lack of staff in wild places had taught Sam that there would be no ranger or deputy to stop them. If by chance they had been challenged after passing the "Closed—No Entry" sign, Chase could argue that as an FBI agent, he had cause to investigate a crime site on federal land.

On the way into the trailhead parking lot, they had passed a lone driver, a man in a baseball cap driving a silver Subaru Forester. Others had come as well, at least as far as the parking lot: an informal memorial had grown up by the trail register. Soggy sympathy cards and a heart woven out of grass nestled among two incongruous teddy bears and a pink Valentine-shaped Mylar balloon that had no business defiling a natural area.

Balloons were notorious for killing wildlife.

Both Kyla and Kim would have been outraged to find one here.

A faint scratching sound made her turn to check the rocks that flanked both sides of her. A Townsend's chipmunk, its tail flicking up and down, edged away from her pack and the remains of their brunch. The striped rodent froze, eyeing her. Its cheeks bulged suspiciously.

Sam pulled the leftover crackers and cheese into her lap. The chipmunk dashed to the top of a boulder a few feet away, where he twitched and chittered, loudly broadcasting the news of these giant intruders in his territory.

"Were you here when they were murdered?" she asked the animal. "Did you see what happened?"

The chipmunk leapt from the rock and vanished into the underbrush.

"That's what I figured." Sam stuffed a wheat cracker into her mouth and chewed. "Nobody saw anything."

Nobody except for Kyla and Kim, of course. And whoever killed them.

If she hadn't been in Idaho with Chase at his family reunion, she would have been hiking here on August second with her friends. After conquering all the familiar trails off the road to Mount Baker, they'd been on a mission to explore the trails further south along the Mountain Loop Highway. If she had been here at Pinnacle Lake instead of partying with Chase's Latino-Lakota clan, would Kim and Kyla still be alive?

Chase matched a cracker with a piece of cheese, inspecting both carefully before raising the snack to his lips. "I'm so sorry about Kyla and Kim. But if you'd been here, you might have been killed, too."

Sam didn't respond. As a child, she'd been sleeping, absent from her mother's deathbed. Absent, out kayaking alone when her colleague died in the Galapagos Islands. Absent, away in Idaho when her friends died right here.

In age, Sam was nearly equidistant between Kyla and Kim. But she shared a special bond with Kyla, perhaps because they resembled each other, at least superficially. Like Sam, Kyla was petite with long white-blond hair, although Kyla had warm brown eyes and a splash of playful freckles across her nose, while Sam's skin was uniformly pale and her eyes were a cool gray-green. Also like Sam, Kyla spent weeks at a time backpacking in the wild, while Kim worked behind a desk, escaping only for occasional day hikes with her daughter and Sam.

Kindred spirits were hard to find. The loss of her friends felt like a bruise that might never heal. Sam touched her fingers to Chase's thigh. "You checked the case file for me, right? What *do* they have?"

Chase covered her cold fingers with his own warm ones. "You really want to know?"

She nodded. "It can't hurt any more than it does already."

Letting go of her hand, he pulled a wad of pages from the pocket of his windbreaker, smoothed them across his thigh, and read. "Kyla Quintana-Johnson was shot in the back with a 30-06 rifle bullet. A second bullet, most likely from a .357 revolver, was lodged in her brain. That bullet entered her forehead."

Sam sucked in a breath that made her heart hurt.

"Kimberly Quintana was killed by a single .357 bullet to the brain that entered through her forehead."

At least, Sam tried to console herself, their deaths sounded like they'd happened quickly. The women hadn't been raped or tortured.

"No bullet casings or other bullets were found in the vicinity of the bodies, and unfortunately, those are very common weapons. The surrounding ground was hard and dry; the only footprints found were near the lakeshore. Imprints were taken of those; bits and pieces of trash collected from around the scene, but there are no links to anything substantive yet. The trail register was checked, but the pages were wet and the pencil was missing and no hikers had signed in on that day."

That figures, Sam thought. The registers, which were supposed to be used by the Forest Service to record trail usage by hikers, were rarely collected. Often the pages inside the crude wooden boxes had no place left to write and there was no implement provided to write with.

"No witnesses found so far."

The lake in front of her morphed into an impressionist painting. Sam wiped at her tear-filled eyes but only succeeded in blurring her vision even more. "Can I see the crime scene photos?"

"No." Chase folded the pages and stuffed them back in his pocket. "Trust me; you don't want to remember your friends that way." He checked his watch, then stood up. "We both need to get moving."

Taking his hand, she pulled herself up from the rock. "Was there anything in there about suspects?"

"Christopher Rawlins and Troy Johnson are regarded as persons of interest."

"No way." Sam shook her head. She'd spent time with both Kyla's boyfriend and Kim's husband. Neither seemed remotely capable of premeditated murder. "Troy's the one who convinced me to take this damn job."

"At least it's a normal job," Chase said.

"Is it?" She'd had so many crazy assignments in the past, she couldn't be sure.

In less than three hours, she needed to be back in Bellingham at the offices of Washington Wilderness Quest. There she would take charge of a troop of troubled teens whose surly attitudes would supposedly be changed forever by a twenty-one-day trek into the backcountry.

"Please, Sam, I'm desperate," Troy Johnson had begged her only a week ago.

Troy was Kim's grieving husband, Kyla's grieving father. Although their talk was supposed to be about business, and they were in a busy brewpub, it was proving to be a painful experience for both of them.

"I can more or less cope with Kim's admin jobs," he confided, sliding his eyeglasses up his nose. The glasses were thickly framed in black, an old style that was all the latest rage. "I can't take Kyla's place out in the field. Our other field guide already left for his teaching job in Montana." He drew a line down the side of his sweating beer glass with his fingertip. "We have several grant applications out right now, and there's no way we'll land a single one if we don't have a full contingent of qualified staff. You'd be a perfect field guide, Sam."

She'd scoffed at that idea. "I am a wildlife biologist, Troy. I have zero experience with counseling troubled kids. Zero experience with kids, period."

If Kim were still alive, she could have told her husband that humans were Sam's least favorite species.

They were seated in a corner of the tap room at Boundary Bay, and the ambient roar was growing as the pub filled with drinkers.

"You have all the skills we need in the field." Troy leaned in to be heard, his elbows on the table as he ticked off the requirements on his long fingers. "You have a college degree. You're a mature, stable adult."

Sam speculated that the "stable" part might be stretching the truth a bit.

"You have extensive wilderness experience in all sorts of weather; and you are a certified Wilderness First Responder for medical emergencies. And since you taught tracking skills for us earlier this year, you already know the system."

"I was only there for a few days," she argued, leaning forward, too.

"We'll teach you some techniques for dealing with the kids.

Maya will be with you. She knows the ropes now. Aidan Callahan will be your other peer counselor. He knows what he's doing. The peer counselors carry gear, help set up and break down camp, keep watch on the client kids, and generally do whatever you tell them to. In the field, you're their boss."

Wow. She'd never had assistants before; she was usually a team of one.

"You'll have the backup of the mental health counselors in the office, and they'll take your place for two days halfway through the session to give you a break and check up on the kids."

Lifting his beer, Troy took a sip. Deep lines carved his forehead above weary gray eyes, and his cheeks were hollowed above his carefully trimmed white beard. Like Kyla's, Troy's hair was straight and pale, although his was more white than blond now. "You can't say you're not experienced in working with challenging teens; I see what you've done for Maya."

Sam still wasn't sure how she'd developed such a soft spot for the tough juvenile delinquent she'd met on a trail crew two years ago. "Maya has done everything for herself. It's not like I adopted her. She glommed onto me like a remora."

Just as Sam had feared, Maya Velasquez had been booted out of her foster home in Tacoma only days after she turned eighteen. She'd insisted on living in a tent in Sam's back yard for a few weeks, until Kim Quintana took pity on both of them and gave the girl the summer job as peer counselor with Wilderness Quest.

The edge of Troy's pale eyebrow lifted. "I have no clue what a remora is."

"It's a fish," she told him. "Remoras suction-cup themselves to bigger fish for a free ride."

Setting down his glass, Troy reached across the table to

place his hand on top of hers. His fingers were cool and damp. "My point, Sam, is that Maya accomplished a lot with your guidance, and that's exactly what these six kids need."

Pulling her hand from beneath his, she fingered the beer-stained coaster on the table in front of her.

"It's only for twenty-one days," he continued. "The parents signed their kids up long ago; they're counting on us. It's the last expedition of this year, and there's no way I can find someone to fill the job now. I'll pay you three times the usual salary."

The last was a hard offer to turn down. Had Kim told her husband that Sam's last writing contract had fallen through, leaving her unemployed? Awkward emotions of guilt and shame wrestled with each other in Sam's head.

"You know that Wilderness Quest was Kim's dream," Troy pressed. "She wanted this to be her legacy, helping troubled kids find the right path."

Oh, yeesh. Of course Sam knew; mother and daughter had often sung the praises of the wilderness therapy program Kim had created.

Cupping both hands around his beer glass, he stared into the amber liquid. "I didn't even kiss Kim goodbye that morning. And I hadn't seen Kyla for weeks; when she wasn't out in the mountains with the Quest kids, she was with Chris." His voice wavered, and he paused to swallow before adding, "Kim left a chicken in the fridge to thaw for dinner."

Sam struggled to bring into focus her final moments with her friends.

Kim, her face damp with perspiration after their climb from Iceberg Lake to Herman Saddle. She'd swept her arm across the panorama of Mount Shuksan to the east and Bagley Lake far below them, saying, "This is what cures the kids: nature."

Kyla, laughing with Sam after they simultaneously turned

the wrong way during a dance lesson at the Kickin' A Saloon.

At least her last memories of her friends were happy ones.

Troy's tired eyes glistened. "I can't let Wilderness Quest fail. Kim and Kyla..." His Adam's apple bobbed down and back up. "They'd be so happy to know you're taking Kyla's place. That you're helping us go on."

No fair playing the murdered friends card.

How could she say no?

"Summer?" Chase's voice shattered the memory, abruptly dropping her back into the present. He always called her by her given name, insisting that Summer perfectly matched her fair coloring and outdoorsy inclinations. "We really need to go, or I'm going to miss my flight."

Sam gazed at Pinnacle Lake one last time. Shouldering her pack, she murmured softly to the atmosphere, "Kim. Kyla. I miss you guys so much."

Putting a hand on her shoulder, Chase squeezed gently.

"We always said that if we died out in the wild, we'd die doing what we loved," she told him. "But we were talking about being mauled by bears or falling off cliffs or getting swept over a waterfall. We never imagined being slaughtered by a madman."

"No one does, *querida*." He tilted his head toward the trail.

They started down the steep path, the soles of their boots obliterating dozens of other prints from hikers who had trudged up and down this trail over the summer.

The authorities had recovered bullets from the bodies, but no casings from the scene. She'd learned enough about guns from Chase to understand that without bullet casings or the rifle or revolver that fired them, the slugs recovered from her friends' bodies were useless except to explain the cause of death and narrow down the types of weapons used. One 30-06 rifle, one revolver. Or perhaps even two revolvers.

Was the killer a man? A woman? One killer or two? So many unanswered questions. Detritus collected at the scene might contain traces of DNA and maybe even fingerprints, but those were useless without a specific individual to match.

She followed Chase's lean figure down the mountainside. Had the killer hiked this same winding trail? Were they trampling vital evidence? The hundreds of bits of rubbish ground into each mile of trail would drive any crime scene investigator crazy. She routinely picked up stray items every time she hiked, a small good deed to keep wild areas pristine. On her way up the trail, she'd bagged a button, two candy bar wrappers, a torn nylon strap with a rusty buckle, and a small packet of tissues that had slipped unnoticed out of a hiker's pocket. She knew other hikers who collected garbage along the routes they traveled. Evidence could easily have been carried away by environmental do-gooders.

Hell, for that matter, half the debris in her trash bag might have been transported here by investigators. Dozens of officials had tramped up and down this trail since that day, photographing the scene, carrying the bodies, or just coming to gawk like humans did anytime something exciting happened.

Why didn't perpetrators ever conveniently isolate their clues from the background mess?

"Too bad the real world is nothing like CSI on television," Chase said over his shoulder, reading her mind again.

She needed to change the subject. "I so wish you lived here, Chase."

"I put down the Seattle office as my OP. But it's a long shot."

Sam understood that meant that Agent Starchaser Perez had requested a transfer from his Salt Lake City FBI office to his "office of preference" in Seattle, but the Bureau seemed to run like the army; agents had little say in where they were assigned. Today, after a three-day visit, her lover was rushing off in typical spook fashion to an FBI explosives training course in a location he refused to disclose to her.

"I'm trying," he added.

Was there was an unspoken "Are *you?*" after that sentence? She still felt guilty about turning down Chase's proposal to move in with him in Salt Lake City. Did he truly understand her reasons, or was he only pretending to be patient because he hadn't yet found a replacement girlfriend?

There was no time to sort it out now. Chase had a plane to catch and she had to get to this blasted job. Just thinking about the assignment knotted the muscles between her shoulder blades. Twenty-one days, she reminded herself. She couldn't save her friends, but she could help save their dream. Three weeks, and she would be done with this commitment to the ghosts of Kyla and Kim.

She paused to pick up a plastic bottle top and a gum wrapper from the side of the trail.

"Summer?" Chase prompted, glancing back over his shoulder. "I know we came in separate cars, but I want to make sure you get back safely to yours."

"I'm right behind you." Sam stuffed the trash sack into her pack and focused on hustling down the mountainside, keeping a wary eye on the thick forest around them, watching for the glint of a rifle barrel or some obvious sign of evil lurking along the trail.

"Think you can find your way out of here?" he asked as they neared the parking lot.

"I got here, didn't I? My trusty GPS lady helped."

He ran a knuckle over the dark whiskers already starting to

shadow his jaw line. "The GPS unit you haven't updated in a decade?"

"Forest roads haven't changed much in ten years either, Chase."

"Touché." He practically galloped to his rental car, but she grabbed him before he slid into the driver's seat and wrapped her arms around him, pressing her ear against his heart and squeezing hard. For a change, he was the first to pull away. "I'll see you again in a few weeks."

"You never know," she murmured. Every goodbye could be the last.

"We'll talk tonight." His kiss was too quick.

They both slid into their cars, and Chase waited until she'd started up her Civic before he peeled out of the lot in a cloud of dust.

Sam shut off her car engine. Walking back to the memorial, she plucked out the Mylar balloon and stabbed it through the heart with a car key before stuffing the deflated remains into her back seat and heading for Bellingham.

Chapter 2

When Sam arrived at the Wilderness Quest office, she found Troy in the administrator's office. The name *Troy Johnson* had replaced *Kimberly Quintana* on the door plaque.

"It's best not to remind clients of our tragedy," Troy explained. "We were lucky to keep the Wilderness Quest connection out of the news." He grimaced. "Probably helps that Kim never took my last name."

Kim had always maintained that Quintana was a much more interesting name than Johnson, but Sam was not going to share that comment with her friend's husband.

Troy noticed Sam staring at the empty spot where Kim's computer had rested. "The police took her laptop. They took mine from home, too. And my cell phone. They already had Kim's and Kyla's."

She didn't know what to say.

His expression grim, he fingered his beard. "Kim had a hefty life insurance policy, with me as beneficiary. I had one, too, but they'll figure I took that out just to make the situation look less suspicious."

Sam groaned. "Oh, Troy."

"The spouse is always a suspect. I should know." Troy Johnson was a retired deputy prosecuting attorney from the Whatcom County court system.

The kids in her expedition "crew," as Wilderness Quest

liked to call each group of client kids, had arrived in town yesterday, along with their parents. All of them had met with the company's counselors, who reiterated the goals of wilderness therapy—healing old wounds, strengthening family relationships, setting realistic expectations for the future, breaking bad habits. A three-week expedition into the backcountry was a chance for teens to escape the distractions of a perpetually connected world and learn to rely on themselves and find joy in the present. The kids were examined individually by a physician and a psychologist while the parents met with Troy for a frank discussion of their issues and expectations.

Today the kids would be counseled; relieved of personal clothing, jewelry, electronics, drugs, and weapons; and issued uniforms for the outing.

While the staff readied the kids and equipment for the field, Troy installed Sam in an empty counselor's office to watch recorded videos of his interviews with the parents.

The staff had taken photos of the kids as they'd first arrived yesterday, and Sam held them in her hands now to match up kids and parents.

The first video segment was labeled *Olivia Bari, Toledo, Ohio, 16*. In her intake photo, the girl wore a green striped blouse tucked into close-fitting jeans. With her olive skin, long raven hair wrapped in a green headscarf, thick eyeliner, and dangling filigree earrings, the girl resembled a stereotypical gypsy. But Olivia had far more lines engraved on her forehead than any sixteen-year-old should.

Setting the photo aside on the desk, Sam started the video on the computer screen. The camera offered a fish-eye view over Troy's shoulder from the corner of his office. Like their daughter, the Baris' builds were on the small end of average, and they both had bronze skin and dark eyes. The father's hair was graying; the mother's was covered by a bright paisley scarf.

"Frequent truancy." Troy read aloud from Olivia's file, which lay open on the desk between him and the parents.

Mr. Bari nodded. "She says she goes, but then the school calls and tells us she doesn't."

"She lies," Mrs. Bari affirmed, her gaze fixed downward.

"She is disrespectful," the father added. His accent—Middle Eastern?—was barely noticeable, but his choice of words were too formal for a native-born American.

"I understand." Troy folded his hands on top of his desk. "Olivia tried to commit suicide by taking pills?"

"It was an accident," the mother assured him, looking up to meet his eyes. "The pills were Tylenol. She had a headache and didn't know how many to take."

Sam leaned away from the screen. *Yikes.* The first kid in her crew was a suicide risk? How many pills had Olivia taken—ten, fifty? She shook her head, already feeling out of her element.

The conversation continued about Olivia's health: good, no allergies, no drug addictions, no smoking, no drinking.

"There will be boys on this trip?" Mrs. Bari looked worried at the prospect.

"Yes," Troy confirmed. "But you have no need for concern. Our field guide and our two peer counselors will keep Olivia safe at all times." He paused, waiting until both parents nodded. "Now, can you tell me what you hope to gain from enrolling Olivia in Wilderness Quest?"

"We want her to be happy," Mr. Bari said. "We want her to go to school."

Pursing her lips, Sam blew out a long breath. It sounded so simple.

Next up: *Gabriel Schmidt, Boise, Idaho, 18.* The photo revealed Gabriel to be a large boy who reminded her uncomfortably of the white flour dumplings she had eaten with stew last night. He wore an extra-large T-shirt and the saggy knee-length shorts that corpulent males everywhere seemed to favor.

The interview video showed that, like Gabriel, both Mom and Dad Schmidt had pasty complexions and were significantly overweight. To Sam's surprise, their issues were all about their son's use of his computer.

"Gabriel won't come out of his room. He stays up all night playing games."

"He lives in an Internet world."

Troy consulted the boy's file. "Gabriel turned eighteen on August third?"

Both Schmidts nodded.

"You realize that means that our staff, acting on your behalf, cannot compel Gabriel to do anything?" Troy asked.

The point seemed irrelevant to Sam. She'd had a day of coaching by the counselors, but she was pretty sure she couldn't *compel* a teenager, especially one as large as Gabriel, to do anything he didn't want to.

Mr. Schmidt squirmed in his chair. His wife spoke for both of them. "He understands that this is *our* condition for him continuing to live at home."

At least Gabriel had received his high school diploma a few months ago; that put him ahead of the other kids. And there was no mention of drugs or alcohol.

"He's got to come out of his bedroom," Gabriel's father reiterated. "If he's not going to go to college, he needs to get a job."

Sam rubbed her forehead. Why didn't the Schmidt family

just take away the computer or game console Gabriel used to feed his Internet addiction? Mom and Dad appeared to be in their late fifties or early sixties, with graying hair. Maybe Gabriel had been a late-life baby. Maybe they were just tired.

If the Schmidts looked worn, Justin Orlov's parents appeared downright elderly. Which was soon explained by their answers to Troy's questions: they were Justin's maternal grandparents. They'd legally adopted Justin at age nine, and changed Justin's last name to theirs. Justin's father had killed their daughter in a drunken domestic violence incident. The father was now eight years into a twenty-five-year prison sentence.

Sam chewed on her thumbnail. Another family coping with murder. In his photo, Justin glowered at the camera, his fists clenched at his sides. He was a tall, muscle-bound boy with a blond buzz cut the Marines would appreciate. A dragon tattoo crawled up the left side of his neck, the beast's snarling head and one clawed foot emerging from the neck of his black T-shirt. Justin was a seventeen-year-old who could pass for twenty-three. Repeatedly suspended from school for bullying. On probation for vandalism and assault.

The Orlovs lived in Los Angeles. They were terrified their grandson was going to end up a professional gangbanger.

With his family history, the kid had probably learned his threatening behavior from the cradle. She made a mental note to keep Justin away from anything that could be a weapon. Sam licked her lips, trying to imagine how she would handle this boy. A stun gun might be a good addition to the standard field guide equipment.

Taylor Durand, Sacramento, California, 16. The teen was a tall angular girl. Her straight blond hair, artistically streaked with strands of burnished copper and platinum, dangled past her shoulders. Her bright red lipstick matched the off-the-shoulder blouse tucked into her skinny jeans. Her face was a matte beige mask that spoke of a layer of heavy foundation.

Sam started the video. Like his daughter, Taylor's father was tall and blond and casually handsome. The mother was of average appearance, with an expensive angled haircut and sophisticated makeup. The problems with Taylor?

"She doesn't think she needs to complete high school," the father said. "All she cares about is becoming a fashion model. And we've found drugs in Taylor's room, too."

"Mainly diet pills," the mother added.

Mainly? Sam leaned back in her chair. Would Taylor be in some sort of quaking, hallucinating withdrawal during this expedition? Sam reminded herself of the promotional video she'd watched on the company website. Kids with drug issues came into the program only after going through rehab. Taylor might be jonesing for a fix during the expedition, but she wouldn't be actively detoxing.

Nick Lewis, Everett, Washington, 15. Sam's youngest draftee, and the one closest to home. Nick's photo showed a slight dark-haired boy wearing a green plaid shirt that was at least two sizes too big, the sleeves turned up into French cuffs, double-buttoned in place around his skinny wrists. As a petite woman who lived in perpetually rolled-up sleeves, Sam knew that trick well. Nick held his hands clasped in front of his stomach as if they were cuffed together. One of the two buttons on his right sleeve was missing; a red thread dangled in its place.

Unlike his son, the video showed Mr. Lewis was a muscular man with thick sandy hair and several days' worth of whiskers on a jutting chin that he stroked throughout the interview. His complaints about his son? Too many school absences. This was obviously a common theme among the clients.

Leaning forward as if to confide in Troy, he murmured, "His mother always said he was 'sensitive,' but really, he needs to grow a pair."

"The file says Nick cuts himself," Troy stated bluntly. "And the doc says some of his cuts appear to be recent."

"Well, yeah, he does that sometimes," Mr. Lewis confirmed. "Why the hell would any kid do that?"

Troy said, "Cutting usually indicates that the child feels a lot of stress."

"Huh." The father's face reddened. He straightened in his chair. "Nick has no reason to be stressed out." He leaned forward again, putting both hands on Troy's desk. "Look, Nick's mom is not in the picture, but he has me. He likes the outdoors, so this seemed like the place to straighten him out. We've been through a rough patch lately."

"Anything we should know about?"

"No." Mr. Lewis shook his head. "No. It was really nothing special. Teenagers, you know?" He grinned, but his smile seemed forced.

Troy nodded. "I know."

"Besides, we can't change the past, right? We all need to put the past behind us; everything is about the future, right?"

"That's what we focus on here," Troy reassured the man. "Acknowledge the past, but embrace the future."

"Nick's basically a good kid. All he needs is to man up."

"We'll take good care of your son," Troy promised.

Sam blew out a long slow breath and twisted her head from side to side, trying to loosen her neck and shoulder muscles. So far, her troop included a suicidal girl, a boy who cut himself, the on-probation son of a violent killer, and a kid who lived inside a video game. Taylor, the would-be model, seemed by far the most normal.

She picked up the photo of the last contestant. *Ashley Brown, Spokane, Washington, 16.* The girl's photo revealed short chestnut hair cut into spiky layers, the tips died purple. Her mascara and eyeliner were so heavy, the girl resembled a raccoon. Her ears were lined with multiple earrings, and a safety pin adorned her left eyebrow. She'd taken scissors to the tight T-shirt she wore, cutting a deep vee to reveal the cleavage between her generous breasts.

Ashley Brown's mother was another single parent. Like her daughter, her body was all curves. The face beneath her blond-streaked hair was pretty. Her words were anything but.

"Ashley is a smart-aleck skank," the mother told Troy. "She dropped out of school. She's run away three times. She's even sold herself on the streets. She's got to straighten up or she's going to end up with AIDS. Or dead."

Sam sucked in a breath. AIDS? Dead? At sixteen?

"Is she close to her father?" Troy asked.

Ashley's mom narrowed her eyes and sat back in her chair with a heavy sigh. "Neither of us is close to her father. He's a snake. I don't know what I ever saw in that man."

Add one teen prostitute to the troop.

The poor parents. The poor kids. With the possible exception of the Durands, none of these families came across as wealthy. Wilderness Quest was a nonprofit, but the costs of maintaining a staff and equipping and feeding all the participants during outdoor therapy were high. Maybe some of these clients had generous health insurance that was paying for this expedition, but she suspected most had scraped together the fee as a last hope of straightening out their kids.

It was depressing.

She didn't want to deal with any of it; she was already depressed enough.

The door opened. Maya stepped in, dressed in her yellow uniform shirt with STAFF printed front and back, quick-dry cargo pants, and hiking boots. "I just wanted to say hi, 'cause we're not supposed to act like we know each other out there. I'm glad you're on this trip."

Sam hadn't seen Maya since the girl started working for Kim. She turned off the computer, stood up, and hugged her teenage friend. "I'm glad *you're* on this trip, because I don't know what I'm doing."

She also realized that she and Maya hadn't had the chance to talk about the murders. Kim and Kyla had been Maya's mentors and colleagues. "I'm so sorry I didn't call you, Maya."

The girl pulled out of her embrace. "You couldn't call, at least most of the time. I worked the trip that ended just a couple days ago."

"I know you're missing Kim and Kyla, too."

A cyclone of emotion tore swiftly through Maya's dark eyes, and she caught her lower lip between her teeth for a second. Then the girl put a hand on Sam's forearm and squeezed. "Shit happens."

She turned toward the doorway, but stopped before exiting to look back. "It helps a lot to be out there, Sam. You'll see." Maya closed the door softly behind her.

Shit happens.

Sam slumped back into the chair. A lot of shit had happened to Maya Velasquez in her eighteen years. She's lost her dad and then her mom to drugs, endured a series of foster homes, and paid for her juvenile burglary convictions through grueling trail work.

Compared to Maya's, Sam's life had been a picnic. When it

came to enduring hardship, Summer Westin was a wimp.

Crossing her arms on the desk, Sam lowered her head onto them, envisioned herself back in Boundary Bay brewpub, savoring a cold ESB and a pile of yam fries.

"You're doing God's work," her father had remarked when she told him she would miss their regular Sunday evening phone calls while she filled in for Kyla at Wilderness Quest.

She'd considered asking him why God wasn't doing his own work, but she knew that Reverend Mark Westin would have an answer that she probably didn't want to hear. She envied him his faith, if not his lifestyle in rural Kansas.

"Ready?"

She jerked her head up, startled.

Troy stood in the doorway with a much younger man beside him. "The kids and the gear are loaded in the van. Ready, Sam?"

"Not really." She stood up anyway.

"Did you watch the videos?"

"Yep. That's why I'm not ready."

Troy covered the distance between them with a few long strides and wrapped her in an awkward hug. "We got lucky this time. None of these kids are too hard core; we didn't have to lock up a single one last night and let me tell you, that's pretty rare."

"Good for them. Good for me."

"You have your notebook with all the exercises; you'll be fine. And Aidan and Maya have done it all before. Speaking of which..." He gestured to the young man to join them. "This is Aidan Callahan."

Aidan's appearance was as Irish as his name. He was nearly as tall as Troy, with reddish brown hair and freckles dotting his face and arms. His cheeks and chin looked freshly shaven.

Troy patted the young man on the back. "Aidan is in his last year of college. This is his third year with us, and we've known him since he was a kid. If he comes back next summer, he'll be a field guide. For now, he's your dependable second-in-command."

Aidan shot Troy an indecipherable look, then turned to her. "I've got your back, Sam."

She shook hands with him. "Glad someone knows what they're doing."

Aidan gave her a little salute, and then turned toward the door.

"You'll be fine," Troy reassured her for the second time. "Remember that you get a two-day break halfway through when the counselors come up to relieve you."

At least she had that to look forward to. With luck, Chase would be able to escape from work again in ten days and they could spend the time together.

Troy gave her a final quick squeeze. "Thanks again, Sam."

"Don't thank me yet. I might march them all off a cliff." Hefting her backpack from the floor, she squared her shoulders and followed him to the parking lot.

~ END OF PREVIEW ~

To find out what happens when Sam leads six troubled teens into the North Cascades wilderness, pick up a copy of *Backcountry*. You can find all the links on Pamela Beason's website:
http://pamelabeason.com

Acknowledgments

No writer can produce a good book alone. I owe a big THANK YOU to the following people, who read the drafts of this book and helped to improve the story: astute readers Jeanine Clifford and Alison Malfatti, author Rae Ellen Lee (raeellenlee.com), and amazing all-round editor Karen Brown. Thanks are owed also to author Sara Stamey (sarastamey.com) for her help in improving the book description.

Books by Pamela Beason

The *Run for Your Life* Young Adult Adventure Trilogy

RACE WITH DANGER

RACE TO TRUTH

RACE FOR JUSTICE

The Neema Mysteries

THE ONLY WITNESS

THE ONLY CLUE

THE ONLY ONE LEFT

The Sam Westin Mysteries

ENDANGERED

BEAR BAIT

UNDERCURRENTS

BACKCOUNTRY

Romantic Suspense

SHAKEN

CALL OF THE JAGUAR (ebook only)

Nonfiction Ebooks

SO YOU WANT TO BE A PI?

There's always a new book in the works. Keep up with Pam by subscribing to her mailing list on http://pamelabeason.com

About the Author

Pamela Beason is the author of the *Neema Mysteries*, the *Sam Westin Mysteries*, and the *Run for Your Life* young adult trilogy, as well as several romantic suspense and nonfiction books. She has received the Daphne du Maurier Award and two Chanticleer Book Reviews Grand Prizes for her writing, in addition to an award from Library Journal and other romance and mystery awards. Pam is a former private investigator who lives in the Pacific Northwest, where she escapes into the wilderness to hike and kayak as often as she can.

http://pamelabeason.com

Made in the USA
Coppell, TX
19 January 2020

14690192R00159